Make Me Dream

COAL HAVEN, BOOK 4

MARIE JOHNSTON

LE PUBLISHING

Stetson Barron has been the center of my world since I was twelve. But with our ten-year age difference and my quirky nature, I didn't think I was more to him than his little sister's color-of-the-month-hair best friend. Until one hot summer night at his cousin's wedding when I climbed him like a water tower.

And then he didn't talk to me for weeks afterward.

A pink plus sign and an "OMG, what am I going to do?" later, the trailer I lived in with my mom burned down. Stetson showed up at the ER like a country knight on a diesel-powered steed, arranged a place for my mom to stay, and took me home with him.

The weeks of radio silence after our hookup have left me wary. Being with Stetson should be a fantasy come to life, but I'm waiting for my prince to ride away. My mom was in the same situation once, and I've learned her lesson. When Stetson is forced to choose between his new family unit and old family expectations, will he prove to be the man of my dreams? Or am I in for a harsh awakening?

One

LYRIC

Opening the clinic lab was normally one of the favorite parts of my job. The lab wouldn't be open to patients for another half hour, and I could work in peace. I could get lost in my work without keeping an eye on the registration window. But today, anxiety crawled through my belly.

I waved my badge in front of the reader by the door, and the lock clicked open. I let my badge go, and it reeled into my lanyard as I shoved through the door. The hinges squeaked as the door caught and slowly swung shut behind me.

I stared at the dark lab with its faint whirring of analyzers and the random clicks they made while sitting dormant throughout the night.

I had thirty minutes to finish what I needed to before the lab officially opened to patients. That meant turning on equipment, taking vials of reagents out of the fridge, running quality control, logging on to no fewer than five computers, and hoping no early bird patients arrived for their fasting blood work.

One other task weighed on my mind, and if I didn't get it done, my nerves would detonate and I'd be nothing but a scrubs-covered dust cloud.

I dropped off my phone, tote bag, and the book I read on my breaks in the manager's office. She should be the next medical technician in. Eventually, there'd be four of us working for the bulk of the day.

I took a deep breath, stepped out of the office, and faced the dim lab. Pressing my hand against my abdomen, I inhaled slowly. This was it. My extra task had to be done while I was alone. I didn't want to risk my job. I needed to work here. The clinic lab was the only place in Coal Haven where I could get a job with benefits using my medical lab scientist degree. I wouldn't get fired if I got caught carrying out my personal mission, but I'd have a blemish on my reputation. And people would *know*.

Shrugging into my lab coat, I began my morning procedure like I usually did. Today was no different from any other. But soon, I'd find out whether my life was going to be forever altered or if the fog I'd been living in for the last six weeks would dissipate and become nothing but a dream.

I went to our hematology department first—a counter with a tabletop analyzer that looked like it should serve a cup of java instead of reporting how many blood cells were circulating in a patient's system.

Nerves fluttered within my stomach as I stuffed my hands into purple nitrile gloves. I logged on to the main computer and set the analyzer to run through its startup while I took out the quality control reagents. Giving them a little roll between my hands, I anxiously tapped my foot.

I had to get this over with.

Next, I went to our chemistry department—a double

line of counters flanking a floor-model analyzer. I logged on to the main computer and let the analyzer start waking up for the day.

I turned on every computer available for the techs to use. Then I trashed my gloves and hung my lab coat on the back of an office chair.

This was it. I wanted to throw up, but that feeling wasn't new. I'd been plagued with nausea for a couple weeks. I snagged a specimen cup from the stock we handed to patients to collect their urine samples and headed for a toilet. I had less than ten minutes before the lab opened.

I ducked into one of the patient restrooms and collected my own urine sample. My heart lodged in my throat. How had I gotten here?

I knew *how*, but how had I let things get away from me like that? I didn't typically land myself in these situations.

This could be just a normal day. A negative result, and life would be back to my low-key normal.

A positive result would mean I was pregnant.

My stomach sank like I was free-falling. Ugh. I should buy some saltines for the mornings.

I put the urine cup in the pass-through cabinet so I could grab it on the lab side for testing. Techs weren't supposed to run tests on themselves, each other, or anyone else if a doctor hadn't placed the order.

Which was why I had to get this over and done with before my coworkers arrived.

After closing the cabinet, I washed my hands, cursing the incident that had brought me to this moment. It was easier to run the test here. Alone. No witnesses to any part of it. Coal Haven was too small for me to pop into a store and buy one. I couldn't risk being recognized. I also couldn't order a kit to be delivered to my house. I lived with my mom, and we shared accounts for everything.

While I could work around that fact, I had lost my patience with wondering. As fast as a kit could be shipped to my home, I'd die a thousand deaths waiting for it. I had to know. Now. Once I'd committed to testing myself at work, I'd decided today was the day.

Over two months ago, I'd been dumped by a guy who shouldn't have earned five minutes of my time. I'd been with him for four months. Four months of being told he could do better—with women, with work, with life—if he got a job in another town. He could do better in another state. He could do better if he lived anywhere but Coal Haven, North Dakota.

As if I wasn't used to hearing out-of-staters trash North Dakota, like we were ignorant backwoods folks who had no idea a big ol' world existed outside our borders.

Yet when I had said, "Well, I'm confident I can find an asshole to date no matter where I live," he'd dumped me.

Jackass.

I could go anywhere. I could blindfold myself and stick a pin in a globe and guarantee they'd be short of med techs, but my mom was in Coal Haven, and she wasn't leaving. Therefore, neither was I. If I left, I'd lose her, and we were each other's only support. It'd been that way since I was six, when my dad walked out and acted like we never existed.

But weeks ago—six, to be exact—I'd made a mistake I hadn't thought I'd regret.

With a long exhale, I left the bathroom and put my lab coat back on. Back to being a tech.

I dug out a box of test kits, set them on the counter, and retrieved the quality control from the refrigerator. I'd put way too much thought into this. Normally, we didn't do QC every day unless we used the test kits. But environmental services came through after the lab was closed and emptied all the garbage and biohazard bins. I worked with too many smart techs. If they saw the biohazards with a used test and no QC marked in the computer, they'd ask questions.

I couldn't risk it. I could explain doing extra QC just because I had time and it didn't hurt. But I'd make sure they never found the extra test.

I unwrapped and lined up three little test cartridges on the counter. Lateral flow tests. Chromogenic results, meaning a color developed—in this case, if the test was positive.

Fancy terms for a pregnancy test.

Swallowing hard, I put on another pair of gloves and grabbed my urine sample from the stainless steel pass-through cabinet. I used the tiny pipettes that came with the kit to set up my test and the positive and negative QCs. I set a timer and forced myself to walk away.

Three agonizing minutes that'd go faster if I wasn't staring at the neat line of tests.

My chest was tight, my stomach bundled into a knotted ball, but I went to the heme analyzer and started the first run of QC. Then I popped over to the chemistry analyzer and readied the orders for its daily controls.

The drone of the machinery grew louder just as the timer went off.

Oh, God. This was it. My heart and all my other organs crowded into my throat.

I couldn't be pregnant. Six weeks ago was the only time I hadn't used protection. My only thought when Stetson Barron had found me sulking in the tack room of Holden's barn and gotten close enough to brush a kiss on my lips was *Finally!*

The man I'd been lusting after since I was old enough to know I liked boys and aware enough to know that big, sometimes goofy, but secretly brooding Stetson was my one and only type had finally touched me in a way that told me he didn't see me as only his little sister's best friend.

And we had done more than touch. We'd gone all the spectacular way.

Then he hadn't talked to me again. Ever since, he'd practically run out of buildings when I walked in.

I approached the counter to see the results, my shoes as heavy as if they were lined with concrete. When I looked down, my heart dropped like an elevator with its cables cut. Like a boulder falling off a cliff. Like my future just went *wham* and flopped at my feet.

Positive. I was pregnant.

My lungs froze, and my breathing came fast. My focus was on the three tests, willing the QC to have failed, for the tests to be faulty.

Oh. My. God. What had I done? Who could I tell?

I hadn't told my mom anything about what was going on. She'd only asked me a million times for the last six weeks if I was all right. She thought my breakup with Cole was messing with my head.

Cole and I still crossed paths, but it resulted in little more than sneering at each other. My worst revenge on him was to get on with my life in a way he knew I wasn't missing him and his mind games.

Was getting pregnant with another man's kid weeks after the breakup enough?

I blinked. A sob rattled out of my mouth. Then another. Tears tracked down my cheeks. I rushed to put the box of pregnancy tests back in the drawer, but I fumbled. Nothing was working right.

A light touch landed on my shoulder. I spun around, scattering the test cartridges across the counter. My manager, Joan, reared back like she was afraid I'd barrel over her trying to run.

"What's going on—" Her gaze landed on the tests.

Joan was astute enough to read the situation. We weren't open to patients yet. The QC on the analyzers wasn't complete. I hadn't even touched the little urine analyzer, and I hadn't gotten as far as taking the fabric covers off the microscopes.

She tapped the end of the sample I hadn't labeled with a plus or minus sign for the QC to get a better look. Her eyes flared, then she yanked a purple glove out of the nearest box. She put it on, gathered the small tests in one hand and dumped them into the biohazard bin. "We'll get the QC entered later."

"I don't know what to do," I wheezed. If this was Cole's baby, I'd know to have custody forms ready. He wouldn't want anything to do with me or a kid. Nothing to tie him down.

Would Stetson be the same? Or would his family rip everything from me to get their hands on his firstborn?

She steered me through the lab as I gasped and coughed, trying to keep my tears at bay. This wasn't me. I was chill. I'd had patients pass out on me while I was drawing blood. I'd had to break into the restroom when they'd fallen. I'd put myself through college by doing phlebotomy in the ER in Bismarck. I'd been wedged between nurses and doctors while they worked on people who'd been in car accidents, stabbed, or shot.

I had once used the main restroom in the hospital where I interned only to find a confused, elderly woman squatting on the trash can to pee, and I'd calmly directed her to a stall.

I didn't panic. Ever. I didn't lose my calm. Health care had a way of raising the unusual circumstances bar until it took a lot to faze a person, even those of us with more limited patient contact.

Joan knew that. She was the same way—unless a spider

skittered across the floor, then she practically played The Floor is Lava for the rest of the day.

She sat me down on her office chair, her brow pinched and her brown eyes glittering with worry. My reaction concerned her.

"I still have my lab coat on," I mumbled. Her office was a clean zone. We could have food and drinks in here. No sobbing, rattled techs still in their lab coats.

"Don't worry about it." She peeked out of the office and set her jaw like she'd come to a decision.

I glanced at the time. I was supposed to open the door for patients, and I hadn't done half of my opening duties. "I'm sorry. I messed up—I shouldn't have… "

She waved her hand, and her chin-length black hair brushed her jaw. Joan had been the lab manager since before I'd gone to college. She was a med tech originally from the Philippines. She'd headhunted me the day I shadowed her when I was a junior in high school. She'd been my mentor, and she'd managed to hold an opening in the lab, so I had a position when I graduated with my degree. Recruiting techs to rural areas was hard, and she'd had faith I'd be a good worker.

I didn't want to prove her wrong.

"You don't abuse the system, and believe me, I know why you're sneaking a pregnancy test in a town with three thousand people." She crouched to meet my gaze. "Are you okay?"

I almost wiped my eyes with the back of my hands but scrunched my nose. Joan had a pump bottle of hand sanitizer on her desk. I used a dollop as I sniffled and regained control of my breathing. "I don't know. I didn't really think —it couldn't happen—I'm…" I was a mess. "I had a one-night stand, and it got out of control."

A loud rap on a door resonated through the lab.

That dried my tears right up. I jumped out of the chair, my pulse skyrocketing. How many people were going to walk in on my private moment?

Joan pursed her lips and glanced out of the office. "Wait here. Don't worry about opening duties. I came in early to submit payroll, but we'll both tackle them when you've recovered. I'll take care of whoever is here." She waved her hand. "Sit."

Plopping my butt in the chair, I nodded numbly. While she was gone, I stared at my pale hands on my lap, stark white against my purple scrubs.

Pregnant.

I supported myself and helped my mother on a small-town tech's wages. I made enough to pay the bills, put a little away in savings, keep up with the multitude of repairs my mom's trailer needed, and take her out to eat occasionally. It wasn't a bad life, but there were no Caribbean cruises in my future.

A baby. Worries started to assault me, but I cut them off.

I had a few obstacles to consider before I dealt with the logistics of being a single mom. The thought that three struggling generations would live under one leaky roof.

That wasn't what I wanted. I was working toward a better future. For me. For Mom. And now I had another's future in my hands.

The anxious anticipation from the morning melted. A new dread set in, but it was accompanied by a heavy dose of excitement.

If I told my teenage self I'd be having Stetson Barron's baby, younger me would be ecstatic. All those teen years longing for him to just look at me, but at the same time knowing I was too young, had stretched into catching glimpses of him when I came home during college.

I'd hang out with my best friend, his sister Isla, and I'd

try to talk to him. He'd grunt and ignore me like usual. He'd call me Ricky, and I'd get a zing of awareness that shot straight through my heart and down my spine.

Then I'd moved home and started working. I was old enough for him. Yes, he still had almost ten years on me, but we were full-fledged adults.

And he hadn't looked at me or talked to me any more than he had before. He hadn't acted differently toward me than when I was fifteen. I was almost twenty-five.

I couldn't wipe away the dawning horror in his expression when he'd realized he'd forgotten protection. And the *Oh fuck, she has to be on birth control* tone in his voice when he'd asked if I was taking something was loud and clear in my memory.

Paying for monthly birth control when I had a mortgage-sized payment of student loans for the next ten years wasn't my priority. Diligently using protection had been my priority.

Until it wasn't.

Now I was faced with having the baby of a man who probably considered me the biggest regret of his life.

Stetson

I swung around and parked my pickup beside the shop. My parents' place, the house I'd grown up in and where Isla still lived with them, lorded over the land. Two large windows under the steep peak of the roof made the house look like an owl, a comment I'd made before I was old enough to be in school, and Mom had broken down in tears.

It was why I'd built my own place as soon as I'd gotten

the oil money trust fund my dad's parents had left me. I'd purposely stayed away from the A-frame design and went with a modern two-story farmhouse vibe.

People had asked me why I chose the design I did. I always said the builder I'd hired had come up with the plans, and he had—after I had shown him several examples of what I wanted.

But the people in town didn't expect me to want a place with a homey feel. A place that screamed warmth and comfort. I was jovial, sometimes goofy if I was trying to make a kid laugh, but I was Cameron Barron's son. I should have a monstrosity of a home that showed the county how wealthy I was.

I was the opposite of my dad. The only land I owned was the two acres surrounding my house, and I'd had to purchase that from the ranch. I made a good living, but I worked hard for the money. My savings held the rest of the trust fund money my house hadn't eaten up, but that was it.

When I envisioned a home, I didn't want to be reminded of my mother's tears, and I didn't need it to scream wealth. I wasn't wealthy. My parents were.

I jogged into the house, using the sliding glass door off the dining room that Mom unlocked every morning. She was in the kitchen, holding out color samples. She had her fingers in so many pots in Coal Haven, I could only guess what the swatches were for.

She frowned, her way of acknowledging I was there. "I'm repainting the living room."

Meaning either Dad was repainting the living room or she'd fired someone she'd hired to do it. Or she thought I would paint. And I would, if she asked. But I wasn't offering. Mom and her painting jobs were tedious. I'd rather watch the paint dry for an entire month than have to slap it on the wall and carefully police all the splatters and uneven lines.

This was a house of perfection. The one constant Mom could control in her life, other than me and my sister. I was aware of how Mom operated, and life was better when I worked with her instead of against her.

"What colors?" I asked.

Her frown deepened, but no crinkles marred her forehead. She never told us what her regular visits to Bismarck were for, but once I noticed her frown lines disappearing, I'd figured it out for myself. I wished they could be laugh lines, and I didn't blame Mom for wanting them immobilized. For her, it was like wiping the bad memories away.

"I'd like to change the accent wall," she said.

The wall was an olive green that had turned out darker than she'd preferred, but surprisingly she hadn't asked me or Dad to change it. Until now. What was she worried about?

"A blue, maybe." She scrutinized several different blues that I wouldn't be able to tell apart if I had a year to study them.

I was about to edge back out the door. She'd asked me to stop in before I began haying. If all she'd needed was to verbally ponder colors, it was my lucky day.

"I'm meeting an old friend tonight." She set the samples down and propped a hand on her hip. She was dressed in her standard uniform of a power suit with a skirt one inch past her knees and a matching jacket. Her blouse was probably silk, and she had ten more lining her walk-in closet. "She's bringing her daughter."

I bit back a groan. "Don't set me up—"

She held up her free hand, and I snapped my lips shut. "She's a nice girl. A *good* girl. She would never give you the same trouble Krystal did."

Krystal's name hit like a jolt of dread had been injected

into my veins. Mom hadn't thought Krystal would give me the kinds of problems she had either. And like an idiot who'd wanted the home I'd built myself to amount to something Mom would be proud of, I'd tried not once, but twice with Krystal.

I could get a pass for the first time. I had no clue that letting her stay over a few nights would amount to half her shit in my closets and dressers. A lack of bathroom counter space and being asked to sell my grandpa's old '37 Chevy to make room in my garage for her car. I hadn't. The Chevy had stayed in the garage.

When she'd demanded to read my texts, have passwords to my email and social accounts, and screen my calls, I'd broken up with her.

And it'd been ugly.

She'd moved away, then moved back. And I gave in a second time. Chalk it up to loneliness or Mom's insistence that I should have nothing to hide from the woman I loved, but either way, it was a mistake. A second ugly mistake.

Even Mom didn't want Krystal around anymore. It hadn't helped when Krystal showed up at my cousin Holden's wedding ceremony after our breakup. I had told her there were plenty of witnesses and I wasn't too proud to get a restraining order.

She'd slunk away, and apparently six weeks was enough time for Mom to think I was ready to move on.

I wasn't, but it had nothing to do with Krystal.

My recent resistance to date, hook up, flirt, you name it, was because of what I'd done before Krystal had arrived at Holden's. If I were a teen, I'd snicker and correct that to *who* I'd done. Hell, I didn't have to be a teen to make that comment. I would've cracked that joke two months ago.

But I couldn't. Not about Lyric. Not about the best sex of my damn life. Not about a woman I couldn't forget.

My blood was recirculating to my irresponsible dick just thinking about her.

I wouldn't ruin Lyric's life. I wouldn't take my sister's best friend away from her. Thanks to our parents, Isla didn't make friends easily. Not as a kid—definitely not as an adult. Anyone she'd met and was friendly with was through Lyric, and even that was limited. Mostly because of our half brother and the laws our parents laid down before Isla was born.

Neither of us was allowed to have anything to do with Liam Barron, and I'd been the foundation holding Mom up after too many of her breakdowns. I couldn't go against her wishes after seeing what she'd gone through.

Liam seemed like a decent guy. He'd been a wild kid, but now he was married, with twin boys and a brand-new baby girl.

My half brother had gotten none of the life I had growing up, but he was living the life I wanted. And I had to suck it up.

Like it or not, Lyric would be forced to choose. She was tight with Liam's wife, Kennedy, and one of Kennedy's coworkers, Aspen, but she split her time with Isla. They'd been best friends since kindergarten. I wasn't ruining that.

Nor was I incurring Mom's wrath for dating the wrong type of girls. Krystal might've been batshit, but she'd hidden it behind a refined shell in public. She dressed nicely, with no rips in her clothing, no visible tattoos, no primary colors in her hair, and she had a respectable job as a nurse.

Lyric worked in the lab. I didn't know what she did, but Mom probably thought she played with potions and got paid under the table for it. Lyric had hair colors that changed more often than Dad bought new pickups, equally unpredictable painted nails, ripped leggings, and tattoos.

She'd said once she'd have more piercings if it weren't for her job.

And something deep inside me dug it. Dug her vibe real damn hard. Then I'd tasted her. And I'd fucked her.

I hadn't been the same since.

Mom was eyeing me. I was lost in my head. A common occurrence since I'd been buried deep in the heaven between Lyric's legs with her commands to fuck her already in my ear.

I bit back a groan. "I'm not ready to date anyone, Mom."

"Stetson, you're almost thirty-five."

I was almost thirty-four.

The door slid open, and Isla entered, giggling like she was sixteen instead of twenty-four. Lyric piled in after her. Her gaze landed on me, and she went pale.

Goddammit. Had I known she'd be coming over, I would've told Mom I wanted to get started on cutting the hay first. I'd been mostly successful at avoiding my personal torment until now.

But I gave myself exactly one second to drink her in. Her hair was pulled back in a ponytail, and the ends were dyed a lovely purple. Isla had dyed her hair once, and Mom had lost her shit even though I argued that it looked nice and Isla was an adult. Isla had stripped the color out. She'd have to take on that fight another day.

Before I tore my gaze away, I also noticed Lyric's lips were gloss-free. Her gloss tasted like watermelon. I had boycotted the fruit all damn summer. Six weeks wasn't long enough to forget what happened between me and Lyric. Sixty years wouldn't be enough time.

"Morning, Stetson," Isla said, cheeriness second nature.

"Morning, ladies," I said and started scooting around them to go out the door. I was a big man, but I could be nimble when I wanted to get away from my family and the woman who wasn't supposed to drive me wild.

"Stetson!" Mom called after me. "Tonight at seven. At Rattler's."

"Sorry, busy tonight." I darted out the door before she could reply. I had to get away from the idea of a blind date. Mom never ate at Rattler's unless she wanted to make a show of something. I wouldn't be paraded around like a prized stud, and I wasn't doing it at a place I normally went to for escape.

I took a big breath of manure-scented air. My chest was tightening to the point where I considered laying off my buddy Remington's wings at Rattler's, but my newfound breathing troubles had nothing to do with cholesterol or cow shit.

How could I have a perfect imprint of Lyric on my brain after being around her for less than a minute? She was wearing a pair of shorts with skulls on them. An ugly-as-fuck style where the front pockets hung out, but they were my favorite pair. They hugged her ass like I wanted to and showed off her curvy, creamy legs.

I'd had those legs wound around me once.

Breathing was proving difficult as I rushed to the shop. I'd have nothing to think about but Lyric while I was cutting the ditches.

Did she ever think about that night?

We'd been out of our minds—so much so that we each hadn't considered using protection. I'd endured six weeks of terror that she'd tell me she was pregnant. That she'd tied herself to my shit show of a life behind a perfectly polished facade. Lyric didn't do facades. And she might be best friends with Isla, but she knew damn well my family didn't have a say over her. Isla craved that freedom; it was what had drawn her to Lyric.

But a baby would be stronger than Gorilla Glue.

Unless my parents treated it like Liam. Then it'd be considered an unfortunate blemish in history in public. The worst degradation and humiliation in private.

A vise closed around my lungs. No way would any kid of mine go through what Liam had. Shame burned hot in my airways. I'd been a willing participant in what he'd endured and how he was still treated. No kid should've had to choose between their parents and their half brother, but I owned my decision. I'd tossed away a sibling for Mom and Dad.

Lyric was too strong for my family. I spent my time figuring out how to bend around the restrictions my family name caused, but with Lyric, one of us would end up breaking.

Two

LYRIC

"Are you sure you don't want to go out tonight?" Isla slipped her sunglasses on as we walked out of the farmers' market area in the park. Tents were coming down around us, and pickups with loaded beds or trailers pulled away.

Isla was the director, thanks to her dad. She wouldn't admit it, but we all knew the market wouldn't exist if he hadn't wanted to give her something to do within city limits. I'd chafe against the restraint, but then, my dad would rather forget me than have me in the same town. Besides, I'd learned long ago that Isla had her own way of maneuvering around her parents.

As for going out tonight, I was one-hundred-percent sure. Naomi had made a point of telling Isla she was meeting a friend for dinner who was bringing her *gorgeous* and *successful* and *single* daughter. A thirty-one-year-old market analyst who probably dressed like Naomi wanted Stetson's wife to dress.

A market analyst sounded exactly like what Naomi would want for Stetson. The girl could probably find work at the coal mine, the gasification plant, or the refinery. She would most assuredly find a husband if blue-collar dudes were her thing, and if that guy was Stetson, I didn't want to watch a love match happen.

I didn't want to sit and wonder how I was going to break the news of my pregnancy to him. It had been two days since I'd taken the test. I didn't have any answers, but I also didn't want to dry heave when I thought of facing Stetson with the news.

My low-grade nausea swirled up a few levels when I thought of Stetson telling his parents. I didn't want to be around for it. I most certainly didn't want to see a baby plan of action form in Naomi's eyes. Would she try to take the baby or snap it out of existence like a Marvel villain?

She was going to make that decision regardless. And Stetson would do whatever his mom wanted.

Normally, I'd admire a guy who was dedicated to his mother's happiness, but their relationship was toxic, and I wanted no part of it.

Too bad for me.

Isla got into her metallic-blue Range Rover, and I slid in the other side. We'd had this arrangement since we were little. She drove because she could afford the gas. I could now too, but the arrangement had stuck.

"Are you going to Rattler's?" I asked, a sucker for punishment. If she went to Rattler's, I'd innocuously find out later whether Stetson had met the golden daughter.

My stomach clenched like I was going to do a sit-up while I was actually sitting up. Morning sickness in the evening or the idea of Stetson and someone else? My belly cramped. No, I wouldn't be going to Rattler's.

"Nah. I'll go home and see if Stetson managed to stay out of Mom's clutches. He's been shifty lately."

"How so?" I'd been shifty lately too. It wasn't possible our one time together had affected him as well, was it? Hope would lead me down a lonely path.

"I dunno. He hasn't really gone to Rattler's. Remington keeps bugging me to see if he's alright."

The urge to heave was replaced by a warm, fuzzy sensation spreading through my abdomen. "Is he worried Stetson won't attract a crowd and revenue will fall?"

Isla snorted. "Right? No, it's something else, but it's not like Stetson to talk. I think he's lying low after the Krystal encounter at Holden's."

I wanted to snarl when I heard Krystal's name. Seeing her at work was bad enough. Having to deal with her in a professional capacity taxed all my patience. Knowing that Stetson, however briefly, had picked her was gut wrenching.

She was a nurse at the clinic and annoying as hell. She'd given me a wide berth since the incident at Holden and Emery's reception. At first I was paranoid she knew I'd been with Stetson, but she was unusually proficient and kind to everyone. Typically, she said what was on her mind no matter how insulting it was, and we all internally rolled our eyes when she started in on a topic she cared way more about than any of us did.

Crossing the Barrons at Holden and Emery's wedding must've scared her straight, at least for a little while. Hard to go against the town's royalty when you lacked support from the rest of the citizens.

"Maybe," I mumbled.

Isla pulled up to the trailer I had grown up in and still lived in with Mom. Flowers were blooming, hiding the peeling deck. The place was paid off, but since I had begun to work full-time, we'd had to repair the roof and fix some plumbing. More roof work was on the horizon. Electrical was next on the list. The house was old but cared for as well as possible. The thrift store barely padded Mom's savings, and I didn't want her wasting her money on futile repairs.

"See you this weekend?" I asked as I climbed out of her car.

"What else am I going to be doing?" she asked wryly, adding a self-deprecating eye roll.

"We can tear this town up on Saturday—after my shift is done." Just not at Rattler's.

She laughed, a happy, melodious sound that was all Isla, and not for the first time I wished I could be more like her. Refined and polished. She often commented she wished she could be more like me. Two girls insecure about who they were.

I thought those days would get left behind in high school. They'd gotten better, and that was good enough.

I trotted to the door, grateful I didn't have to make an excuse for why I wasn't having more than a cranberry juice at the bar. A girl could claim only so many bladder infections and dietary restrictions before her friends knew something was up.

What would my ailment be this weekend? I had a couple of days to figure it out. Eventually, I'd have to tell Isla I was pregnant—which also meant I'd have to tell her who the father was.

The heartburn that had plagued me for three weeks flamed hotter. I went inside and grabbed a Tums. The oven clicked, its subtle warmth emanating with savory smells of a casserole Mom had thrown in for supper.

Warm fur slid across my leg. "Hey, Floof." I picked my cat up.

He'd been a rescue from the pound, unknown years old,

left behind by a guy who'd worked at the refinery and moved, and my first pet as an adult.

He'd been left by his dad and so had I.

I buried my face in his long fur. Mom called him Fancy, but I had settled on Floof, thanks to the way his fur swayed when he walked. A Maine coon had to be somewhere in his bloodline: long fluffy tail, furry paws, and a love of water like nothing else. He was attached to me, and when I took baths, he perched on the edge.

"Tater tot hot dish?" I called, knowing Mom was inside somewhere. She shut the thrift store down early on Thursdays. It had been our designated meal night since Dad had left. Even when I'd gotten a job at the Tastee Queen, I'd told them I couldn't work Thursdays. I didn't have as much sway at the clinic. The walk-in portion of the clinic was open until nine and I usually didn't get out of there until almost nine thirty, but I still made most Thursday suppers.

She came out of her bedroom, an older, more worn version of me. Her hair was a light brown with a good portion of her temples gone gray, and she wasn't interested in keeping up with dyeing it. Erin Finnegan had raised me to not care what people thought, and that attitude had bitten me in the ass as much as it'd helped me over the years.

She smiled and her eyes crinkled at the sides. "I added cheese this time."

My stomach rumbled. My boobs were starting to hurt, but Floof's warm body was like a hot water bottle. I'd need to buy new bras. Probably some new casual wear. Soon, I'd need maternity clothes.

A spear of excitement shot through me, but it was too early to be excited. This wasn't my little secret. I had to tell Stetson, and then... I wasn't sure how excitement would fit in once the rest of the Barrons found out.

Mom shuffled to the oven and peered through the

window. I opened my mouth to tell her I was pregnant, to just say the words and get them out. The only other person who knew was Joan, and she hadn't told anyone else, as far as I knew. Joan knew in a professional capacity. Telling Mom was so very personal.

I snapped my lips shut and continued to scratch Floof's chin. I couldn't escape the feeling that I should tell Stetson first, and I should probably say something soon before he found out some other way. Wasn't that why I had risked testing myself at the lab? Or was I just stalling because I was avoiding him and he seemed to be avoiding me?

Mom straightened and brushed her hair off her face. She peered at me. "Everything okay, honey? You've looked so worn out lately."

"I haven't been sleeping well." Sore boobs. Heartburn. And stress. I set Floof down. He crossed to twine through Mom's legs. I ignored the weight of guilt from not sharing my big news with her and changed the subject. "How was the store today?"

My dad's parents had owned the store, but when my parents married, Dad had taken over. The place had been in both their names, as Mom had learned when Dad decided he was going to have a midlife crisis in his early thirties and use the store to rack up a ton of debt.

She'd held on to the store after the divorce to keep from going under and had clawed her way back into the black. She was finally at a point where she could pay herself a real living wage instead of earning scraps and little more.

"Busy for a Thursday." She went to the cupboard and pulled out some plates. "I think tomorrow will be even busier. I might go in a little early and get new product on the shelves."

I used to love going through donated boxes of items.

Mom would let me have first dibs. "I can help on Sunday. Isla probably could too."

Isla loved going through the donations more than I did, but she never accepted anything. I didn't have to ask to know that Naomi Barron would go apoplectic if her daughter wore something secondhand.

"That would be nice."

I'd tell Mom I was pregnant then. I'd tell them both.

So, I'd have to tell Stetson earlier. I'd give myself until Saturday, then I'd call and ask him to meet me. I'd get a small amount of satisfaction from tearing him away from whoever had latched on to him at Rattler's. The thought would power me through the anticipation and trepidation of talking with him alone.

My heartburn died down. A couple of days away wasn't today, and I could relax for a while.

* * *

A piercing shriek roused me from a deep sleep. I peeled an eye open and frowned. What the hell was that noise? A rhythmic alarm made me sit up, adrenaline flooding my veins. The deep sense that something was wrong dug its claws into my chest. An acrid smell assaulted my nose.

Oh, God. Was the place on fire?

Going against everything I learned in school about what not to do in a fire, I crept to the door and cracked it open. Had Mom baked something after I went to bed and burned it? That wasn't like her. I blinked and squinted. The hallway was foggy, but it wasn't my vision that was blurry. Smoke.

Was the trailer in flames? How bad was it? Fear more than the smell threatened to close off my air. My heart pounded harder. Was Mom awake? She was such a deep sleeper.

Tendrils of smoke curled through the hallway, inciting a cough. My pulse spiked. "Mom!" I hollered. "Floof?"

I kept my door shut at night, and my cat slept with Mom. Her door was open.

"Mom!" She had to be okay. "Floof?" I couldn't be too late.

I edged out of my room. In the dark, I couldn't make out as much as I usually could in the kitchen. Letting out another cough, I rushed to Mom's bedroom at the end of the trailer.

She met me at her door, tying her thin robe shut, her eyes wide and her hair wild from bed. "Fire," she gasped.

My jab of relief was short lived. "Where's Floof?"

She spun and looked around. I coughed again, air getting caught in my throat until I choked. Wasn't I supposed to be low to the ground?

Grabbing my arm, she shut her bedroom door and dragged me to the larger window at the very end of the trailer. The centerpiece of the master bedroom that should've been replaced ten years ago. "We've got to go."

"I need to get Floof." My lungs tightened. My throat was so dry, and I tasted smoke. Another cough erupted from me. I wasn't abandoning him like his previous owner. I had to find him.

How would I do that when his fur was the color of the smoke?

Mom was starting to cough as she wedged the main panel of glass from the window. "He'll take care of himself better than us. Come on."

I hesitated. I'd go down with the trailer to find him. But I no longer had just me to think about.

I stepped in to help her. "Here, kitty, kitty, kitty!" I kept calling as she pushed out the screen.

"You go first."

The streetlight shone in on her, highlighting her hair with yellow streaks.

"My cat," I sobbed, not realizing I'd been crying, and it wasn't just tears from smoke irritation. Where would he be? In the living room? "Is he under the bed?"

"He can get through the window too. We can't save him if we're dead, Lyric. Go."

My delay was costing Mom. This smoke wasn't good for either of us.

She helped me crawl out the window. The drop to the bottom wasn't more than four feet, but when I landed in the mulch around Mom's peonies, I yelped. Shit. I was barefoot and wearing only my T-shirt and thin shorts. The days had been hot, but the concrete had cooled overnight with the temperature. Goose bumps prickled over my skin.

Strong hands wrapped around me, and my heart nearly imploded. How much more shock could I take tonight?

Our neighbor Francis shifted me to the side. "I'll help your mom. Have you called 9-1-1 yet?"

God, no. All I'd cared about was Mom and Floof. "M-my phone's inside," I said as he darted away to help Mom climb out the window.

I rubbed the back of my hand against my face as I coughed. My throat was itchy, and my mouth tasted like I'd been licking smoldering electrical tape, but breathing was immediately easier.

Francis ushered both of us to the sidewalk. The concrete was cool under my bare feet, and the shrill alarm was still audible as he herded us farther away, past even his house. Smoke grew thicker as it billowed out the bedroom window.

"Floof," I mumbled. Tears tracked down my face.

Mom hugged me to her. "He'll take care of himself. He always does."

I squeezed my eyes shut as sirens filled the night. We

were helpless as the home I'd grown up in erupted in orange flames that lit the neighborhood. Other neighbors circled us as the fire department and police arrived.

I didn't see who draped a blanket over us, but I hadn't realized I was shivering until the fabric protected us from the cool night air.

Mom's face was set in stone, and she didn't let me go as Francis talked to a cop and they both walked toward us.

"How are you each doing?" The officer's black hair was pulled back in a ponytail, and her name tag read Bird. She was a few years older than me, and we'd always smiled and said hi when we passed each other on the street. But she was inspecting me and my mom now with a shrewd gaze, worry deep in her brown eyes.

"Fine," I said on a cough. Okay, I wasn't totally fine, but I could've been caught in the blaze that was stealing everything from me. Mom nodded like her answer was the same.

An ambulance rumbled down the street.

"I'll be right back." Officer Bird left only to point us out to the paramedics.

Mom coughed, which reminded my throat it was irritated, and I started coughing too. The lingering taste of smoke on my tongue was gross.

The next few moments were a blur. Paramedics checking me and Mom over. Shuffling us into the ambulance. I could walk to the hospital and clear out my lungs—it was only a few blocks away—but I was barefoot in pajamas.

"Is there anyone I can call?" Officer Bird asked. "Someone to meet you at the hospital?"

I rattled off Isla's number. I knew it better than I knew my own; we'd memorized each other's as kids. Isla would be frantic, but she'd race to the clinic. She could handle more than her family estimated.

They put me on the cot since I was coughing, and I gave the blanket to Mom. The male paramedic—Dylon, a few years older than Stetson, with a teenager I'd drawn blood on for a hemoglobin test last week—produced another blanket for me. I gratefully cuddled under it. Mom's face was streaked with dirt. Did I look the same? It wasn't every day I climbed out windows and jumped into flower beds.

At the hospital, they wanted to put us in different rooms, but Mom refused care. "I only caught a ride. Check her out. She got a bigger dose of smoke."

She perched on a hard plastic chair while Dylon helped me move from the cot to the exam bed. If I took a right out of the room and followed the long hallway, I'd be at the lab. On the other side of the lab was the clinic. The hospital had eight beds and two small rooms used for the ER. I'd been a patient in the clinic but never on the hospital side.

The nurse shut the door. Meghan was Mom's age and the best person I could've asked for. She'd known me as a kid, and she was a regular of Mom's.

Her smile was kind, reassuring. "Hey, Lyric. Erin. This isn't how we should meet up."

I smiled, but reality was sinking in. Mom and I had lost everything. I was in a hospital with nothing but the clothes on my back, and I had nowhere to go. A shudder ripped through me. *Hold it together.*

Meghan shoved an oximeter onto my finger and wrapped a blood pressure cuff around my upper arm. "I'll get you a warm blanket after I get your vitals. I'm going to go ahead and draw blood so when lab arrives, they can run it right away."

Arwyn was on call. She lived in town and would be here in minutes. I sighed. What a debacle. Mom and I didn't need medical bills, but we had nowhere to go. Paying for lab tests would cost the equivalent of rent right now. My money and cards were with my phone on my dresser in a bedroom that might not be there anymore.

I hiccuped through the tightness in my throat. The sterile smell of the hospital chased away the cough. My throat was irritated, but I was fine. I shouldn't have been exposed long enough to affect me or the baby.

Oh, no. The baby. The stream of automatic ER lab tests ran through my head. The staff would need to know my pregnancy status for possible tests and treatment. More people would find out, and I hadn't told the father yet.

Voices sounded outside, including a distinctive male voice that had been traced into my soul.

What was Stetson doing here? I wanted to sink into the bed. The delight of hearing his voice was quickly turning into a sobering realization.

"I think your friends showed up," Meghan murmured as she punched in information at a computer stand. "I can let them know to stay in the waiting room until you're ready."

I couldn't delay any longer. I was in the hospital, and I knew the standard blood panel ran in the ER. I trusted many of my coworkers, but I couldn't face both Mom and Stetson and confess I'd been too scared to tell them. Mom was the most important person in my life. She had to know.

And Stetson would be one of the most important people in the baby's life. Just because I couldn't have him didn't mean he didn't deserve to know before the night staff of the ER. "Actually, can I talk to them really quick? Just let them know I'm okay?"

My stomach twisted so hard I put my hand over my lips. This wasn't how telling Stetson or my mom or Isla was supposed to happen. It was supposed to be private. It was supposed to be on my time.

But then I was supposed to have used protection to keep from getting pregnant.

Meghan patted my arm and gave me a wink to let me know she'd bend the rules for me. The perk of being coworkers. "Just a couple of minutes. I've gotta grab the blood-draw cart anyway."

I nodded as bile rose in my throat. As soon as Meghan breezed out, saying, "You have two minutes, and I'm kicking you out when I come back," Stetson shouldered through the door.

A small ER meant the waiting room was around the corner. Too short of a walk before I was faced with the man I'd dreamed about for way too long. His dark-blond hair was mussed and ruffled, like he'd worn a hat all day and shoved his fingers through it all night. How could he wear ragged jeans with frayed hems and a hole in the knee and a tight black T-shirt and still be the best-looking man I'd ever seen?

Isla poked her head out from behind him and tried to shove him out of the way. "Oh my God, Lyric. Are you okay?" She swung on Mom. "Erin, oh my God. Are you okay?"

Stetson's gaze flicked away long enough to check on Mom, then he pinned me again. He took in my rumpled appearance, his gaze darkening as it swept down my body. I was huddled under the hospital blanket, but it was like he had laser vision. "What happened?"

"The trailer's gone." Mom's voice was hoarse. "Burned before our eyes."

Stetson's brow dropped. "Shit."

The rumble of the blood-draw cart sounded at the end of the hall. Meghan would be back soon. I swallowed, and my voice was hoarse when I spoke, but it had nothing to do with the fire. "I have to tell you all something before she gets back. They're going to draw blood, and they're going to do a pregnancy test." It might be standard, but I wanted them to.

I wanted the doctor to make sure everything was okay. "And it's going to be positive."

The air was sucked out of the room in a heartbeat. I couldn't move. Stetson went perfectly still, his gaze glued to mine. His normally chiseled face was as motionless as granite. Even his eyes, which hid a lot of his emotion if you didn't know what to look for—and I'd become an expert at reading them—were shuttered.

"Lyric?" Mom's disbelief was audible. "Wha— Who?"

From the corner of my eye, I saw her look between me and Stetson. Mom might've let my dad walk all over her, but she was far from clueless. She'd made it her goal to be savvy and read people. Her sharp inhale told me she'd interpreted the situation correctly. A small gift, not having to spell it out.

Isla's eyes widened. "Seriously? Oh, no. It's not that jackass who dumped—" She finally caught the charged stare between me and her brother. I didn't have to see the pieces click into place in her expression. Stetson acting shifty. My lack of alcohol. The way I couldn't take my eyes off him.

What was he thinking? I couldn't tell.

"Oh my God. Oh. My. *God*." Isla shoved him with both hands, the only thing that could break our eye contact. "You selfish bastard."

His attention on me broke long enough to flick his sister's hands away like they were fifteen and five again and he was teasing her. "We don't know it's mine."

He might as well have ripped my heart out of my chest. Tears burned my eyes, and I sniffled. "It's yours," I muttered. "Unless you want a rundown of my very reliable cycle."

"You were with a guy just weeks before—"

I shot him a glare that could cut marble. It was enough

to make him snap his lips together. "And you were with who? Should I ask them for pregnancy tests?"

Mom rose and smoothed out her robe. She touched Isla on the arm. "Perhaps we should give these two some privacy."

"How could you?" Isla stomped her foot, then adjusted her stance like she realized she'd pulled the spoiled brat move.

"Isla, let's give them some privacy for now." The two shuffled out the door, with Isla glaring at Stetson's back.

I wanted to flop back onto the thin pillow and cover my head with the blanket. This was the conversation I didn't want to face. "I'll get a paternity test done." I tried to be logical. If I was in his place, would I want the same thing? But in the end, it meant he didn't trust me and that... hurt. "They can do it while I'm pregnant."

"Are you sure it's mine?" he asked quietly.

"Certain. But I'll still do the test. I know how your parents will be." And there was the rest of the issue. The whole damn town would speculate otherwise. I didn't care, but Isla would. Naomi. Cameron. I didn't know what they would do if they didn't think the baby was Stetson's. But worse, I feared what they'd do when they learned it was. Would Liam 2.0 ensue? Or would Stetson's baby make them want to take over?

I shuddered. Neither option was ideal.

He sank onto the edge of the bed, nearly sitting on my feet. "Fuck, Lyric."

"Yeah." I curled my legs under me. Two months ago, I would've dreamed of being in the same bed with Stetson. This was not it. His spicy amber scent surrounded me. He'd used the same aftershave since I'd known him. So familiar. Comforting. But his shocked expression kept me rooted to my spot.

Meghan entered and went through the process of collecting blood as if she'd heard everything and was choosing to ignore it. Stetson switched to the chair Mom had been in, his big body swamping the thin piece of furniture.

"Dr. Klevin is on call, and he'll be here in a few minutes." Meghan wheeled the cart back out the door.

Dr. Klevin was professional. I trusted him to be discreet. I'd never been so grateful for a small hospital. I wanted the time to figure out how to hang on to what I had left of my life. I pushed on the bandage from the blood draw and flexed my arm. Well, the news was out. How far would it travel beyond the ER?

"What are we going to do?" Stetson asked, his words strained.

I met his deep-brown gaze. The traitorous fantasy I'd been harboring and refusing to acknowledge reared its head. He'd rejoice, go down on one knee, tell me I was the only girl in the world he wanted to spend the rest of his life with. Then he'd gush about the baby and the life we'd have together.

Happily ever after. Like the fairy tales.

Only, I was a broke med tech who lived with her mother and our home had just burned down. His first thought had been "Is it mine?"

Not the stuff of fairy tales.

I wanted him to have it as bad as or worse than me. The yearning. The constant desire. I wanted him to tell me I was his everything.

I couldn't change the way he was. I couldn't make him love me. So, yeah. Now what?

The fire gave me different circumstances to focus on. It wasn't much of a bright side, but I'd take it. "I have so much else to figure out. Mom and I lost *everything*. We don't even have anywhere to go after this. Our car keys were in the house. Our money. Our clothing." Tears sprang into my eyes and cascaded down my cheeks. "And I couldn't find Floof. What if he's dead?"

I didn't mean to wail, but of all the unfairness of my situation, losing my cat toppled my resilience.

A warm body crowded me on the bed, and I was drawn into his arms. "God, I'm sorry, Lyric. I was so stunned I almost forgot about the fire."

The comfort I'd been yearning for was mine. It wasn't about the baby, but the fire was traumatizing and I'd lost my cat. I needed someone in this moment, and he was there for me. I didn't know for how long, and that was almost as heartbreaking.

"He's gone, Stetson." I let myself sob into his hard chest. I was tired of my heart hurting.

* * *

Stetson

I pulled up in front of my parents' place at three in the morning, as close to the door as I could. Fuck the lawn.

"Wait here, all right?" I said to a wan Lyric in the front seat.

Isla hadn't spoken to me more than to agree about housing arrangements. Erin could stay in my old bedroom. The lower level had a kitchenette, so she wouldn't be on top of Mom or Dad. Isla could loan her clothing and take her to the trailer and do what she needed to do to reconcile the trailer house and the damage.

Lyric was coming home with me. If the situation wasn't so dire for her and her mom, I'd be giddy for a reason to have her close to me without admitting I'd been lusting after her for so long.

Mom was in the kitchen, dressed in black yoga pants and one of Dad's old T-shirts. I was surprised she'd let Dad sleep.

Isla and Erin stepped in.

"Thank you," Erin said to Mom. "I promise I'll be out of your hair as soon as possible."

Mom's expression was just shy of glacial. She at least covered the irritation I was sure she felt. "We'll get you on your feet again."

Isla ushered Erin downstairs, explaining the layout of the house and how she'd find clothing while Erin showered.

When they were out of earshot, Mom tipped her head toward me. "Why couldn't she stay at your place?"

"Lyric is staying with me. She's pregnant." This was the first time I'd said it out loud. It didn't feel real. More like I was telling Mom about an acquaintance's news. Lyric was a casual friend, and it was best to throw the verbal punch instead of warning Mom about it. I'd learned the hard way. She didn't like being lied to or misled, and I was old enough to remember her reaction when she'd learned about Dad's affair. "It's probably mine."

Silence roared in my ears as Mom digested the news.

"Probably?" Her hiss could melt ice.

If I had a hat on, I'd clutch it in front of me. I didn't know how I felt. Disappointment balanced on a precipice, ready to topple at the news the baby might not be mine, but I couldn't admit that. Not to Mom, not to myself. I trusted Lyric, but when it came to relationships, I knew her activities probably as well as she knew mine.

I'd seethed inside every time she met some asshole at Rattler's. I didn't care if they'd cured cancer and solved the world peace problem. Assholes. All of them. None topped six months with her, and I'd been dreading watching her find "the one."

I'd been ready to step in if her ex Cole passed the six-month mark. When they were at Rattler's together, he'd eye up other women behind her back, and I didn't like the constant threat of *I can do better* in his voice when he talked to her. My restraint at not throwing him out of the restaurant should've won a medal.

"I just found out," I finally said. "Lyric and I have a lot to talk about, but she has to find a place to live, a way to replace her belongings, and then we can talk about...the baby."

"The baby," Mom echoed, blood leaching from her face. "Again with what to do about the baby." She shook the past off her shoulders, her expression back to business. "Fine. Get her on her feet so she can get out of your house. Then once we know if the baby is even yours, we'll move forward with what to do."

Everything Mom said rubbed me raw, but it was the middle of the night, and I wouldn't change her personality at three in the morning. "Hope you can get back to sleep." I ducked outside.

Lyric was curled in my front seat, and damn, I took a few extra seconds to watch her. She was in *my* pickup, her head resting against the window, her hand tucked under her chin.

She straightened when I got inside. The faint smell of smoke lingered on her and filled the cab. I didn't say anything as I took the driveway to the road and drove the half mile to my place.

I'd built this house at the highest point of our land. The stunning view to the south and east was the tradeoff for taking the brunt of the brutal wind before the three rows of trees flanking the north and west sides of my property grew tall enough to offer protection. Lyric had been one of the first to see the place with Isla when she was nothing but my little sister's best friend.

But taking the driveway in the dead of night with her felt right. She knew my place. I could help her be comfortable and recover.

I parked in the attached garage, using the stall closest to the house. The Chevy was in the other stall.

She was slipping out when I got around to her side. I picked her up, trying hard not to enjoy feeling her in my arms again. Not the right time. Would there ever be?

She squeaked and flung her arms around my shoulders. "What are you doing?"

"You don't have shoes on."

She went lax, and I cradled her closer for no damn good reason. "Thanks," she mumbled.

I would've done this at the hospital, but Meghan had pushed her to my pickup in a wheelchair. Lyric had given her mom the gripper slippers reserved for patients.

I took her to my bed. Yeah, I had a guest bedroom, but I couldn't have forced myself to go down that hallway if I'd tried. And I didn't try.

I set her on my California king bed. She rubbed her hands over her face. Fatigue hung from every inch of her body.

"You're not going to work tomorrow." I wasn't asking. She didn't have her phone, and I'd keep the house quiet so she could sleep.

"Arwyn messaged Joan, and Joan told her to tell me to stay home until Monday. She'll take my shifts." A small smile lifted her lips. "HIPAA only goes so far when your coworkers are considerate."

I waved to the giant chest of drawers against the wall.

"Go ahead and shower and grab whatever you need out of my dresser."

The smile vanished, and she blinked like she'd just realized I'd put her in my room. It'd felt so natural. She'd been in my house before, just quick stops with Isla. I didn't like big gatherings at my place. I left that to Holden. I already had enough people in my business; I wanted my home as my safe space.

"I'm not wearing any of Krystal's shit."

"I cleaned all that out," I grunted. She'd had crap squirreled away everywhere, without asking me first. "I've got shirts and shorts. You'll swim in them, but they'll do until Isla and your mom get some clothing from the store."

Some tension left her shoulders. "I've gotta—"

"Do nothing but clean up, and only so you can sleep better and feel better when you wake up."

"Stetson." She said my name on a sigh. I didn't know if she wanted to argue about my bedroom or talk about the baby or tell a joke—it didn't matter.

"Get some rest, Lyric. That's all you need to do for the rest of the night and tomorrow. Need a bite to eat before you go to sleep?"

She wrinkled her nose. "No. Maybe some water?"

I jutted my chin toward the bathroom. The barn-style door was open. For a bathroom door, it was my favorite decor in the room. "I'll bring some in when you're done."

In the kitchen, I listened for the shower. It kicked on, and I nodded. Good. I got her ice water and a few saltine crackers, just in case. I didn't know shit about pregnant women, but I'd have to learn. I was determined to.

Lyric was pregnant. And the baby was likely mine. It made sense. I'd seen her face when she realized we didn't use protection. The stunned shock wasn't the look worn by someone used to going bareback.

Did I want— No. The middle of the night wasn't the time to ponder my feelings and wonder how my family would deal with it. I'd gotten Isla's negative reaction. Mom's wheels were already turning. All that shit could wait for another day.

When the water turned off, I gave her a few minutes to dry off and get dressed. Thankfully, with the events of the night, it was easy to ignore a naked Lyric in my bathroom. Wearing my clothing.

I hadn't closed the bedroom door. Neither had she, but I knocked on the doorframe.

"Yeah?"

She was pulling back the covers and lifted the blankets like she was inspecting the sheets.

"I wash them regularly." I might've been able to keep from thinking about her in my bedroom, making herself comfortable, but when her bare legs were sticking out from my gray Coal Haven Drillers T-shirt she swam in, I couldn't dwell on anything else.

Under the loose material, her ass swayed with her movements. The floral tattoos on her ankles, which I'd staunchly avoided studying, were vibrant and on display. Same with the twining rose around her forearm and a tiny point of the mariner's compass sticking past the collar of my shirt on her back. The purple ends of her hair hung damp over her shoulders.

"How regularly?" she asked, her tone dubious.

"Last weekend." I might be a bachelor, but I refused to let my home fall into the stereotype. Getting dirty was part of my job, but I didn't let it contaminate my space. "I haven't been with anyone since you," I added quietly.

If anyone else had noticed, they hadn't mentioned it. My sex life was no one's business, but I just really wanted

Lyric in my bed, and if my confession helped, I would repeat it a hundred more times.

She glanced over her shoulder, a dark brow arched. "You gonna be okay?"

A laugh burst out of me. Her comment was the last thing I'd expected, but I should've. This was Lyric. "Smart-ass."

She must've been satisfied with my answer. She climbed into the bed, stayed sitting, and draped the blankets over her lap.

I handed her the water, hating how badly I wished I could crawl in next to her.

She drank the whole glass in a few long pulls.

"Want more?"

She shook her head and set the glass on the side table. "No. I have to pee enough as it is now."

"Now?" I'd really have to learn about pregnant women. How big was the baby?

"I think it's the hormones this early. Then it'll be the size and position, but I haven't read up on it much. Honestly, it's still sinking in."

"How long have you known?" Six weeks. When was the earliest women could tell?

"Only a couple of days. I suspected..." Her face was drawn like the stress of wondering had been placed on top of everything that had happened tonight. "But I had to figure out how to take a test without anyone being in my business, and then I had to get the guts to do it. And once I knew, I had to figure out when and how to tell you. The fire took care of that."

I didn't ask her the specifics. I already felt shitty that she'd been dealing with all that alone while I'd moped around town.

Pressure squeezed around my lungs. We hadn't talked a

lot in the hospital room. There'd been long stretches of waiting, but her labs had been normal, her oxygen levels were fine, and the doctor had let her go. Still, we had decided little more than that she'd stay here until she got back on her feet.

And after … I didn't know. I didn't want to think about her leaving my house, and I'd meant what I said. She didn't need to worry about it tonight.

"Thanks for telling me," I said, losing the game of sounding chill. She needed rest anyway, and I needed … I wasn't sure. "Want the light on or off?"

She lay back and burrowed farther under the covers, snuggling against my pillows. Something inside me shifted, altered, and I wasn't sure it'd ever return to the way it was. "Mind leaving the hallway light on? I usually shut the bedroom door so Floof wouldn't wake me—"

Her eyes misted over. Ah, hell. The cat.

"Yeah," I said, my voice gruff. "I'll leave the hallway light on."

"Thanks." Her voice was tiny, but I turned away and forced myself to march out of the room.

I went to the guest bedroom. My feet would hang off the end of the queen-size bed, and I didn't have any clothes to change into. There was probably a load in the dryer if I was in a bind. Bothering Lyric by going into my bedroom wasn't an option.

Besides, as tired as I was, I wasn't sure I could sleep. Restless energy coursed through my body. The need to do something wouldn't let me shut my eyes for long.

I waited several minutes, sitting on the edge of the bed and staring at the taupe carpet. When I thought enough time had passed and Lyric was asleep, I walked as silently as I could through the house and out the front door. I hopped in my pickup and drove away.

Three

LYRIC

I suffered through the few moments after waking up in which everything that happened the night before registered. The awareness of being curled up in Stetson's bed sank in, and I buried my head deeper under the covers.

Light streamed through the large picture window. Who had a picture window in their bedroom?

I stuck my head out and blinked.

What a view. An obnoxiously bright view, but gorgeous. Green pastures with small rolling hills greeted me. Black dots of grazing cows and the twinkling blue of a stock pond consoled me more than anything else had so far.

I let out a long breath. Stetson had left shortly after I'd gone to bed. My mind had been whirling way too fast to succumb to exhaustion. Then he'd left.

Where would he go just hours before dawn?

Jealousy acted like an unruly puppy, gnawing at my belly. I sat up and pushed the covers away. Stetson's shirt was twisted around me. I straightened it. I had just opened a drawer and grabbed. The whole act was too intimate for my taste, and I had wanted to get it over with.

Where would he go?

I haven't been with anyone since you.

Those words shouldn't satisfy me so thoroughly.

I swung my legs over the side and took my time standing. I stretched sore muscles and ran fingers through unruly hair while I checked out the surprisingly simple but tasteful decor.

The window had blackout shades that he probably didn't need to draw very often. He was up before sunrise and outside working most of the day. Isla had said he shunned all things corporate. Stetson's own rebellion against his father.

Cameron had wanted him to follow in his refinery CEO footsteps. But Stetson had refused. I doubted he even used an alarm clock.

Then there was the trendy barn door for the bathroom and a stunning photograph of racing wild horses. The furniture was a set and matched the dusky wood of the bathroom door.

I used to dream of living in a house like this. A home with real walls and space for decent-sized furniture. Mom and I used to joke it was a good thing we were short and didn't need a big couch or more than full-size beds.

After using the bathroom and stealing a fingertip full of his toothpaste, I dug back into his dresser. His shorts would be ridiculously large on me, but I couldn't go parading around his home in nothing but a shirt.

I haven't been with anyone since you.

My mind kept wanting to scream *What does that mean?* Was he too hung up on me to date? Had I captivated him and no one else would suffice? But I had more to worry about. Stetson's comment didn't have anything to do with rebuilding a place to live or the baby, so it wasn't my concern.

I dug through the drawer I'd gotten the shirt from, but it was packed full of T-shirts. Without thinking, I leaned in and inhaled. Fresh breeze-scented fabric softener and a hint of his spicy amber aftershave. Stetson's smell.

I caught myself inhaling to catch more of his scent and shoved the drawer closed and checked the next one. I pulled out a pair of basketball shorts and held them up. A giggle escaped. Not a chance they'd stay around my waist. I put them back and dug around. A scrap of red caught my eye.

With slightly more thought than when I sniffed his laundry, I tugged it out. Lacy underwear. I frowned and turned my head. One side was snapped apart. The jealousy I dreaded when it came to Stetson ignited in my belly.

Wait. My stomach untwisted as I recognized the fabric.

This was my underwear. From the day we...

I thought back. Every moment was stamped into my brain. The way I'd climbed his body like my own personal Mount Everest. How completely he'd filled me. The care he'd taken getting me ready for his size.

He'd torn these off, but he hadn't tossed them on the floor. He'd stuffed them into his pocket.

And he'd kept them. Laundered and neatly folded and tucked in the bottom of his drawer.

Had he planned on giving them back? They were ruined, but he kept them. What did it mean?

I put them where I'd found them. Where was he?

I walked through the house to get to the kitchen. The rest of his house was decorated like his bedroom. Photographs of horses and nature artfully graced his walls. The furniture was sturdy, quality, and matched the wood-work of the rest of the house like it did in his bedroom.

When I'd first seen his place complete, I recalled thinking someone had put a lot of thought into the design.

The overstuffed couch was as inviting as the plush love seat. A glider rocker topped off the *U* of furniture facing a large-screen TV mounted on the wall. The kitchen always left a yawning emptiness in my chest.

I loved baking. Mom and I had gotten creative while cooking in the trailer house. We had been limited on storage, but we had our system.

Stetson's kitchen counter held labeled bins for coffee and tea pods, for fuck's sake. Who had space for that?

My stomach gurgled. Mentally I didn't have an appetite, but if I didn't eat something bread-like, the heartburn would flare up.

I made myself toast and munched on it. It was almost nine. I hadn't gotten much sleep, but I would've been at work for almost two hours already if this were a normal day. But it was the furthest from a normal day I'd ever had, including when my dad had walked out.

I had nothing to do but wait in Stetson's large shirt. I wandered around his house, growing frustrated about not hearing any news, being unable to receive any news, and wondering why Stetson had taken off in the middle of the night. I had no phone. Stetson had no landline. All I could do was watch TV and wait.

It was way too easy to curl up in the corner of his big couch, toss a blue plaid fleece blanket over my lap, and get lost in all of his viewing options.

Nearly an hour had ticked by when I heard the drone of an engine. I wrapped a blanket around myself and walked to the window. Stetson's pickup pulled into the garage. I sucked in a long breath. This was it. Daylight shone outside, and it was time to discuss the revelation from last night. Nerves knotted in my stomach as I went through the kitchen to the mudroom just as Stetson opened the door.

A furry bundle was trapped in his brawny arm. I gasped. "Floof!"

Elation swept through me as I dove for my cat. He was squirming in Stetson's hold and meowed when he noticed me. I grabbed him in a bear hug and buried my face in his smoky fur, not caring that I was sobbing.

My cat was alive.

"I'll grab the rest of his stuff," Stetson said.

I popped my head up. "What stuff?" Did something survive the fire?

Stetson was dressed in the same clothing he'd been in last night. Fatigue lined his eyes. "I didn't find him until it was daylight. I couldn't go into the trailer, but I waited by the sidewalk, randomly calling for him. A couple of hours ago, he finally jumped out the window, but I don't think he'd been in there all night. Then we had to wait for the farm supply store to open to get food and a litter box."

He'd done all that while I was sleeping? Touched, I stated the obvious. "You don't have indoor pets." He had barn cats he fed and took care of but none of them had migrated into the house no matter how many times Isla and I had caught him with a kitten tucked in the crook of his elbow. Same with his dogs over the years. He loved his dogs, but they'd been outdoors only. He'd claimed animals had jobs on a ranch.

Stetson lifted a big shoulder. "Floof is used to being indoors. It's not like bringing a barn cat in and not knowing if they'll use the litter box—which I bought new."

A tidal wave of relief slammed into me. Floof had survived and seemed healthy. He must've been hiding under the bed and jumped out after Mom and I had escaped.

And he could've been lost, but Stetson had stayed awake

all night to get him. I set my cat down and threw my arms around Stetson. His arms immediately banded around me.

"Thank you," I murmured into his neck.

"He's important to you."

I looked up, past his strong jawline to those brown eyes I'd only been this close to once. Everyone talked about how hot Stetson was. He was big and good-looking, with a great personality. But I'd fallen in love with his eyes. They told a deeper story. They were the glimpse inside to the real him I doubted he'd shown anyone.

I stroked the side of his face, and his eyelids hooded. "I found my underwear in your drawer."

Stetson didn't blush. The man pretended like nothing embarrassed him, but it was in his eyes, for those who bothered to look. "I didn't want to throw them out."

I rose on my tiptoes, and he leaned his head down. I cupped the side of his face. "Why not?"

"That day was fucking hot, Ricky."

Only he called me Ricky. And he usually did it to annoy me, but all it did right now was coat my insides like warm butter. "I thought you'd forgotten about it."

"I'll take that day with me to my grave. The way you—" He cut off with a growl and claimed my mouth.

I launched into his arms, wrapping my legs around his waist, and got a hard denim reminder that I never did find shorts to wear.

He groaned and licked into my mouth. He tasted sweet, like Twizzlers and the Coke he'd chased it with. *Breakfast of champions*, he'd joked once, and I never thought I'd be a firsthand witness to the flavor on his tongue.

He backed up and turned, setting my ass on the counter. Fire whipped down my spine, and the energy coiled between my thighs matched the power I had them wrapped around.

We weren't doing this again, were we?

I hoped so. Just like our first time together, I didn't want to think; I just wanted it to happen. But he didn't rush like he did then. He took his time exploring my mouth. He lapped against my tongue while his thumb strummed a steady beat against my peaked nipple through his shirt.

I ground against the fly of his jeans. My hormones had been all over the place for the last six weeks, but they were focused on the man in my arms. When I groaned, he broke the kiss to trail down my neck. I tipped my head back, and when he dragged up the hem of my shirt, I whispered, "Yes."

He nibbled at my neck as his rough fingertip grazed over the nipple he hadn't been stroking. I anchored my hands onto the countertop and arched my back into him.

"You need this?" His rough voice was everything I'd dreamed of. When he would talk to me, his words were always laced with a teasing sarcasm, but not now. He sounded as off-kilter and needy as I felt.

A vibration broke through the haze of lust I was under. I swallowed, trying to catch my breath. "Is that your phone?"

"Fuck my phone."

Reality started to sink in, and I tensed. He paused, his hand over my breast, my lower body bare and pressed against him. "Whatever it is, it can wait two minutes for me to get you off. You need this."

I wanted that more than anything. The outside world could wait. I licked my lips, and he tracked the movement of my tongue. "What about you?"

"I need this too." He released my breast to brush his hand down my belly, pausing slightly at my abdomen. Just when I thought things would get heavy and not hot and heavy, he continued, slipping his thumb down to stroke over my clit.

"Remember when I got you off last time?"

I moaned. His soft touch was an intoxicating contrast to his rough skin. "How could I forget?"

"You came so fucking fast, Ricky. All over my tongue."

"Oh, God." I leaned back, giving him better access, needing more.

He continued his lazy circles, not caring how wet I was getting against his clothing. The bulge in his pants was enough to ride, creating delicious friction where I needed it the most.

"You can be loud this time. I want to hear my name when you come."

I strained against him, meeting his hot gaze. His focus was solely on me. *Me.* I had Stetson Barron all to myself. We weren't hiding, doing it fast in the back of Holden's barn. "Stetson."

"That's it, baby. Louder." He increased the pace, and I welcomed it.

"Stetson," I groaned.

He switched the position of his hand and slipped a finger inside. "You're so fucking wet, Ricky."

I exploded. "Oh, God, Stetson!"

"Yes." The word was guttural.

I rode his hand, greedily taking every ounce of pleasure he could give. He was using only one hand, but it was more than I'd ever gotten. Except that one other time. With him.

I shuddered when I came down, but his other arm was secured around me. The front of his pants was wet, and his erection pressed angrily against the fly. It had to be uncomfortable. Yet the smug satisfaction in his face contradicted the pressure behind his zipper.

"Stetson." I didn't know what I wanted to say, but understanding filled his eyes.

He leaned back and traced a line from my wet center to my belly button. "This isn't over. We have a lot to talk about, Lyric." He flattened his hand on my belly. His fingers were still wet. The sight made a lump form in my throat. There was a sense of rightness that was almost heartbreaking. "But that's for later."

He used his clean hand to dig his phone out. Isla's name flashed across the screen. He set it on the counter. "Go ahead and call her back while I get the cat's things and shower."

He stepped away. The hem of the shirt fell to cover my lap, and I thought we were done. But he pressed a hard, quick kiss to my lips before he turned away. I watched his broad back disappear into the mudroom.

I was left bereft. How could I have gone from wondering how he'd react to my pregnancy to coming on his counter? Something I didn't think would happen again, not before or after the talk we hadn't yet had about the baby. Not after his distanced reaction in the ER. I blinked at the cabinets on the other side of the room until Floof twined around the corner, rubbing his tail against the wall. Stetson had saved my damn cat. That was going to mess me up more than anything.

* * *

Stetson

"What the hell, Stetson?" Holden was staring at me like we'd never met but I'd just told him when his birthday was and what he wore when he slept.

I happened to know both details, but only because he was my cousin and best friend.

I shoved my hands into my jeans pockets and rocked back on my booted heels. The hot summer wind kicked past me, buffeting my shirt. Lyric had gone with her mom and Isla to run to the thrift store and to find out what they could recover from the trailer. I had stopped at Holden's to ask him to help me out with chores so I could be freed up for Lyric.

The poleaxed way he was staring at me wasn't right. Holden got me. He was taken now, going from a raging bachelor to the ultimate family man within months.

His newfound love romance had cost me a lot of time with my best friend. Holden was my cousin, but we'd been attached at the hip since he was old enough to walk. He was the only other person who got what it was like being not just a Barron, but the oldest. To have powerful parents who often didn't care who they stepped on. To have expectations and be scrutinized: where we did business, how we did business, who we did business with. Our family had weaponized its wealth so often that sometimes buying a candy bar at the Cenex meant my next stop for a Coke would be at the other gas station across the street. I couldn't appear to favor one business or the owners would think they'd upset the Barrons and lost their cash flow.

"I know," I said. "She thinks it's mine." I wanted it to be. The idea had been planted and was flourishing at an alarming rate. A kid. With Lyric. Fuck, she'd be a good mom. Not too uptight. She wouldn't get wrapped up in drama. And smart as hell.

Would I be a good dad? I didn't have much to offer other than a house, a pickup, and the urge to be more nurturing than my parents were.

Being a good provider and a good parent wasn't always the same. I wanted to be both. I thought I could be both or I wouldn't have built a house to make my family's home.

"Do you think it is?" Holden asked.

"I mean..." I shrugged. I'd sound like a dick if I doubted

it was mine. I took off my black ball cap with a refinery name from two buyouts ago, stuffed a hand through my hair, and replaced my cap. "I've never skipped using protection, and she'd been broken up with her jackass boyfriend for a couple of weeks. Makes sense, you know."

He blinked at me. We dressed similarly. We resembled each other. I was like the zoomed-in version of him with darker hair. Older and bigger, but our expressions were often similar. "Is the big deal right now the fact that everyone knows you two were together?"

"I don't know who knows. Us. My parents and Isla. Lyric's mom. The doctor and nurse from the ER. She would only be six weeks along." The explosion of gossip when outsiders found out would be like an annoying mosquito buzzing around my face. I wanted to swat it before it could bite me.

He glanced back at his house. The kids were at their dad's in Arizona for a couple weeks before school started, and Emery was at work. Would she have heard? I know confidentiality was big in the clinic and the hospital, but this was Coal Haven. Top-tier gossip took priority.

"You two did it at my wedding?" His tone was scandalized—but also impressed.

"It just happened," I grumbled, my face heating. I didn't usually get embarrassed talking about my exploits with Holden.

"Apparently. No wonder we couldn't find you when Krystal showed up."

I winced. Aw, hell. Krystal worked at the clinic.

I was so done with her bullshit. She'd finally left me alone after I told her we were done. I'd made a mistake getting back together with her, and it'd never happen again.

But then I'd said that before, so she'd considered it nothing more than a mere speed bump.

I took my hat off and worked my fingers around the rim. "If I'm being honest, I've been... Lyric is... I wanted her, man. I really fucking wanted her. I have for a while."

His dirty-blond brows lifted, going higher as my confession sank all the way in. "You hid it well. I knew she had a thing for you."

"What?"

"Seriously, Stetson?"

I shook my head. "What do you mean?"

"She's crushed on you for years. *Years*. Haven't you noticed?"

I cleared my throat. "I've been trying not to notice her since she came home from college that one year."

"What one year?"

I scowled and worked my fingers harder against the material of my hat, like I was trying to flatten wrinkles that weren't there. "When she and Isla were finally old enough to drink and I let them come out to the cabin at the lake. And she wore that damn red bikini." Red, like the underwear she'd worn the first time we were together. "I took some fucking notice that day."

"Then why didn't you do anything?"

"She's Isla's best friend. I didn't even think she was coming back to Coal Haven." The girl was intelligent. She could've gone anywhere in the country. Maybe even the world. But she came home to be with her mom. "Then she did, and well, Isla doesn't have anyone."

"Doesn't mean you'll take her away."

Which was exactly why the hookup shouldn't have happened. My parents barely tolerated Lyric as Isla's friend. How'd they react now? "Mom. Dad."

Holden opened his mouth and slammed it shut, then nodded. I didn't have to explain. "How are they taking it?"

"Dunno." I didn't care. That'd come soon enough—

when Mom told me how I was supposed to care. "You know they won't want me with Lyric. Mom only tolerated her 'cause Isla couldn't make any other friends, and Dad does whatever Mom wants."

My sister was painfully shy and a Barron. Two personality traits that pulled against each other, leaving her immobilized between wanting to hide in a corner or stomp her foot and ask for the manager. I'd made it my mission to help her with whatever she needed, and as she'd gotten older, she hadn't asked for much.

"You're afraid your mom's going to make your life hell?"

"I'm afraid she's going to make Lyric's life hell." Lyric was used to my cold, insinuating mother. But what if Mom decided to open her mouth? What caustic insults would she sling around? And how long before Lyric distanced herself from me because of it? She wouldn't be the first girl to do that.

"Shit, man. I don't know." He toed the tip of his boot in the ground. "You can't let your parents treat the baby like Liam."

"No fucking way," I said, my tone as hot as the sun on my forehead. I crushed my cap back on. "No way."

He didn't say anything, but then he never did about me and Liam. Holden and Liam were friendly. Growing as close as family every year, but both of them were conscious of me and my parents. I was grateful for their burgeoning relationship, but my envy was slowly building.

I hated the arrangement, but suffering the alternative once was enough.

"Whatever you need," Holden finally said. "Give me a call and I'll help out."

"Can you hay the ditch to Allen's place?" Funny we still called it that. The uncle I never met. My dad had two brothers and one sister. Kira was Holden's mom. My uncle

Bruce was on the other side of town—our family's land stretched that far. And Allen, the uncle Dad drove away to Texas. The land was no longer his, but Dad had always called those sections Allen's land. They were in Dad's name, and they would become mine. One day.

Didn't feel right with Allen's oldest living by Uncle Bruce now. Archer had married a local girl, and my dad had been an asshole to him. I didn't get a chance to talk to Archer much, but at least he was friendly with me. However, he was closer to Liam's family.

The great dividing factor: who talked to Liam and who didn't.

Foreboding hung on my shoulders. Would my kid be born surrounded by fences with their grandma whispering in their ear about who they could and couldn't talk to?

Four

LYRIC

Mom went into the Barrons' house. It was hard for us to quit calling it the owl house while she was staying there. She'd almost slipped once. I had told Isla once that I thought her house looked like an owl from the outside, and she told me her mom would carve my tongue out with a spoon if I said it around her.

How had I survived a lifelong friendship with Isla?

Naomi had terrified me as a kid. As an adult, I tolerated her like an ornery old horse Isla once had as a kid. We were all instructed to give the mare a wide berth. She had dominated the pasture until she passed. Horses and people were finally able to tread in that area without fear.

Sad to compare Naomi to the mare, but accurate.

I sat on the porch swing next to Isla. For the last twenty years, we'd sat on the same swing, letting the chains squeak as we rocked and pondered our lives.

"Thanks for running us everywhere today." It was the

third time I'd thanked her. She'd picked me up three hours ago from Stetson's. Mom had managed to grab my phone, keys, and purse from the bedroom, along with a laundry basket full of randomly grabbed clothes for me and one for her. Hopefully, I could get the electrical smoke smell out.

I had been surprised she was allowed in the place, but she'd gone shifty when I commented. I could picture Erin Finnegan climbing through the bedroom window she'd fled from last night. I got my streak of rebellion from somewhere, and it wasn't my deadbeat dad.

She and Isla had already procured two tote bags of clothing from the thrift shop for each of us to wear until we replenished our stock. Mom had driven my car here and planned to do laundry all day.

"Stop already," Isla said. "You know you'd do it for me."

We fell quiet. Today had been nothing but logistics. We hadn't gone deeper than what we'd needed to get done. I'd ignored stares as I wore Isla's too-tight linen shorts and college sweater to the small department store in town and picked up toiletries to get me through until my online order arrived.

What had people heard? Everyone in town had to know about the fire, but what else?

Since I'd been with Isla, no one had approached me to talk. A common occurrence that normally made me feel for how isolated Isla was but a relief today.

I'd used Stetson's phone to order the essentials, shoes, and some clothing. The packages would land on his doorstep early next week. I didn't know where I'd be by then. So much to think about, but I was putting it off until later.

The necessities were taken care of. We had shelter, food, and clothing. The trailer house was in Mom's name. She'd have to do all the insurance claims. I had enough to get me back to work.

So that left the brooding elephant in the room, the guy who'd given me a body-numbing orgasm this morning. My best friend's brother. "I'm sorry I didn't tell you. And I'm sorry I slept with him."

She slid her gaze to me. "Are you sure about that last part?"

"What do you mean?"

"You've been into Stetson since we were thirteen," she said dryly.

"You knew?"

"I think everyone knows, Lyric."

My cheeks burned. I'd have loved for the porch to turn into a black hole and swallow me up. "I didn't think he'd ever ... I didn't think he thought of me as more than his little sister's annoying friend."

"I didn't either."

She was uncharacteristically quiet about the subject. If Isla said a guy was a loser, I asked her if it was a little *L* or capital *L*. She was right more than she was wrong. For the first time, I hadn't listened to her about Cole, but he'd definitely been a capital *L*.

"I'm worried, Lyric," she finally said. "He's almost ten years older than you. He's been a bachelor for a long time. Krystal has an *aggressive*"—she put a hand up to punctuate her description—"personality, but her tipping point, what made us go from 'get a load of this girl' to 'whoa, you should get a restraining order,' was his lack of commitment. Not that she should've acted like she did. That part wasn't Stetson's fault. But he still had a role in why that relationship failed. He's the common denominator in all his failed relationships. Don't get me wrong— he won't cheat on you. But he won't do more than coast with anyone, and that's not what you want from him. And it's not what you deserve. Especially with a baby involved."

Hearing my fears confirmed chased away any lingering glow from this morning. He was her brother. She loved him, she wanted what was best for him, but she also knew him better than almost anyone.

Except she was wrong about one thing. "I think what bothered the women he's dated is that he does commit. He commits so hard." Isla's brows drew together, and I nodded. "But it's to his family, and he didn't make those women his family. I don't know what I'm saying other than I see it. I don't think I'm different from them other than that I know. I might've had a huge crush on him, but I'm not in crush territory anymore. I have a baby to think about. My own welfare. I'm not going all moony-eyed over Stetson." No matter how much I thought of him, dreamed of him, fantasized about him. Reality was keeping my feet grounded.

"I get it, Lyric. I'm just worried."

Me too.

If he had rescued Floof and then went to shower, would I have been more resolute? Or more confused?

He'd said he hadn't been with anyone else, and then he'd made me come in his kitchen. Yet I wouldn't call him my boyfriend, and we were *way* out of roommate territory.

I checked the time on my phone. Stetson had asked if I was going to eat supper at his place. I'd had no plans for today other than to piece together what the fire hadn't burned away. Curiosity had made me tell him I'd be back by six. Was he going to cook? Did he expect me to cook?

What even were we?

He'd said we had a lot to talk about. I definitely had questions. Did either of us have answers?

It was after five. The countdown until I could see him

again was on in my head. "I should get going. I need to get all my laundry—new and old—washed tonight."

"I'll take your mom to pick up her car."

"Thanks for grabbing mine."

Isla stopped the porch swing by planting her toes on the deck. "No problem. We figured you'd need a way to leave quickly when Mom gets back."

Naomi wasn't home. She worked in the city offices. Most city employees were probably gone this late on a Friday, but Naomi was either super dedicated to the upcoming Labor Day festivities of Coal Haven or she was avoiding me and my mom.

"How's she taking it?" I asked. A chill crept over my skin. How would her reaction affect me? Naomi was going to be my kid's grandparent. I refused to be scared of her anymore. I respected her fearsome reputation, but that didn't mean I respected her. I also had to care about the mom of my best friend. How were things going to change?

"I don't know. I doubt she'll talk to me about it." Bitterness stained her tone, like it often did when she thought her mom treated her like she was hapless and helpless.

"I'll find out soon enough. I'm not going to worry about it now." I rose just as Mom came out of the house like she was looking for something, anything, to do. Downtime made her antsy.

"Are you leaving?" When I nodded, she said, "I'll grab as much as I can when Isla takes me back to the trailer. When I finish laundry, I'll spend the evening clearing the loft above the store."

The little apartment was a small place. We'd be cramped in the loft that could fit into half of Stetson's upper level. I shoved the thought away. I'd miss his place once I had somewhere to go.

I gave her a quick hug and took the porch stairs down to my car. The little blue Toyota Corolla had been my first purchase once I had a steady paycheck. I was still paying it off.

When I slid in, I opened the window. Hints of smoke that I hoped would eventually fade filled the interior.

On the way to Stetson's, my belly flipped and flopped. How had I acted normal around Isla all day after this morning?

Our one-night stand had resulted in a baby. I'd thought that was the end of it. He hadn't talked to me since. He'd actively avoided me. And then he'd refused to let Isla go to the hospital alone. He hadn't known I was pregnant then. And he hadn't been with anyone since me.

God, I was confused. He was displaying un-Stetson-like behavior.

He was more like the Stetson from my secret fantasies. A guy who looked at me like I was the moon and stars. A man who was so dedicated to me he'd never think of leaving during our sixty years of marriage. Husband and father material. Not like my dad.

His pickup was parked outside the garage, but he'd left the garage door closest to the house open. The bay was empty. Assuming it was for me and trying not to read into the considerateness of the action, I pulled in.

Before I'd even climbed out of the car, Stetson had opened the door to the house and gone to the trunk, where I had stashed the belongings Mom had rescued and my bags from the store. He loaded his hands up with the bags and still lifted the laundry basket, his biceps bulging like he was doing a photo shoot for *Hot Man Candy Monthly*.

"I can get something," I said.

"Go on in."

The haunting normality of the situation crept in, turning my belly flips into a tantalizing heat. Could we have a replay of what happened on the counter? My car in Stetson's garage. Him hauling my belongings in. I sniffed, and my stomach rumbled. Savory smells emanated from inside the house.

I was in my dream. This was what I'd envisioned when I was fifteen and I heard he'd broken up with girlfriend number... Well, we'd all lost count by that point. He'd been planning this house, and my first thought when I saw it was *I want that.*

The place of my dreams. The man from my dreams.

Almost ten years had passed since that day, and here I was.

Only, the circumstance was so different from what I had imagined.

I shoved all that to the back of my mind. Laundry and food. Those were my only two priorities for the night. They were safe topics. "Are you cooking something?"

"The meatloaf is almost done."

I nearly groaned. "With baked potatoes?"

"You like them extra crispy, right?"

"Basically a whole potato french fry, yes."

He grinned, and *God*, it was devastating. The way his natural mischievousness gave way to pride. He thrived on taking care of the people he loved. I could pretend I was in that category for a hot second.

"They've been baking for two hours."

On a moan, I went into the house. Homey smells wrapped around me like a comfortable blanket. I stepped back into the mudroom. The washer and dryer were tucked into the corner.

He set the basket on the counter. "Where do you want the bags?"

I sorted through the clothing, tossing my scrubs in for the first load. "I'll keep the tote bags so I can take the tags off the clothes and wash them. The rest can go…" Where? I had slept in his room last night. Where was I going to sleep tonight?

He peered into one of the shopping bags. "I'll put them in my bathroom."

"Stetson…" I didn't know what to say, familiar trepidation creeping into my voice.

He must've heard the gravity in my voice because he stopped to watch me. My gaze stroked over the dark stubble along his jaw. His whiskers didn't have the burnished highlights his hair picked up from working outside. My palm itched to stroke over his face. I'd been this close to him before, but never just us, just talking. And we needed to talk.

"What are we doing?" It came out as a whisper.

"Nothing you don't want to."

I wanted all of it—that was the problem. But I didn't want to be destroyed by a fantasy that would stay just that for only so long. Hadn't I just told Isla I knew where Stetson's loyalties lay? "I don't want to be hurt."

"Aw, Ricky. I don't want to hurt you." He stepped closer and feathered his hands over my hair. I'd left it down, and he curled his fingers over the purple ends, letting them slide over his skin like he'd been secretly wondering how they felt. "Look, I don't know what we're doing either. But you slept in my bedroom last night, and I don't like the thought of moving you. So, stay."

Like he'd asked a question, my brain yelled *yes*. I couldn't read into this. "And you?"

He continued gently playing with the ends of my hair. "I don't know, Lyric. Where do you want me?"

His proximity made it easy to forget reality. Being so close to him came with its own special fear. Would I be the mom telling her daughter that Daddy didn't want to be with them anymore?

His question resonated as if he was asking about more than where he was going to sleep. I didn't like the thought of leaving his bedroom either. But now that I was faced with claiming my prize, I was tempted to run. "How 'bout you just feed me and lie with me? No more. I don't know if I could take it."

I didn't know if I was talking about both sex and a relationship, and he didn't clarify. Did he feel as unbalanced and uncertain as me?

He dropped a kiss on my lips, like he'd done this morning. Like it was natural. Like he couldn't help himself. Since I was pretending everything I knew wasn't disintegrating around me, I could also pretend he couldn't resist me—even though he'd spent years doing just that.

* * *

Stetson

Lyric deflated as she ate. Exhaustion hung over her shoulders, and she blinked slowly, like she was ready to fall asleep.

I had watched her all through dinner. Somehow, I stayed out of the chair next to her and prevented myself from hand-feeding her, but I listened closely, hoping to hear her moan like she had when she'd entered the house and smelled my cooking.

She ate and complimented me on how good it was. I knew it was fucking good—I also knew she liked Mom's meatloaf recipe and super crispy baked potatoes. I wanted to hear the moan.

I was left disappointed and a little concerned, but I'd been around enough women to know that telling them they looked tired was the equivalent of saying, "You look like hell," and in many folks' minds, that translated to "I think you're ugly."

No one was ugly. Definitely not Lyric, and not with the way her hair had started to curl at the ends since she hadn't done more than shower. Or how the curve of her tits could be seen through the material of her borrowed pink shirt. But instead of black eyeliner that winged off her eyelids, there were dark circles under her eyes. Watching her was like watching energy be vacuumed out of a carcass. A hot carcass, but a nearly lifeless body nonetheless.

Just as I was about to ask if she needed anything, she set her fork down and rubbed her face. "How could I go from staying out all night to needing to go to bed before eight?"

"You've been through a lot. Don't worry about cleanup. I got it."

She frowned, her full lower lip pouting. "You cooked. I can help."

"Or you can go to bed."

A small meow sounded from the floor. What the hell—? The cat. I had a furry houseguest in addition to a sexy one.

She twisted in her chair and picked Floof up. My mom would've shit a perfectly square, shiny brick if Isla or I held an animal at the dinner table. I had been determined to keep all pets outdoors. I liked animals, but I needed them more for work than for fun. Dogs to keep bigger predators away and be cattle dogs. Cats for mousing and driving off small predators. Horses to work cattle and— Okay, those were also for enjoyment, not that I rode as much as I used to.

Seeing Lyric coddle her cat was changing my mind. If the cat put a contented look on her face and drove away the fatigue and stress, then the cat was going nowhere. Even if it did eat so fast it hacked up a line of phlegmy food right after it ate.

She put Floof down and carried her plate to the sink.

I followed with mine. "Go to bed."

"I'll help with dishes."

Since dishes was just putting our plates in the dishwasher, I didn't argue. I had done most of the cleanup before we ate.

When we were done, she stuffed her hands through her hair. "It's just too early, and since someone picked up my shift tomorrow, I don't want to switch my hours around. Mind if I watch a show?"

"What are you in the mood for?"

She narrowed her eyes and crossed her arms. "It's Friday. Aren't you going to Rattler's?"

Why would I go there when I had her here? "I go to Rattler's because I have nothing else to do but work. So I leave the house, otherwise I'd be starting another project that's really just more work. Besides, you're here."

"You go to Rattler's even when you're dating someone."

Yeah, I did. It had been a point of contention more times than I cared to count. Yet it hadn't stopped me. I liked hanging out with my friends, but I wanted to be with Lyric more. That should have worried me, but I was more concerned her question wasn't about me. "Do you want me to leave?" I wouldn't blame her if she needed some time to herself.

"No, it's just... I don't want you to feel like you have to stay."

I didn't care to go anywhere since Lyric was in my house. I'd known her most of her life, but her shift from being my sister's best friend to the unforgettable woman carrying my baby was happening—had happened.

"Watching a movie sounds nice. Then we can talk about what we need to do tomorrow."

"I'm going to Bismarck to get more things."

"I'll take you."

The guarded look was back. "You don't have to."

I wanted to. "Is Isla going?"

"No, she has the market."

"Then I'll take you. Unless you really don't want me to." I waited for her to tell me no, ready for the disappointment. Lyric wasn't one to hold back, so when she didn't tell me to mind my own fucking business about what she did in Bismarck, I started for the living room. Then she wouldn't see the satisfied look that was probably on my face. "What should we watch? Do you feel like a comedy? Horror? Drama?"

I didn't think she'd follow me. I thought maybe she'd make an excuse to go to the bedroom and shut the door, forcing the unspoken decision that I'd sleep on the too-short guest room bed.

But she settled into the corner of the couch and pulled the blue-plaid throw over her bare legs. I had the strongest urge to sink down next to her and cuddle under the blanket with her. Instead, I took the other side and scrolled through shows until she said stop. She picked a gritty crime drama that matched the books I always saw her carrying around.

We made it an hour into the movie before she laid her head on the arm of the couch. Another half an hour, and her eyelids drifted closed. Before the movie wrapped up and the suspect was caught and arrested, Lyric's breathing had evened out.

I debated what to do for all of five seconds. The idea of waking her to watch her stumble to a bed that wasn't hers was too much for me. I shut the TV off, turned off the lights, and picked her up, blanket and all.

She came awake, lifting her head from my shoulder. "Are you carrying me to bed?"

"Yep."

"Oh."

She didn't exactly relax against me before I laid her on my bed and helped her pull back the covers and wiggle under them. I pulled the blankets up to her chin and hovered, lost for what to do next.

Kiss her? Walk away? My feet wouldn't move.

"Where are you sleeping?" she asked in a quiet tone that didn't help me decide. Did she want me with her?

"I've gotta be honest, Ricky. I want to climb right in next to you." I rubbed a silky lock of purple-dyed hair between my fingers. The last few years, I'd wanted to know whether her hair was as soft as it looked. She'd been untouchable then. And now I couldn't quit putting my hands on her.

"I can't have sex messing with my thinking."

"I understand." I had known exactly what she meant when she asked what we were doing earlier. Sex could cloud a relationship. I'd experienced it too many times. Instead of getting to know each other, past girlfriends and I had moved fast. And when I'd gotten to know them, I wished I had walked away well before our underwear had dropped too far. Several of them had thought the same.

I'd already moved quickly with Lyric, both in the tack room and earlier in my kitchen. I didn't know what I wanted out of her, but I couldn't afford to mess it up. Or maybe I knew what I wanted but couldn't admit it. Better not to know what I lost than to watch her slip through my fingers.

I was about to straighten when she said, "But I don't want you to leave either."

Fuck, that was exactly what I wanted to hear. Yet I didn't want her to feel rushed. "Can I just hold you?" I curled more hair through my fingers. "We should probably, you know, get to know each other."

Her soft chuckle was lost in the rustling of blankets. "Weird, isn't it? Getting to know each other?"

"Yeah, Ricky. It is."

I rounded the bed and dropped my pants. I folded those and put them on the wingback chair in the corner of the room, then stripped off my shirt, which joined my pants on the chair. My socks went into the laundry, leaving me in nothing but my black boxer briefs.

I got under the covers with her, sliding in like she was a feral cat in a dead sleep. If I moved wrong, she'd be gone and claw my heart out as she went. My muscles slowly relaxed as I sank into the mattress. When she wiggled close, I had to sternly order my dick to behave. If I could make it until one of us drifted off, this night would be a success. Sleep should've come immediately for me since I hadn't slept a wink last night, but I was wired.

Lyric Finnegan was in my bed, and both my mind and body were ridiculously excited to get to know her. Wired was right. This wasn't anticipation over the physical element. Yeah, I had loved being buried inside her, and I couldn't fucking wait to do it again. Making her come on my counter had only given me more ideas.

But I had strived for a high level of disinterest when it came to her for so long, I couldn't wait to just...talk. And that was not like me.

Wrapping an arm around her, I marveled over how natural this felt, but I kept away from her abdomen, sensing the topic was too complicated for what we both needed right now. "Ask me anything."

"Why haven't you married?"

A hard breath whooshed out of me, ruffling her hair. "Nailing the tender target first."

She shrugged against me. "If I didn't speak so bluntly about the hard stuff, I'd probably be married by now too."

"Oh, yeah?"

"Good try, but I asked you first."

"Damn." She giggled, which encouraged me to talk, as if this was our very own judgment-free zone. "You wouldn't be surprised by any of the reasons, but the root of them all was a lack of compatibility. They thought they were getting one thing, but I wasn't it. My parents weren't it. My life wasn't it. I could've forced my way through some of it, changed myself or my ways, but ultimately, I deal with enough bullshit in and out of the ranch, I refused to go home to it."

"Harsh, but fair. This is your safe place."

I nestled closer to her, keeping my hips pushed back so I didn't nudge her ass with my growing erection. There was no helping it. Her lush body was in my arms. I wedged my hand through her arms and placed it over her boob. A perfect fit. Instead of pushing my hand off, she rested hers over mine.

"Your turn," I said to keep my mind off the warm flesh in my palm.

"I mean, I'm like sooooo much younger than you."

I nuzzled her neck. "Harsh—and not at all fair."

"Aw, Stoney."

When I first called her Ricky, she'd tried to shoot back with Stoney. "You think I'm going to ask you to stop, but that stupid nickname is a turn-on." Most things with Lyric were becoming a turn-on. *Stoney* described my dick right now. "Spill it. Why haven't you gotten that serious with anyone?"

Her chest deflated as she exhaled. Was the topic too serious, or should I prepare myself for something I didn't want to hear?

"Oh, God, I hate to say this." She inhaled and said in a rush, "None of them were you."

Holy. Shit. I'd been ready for her to talk about how her dad left her and she had trust issues. I was sure she did, but daddy issues were different from me being the main reason she was single.

Grateful she couldn't see my dumbfounded expression, I still asked, "What?" Holden was right? I would've bought a little infatuation, but she'd really had a thing for me? "You aren't the type to hold back on account of me."

"I wasn't going to be that girl. I wasn't going to lust after you while you dated everyone with ovaries between the ages of twenty-five and forty. I'm not even twenty-five!" She huffed. "So I dated around. If you were going to pick up women, I was going to pick up dudes."

Unluckily for me, with the energy industries surrounding the town, Coal Haven attracted a lot of young dude traffic. "I cockblocked you as much as possible."

She twisted to look over her shoulder. "You totally did. I *knew* it." She chuckled and snuggled back into her blankets, and into me.

"Cole was a douche." I wanted to snarl saying his name.

"You were such a dick to him."

I was. I'd stop by their table when she was in Rattler's with him and Isla, and if I saw them in the grocery store, I made sure I had a sudden need for whatever products were on the shelves around them. And then I took every opportunity to diss the guy. "He deserved it."

"Yeah, but I didn't think you knew how he treated me."

"Guys like that are like the neon sign of red flags. It's in the cocky, know-it-all grin and the jacked-up and decked-out pickup."

She let out a soft snort. "It was a nice pickup...for a high schooler."

"I don't think Cole will ever grow out of his teenage years. Most teen boys aren't even that bad."

"I thought it was just my silly fantasy playing with me," she said quietly.

"Your fantasy isn't silly. But, Lyric, between our age gap and..." I hated bringing this topic up. We were supposed to get to know each other, but I came with familial baggage. "My parents."

"I'm aware." She squeezed my hand. "Your dad looks like he blames the person he's looking at for his constipation. And your mom—holy shit, Stetson. Laney once said that your mom eats the souls of small children, and I know what she means." She cringed against my body. "Did I go too far?"

Never. "Yes. Mom can't stand small children long enough to steal their souls."

Lyric giggled and wiggled that fine ass of hers before asking her next question. I shifted again to keep my hips from thrusting forward and rubbing some pressure off my dick against her cheeks. "So you see it?"

"Ricky, I live it. Not many people would know what I mean when I say my parents have been an obstacle in my relationships. Only a few of my cousins. Mom and Dad are a part of my life. My job. I can't just walk away from them, and anyone I'm with will have to learn to live with them in my life." Because my parents weren't going to learn to live with someone they didn't want in their lives. And I'd been complicit once. I was still that way. Anxiety gnawed at my chest.

"Why can't your parents be the ones to adapt?"

If only it were that easy. "Dad was raised like he was going to be king. You're probably too young to remember his dad, but he was a harsh man, and he was all about the oldest son. Besides, they're almost sixty. They aren't going to change."

"Only because they've never had to. People can change at any age, Stetson."

I grunted, not bothering to argue.

She tightened her grip on my hand. "It's okay to put you and the other people important to you first, Stetson. Their reaction is theirs to deal with. No matter what age you are, you're the kid in the relationship."

I didn't have a reply. I didn't disagree with her, but that wasn't how my family worked. "When Dad..." The words were hard to say, swelling until they clogged my throat. My childhood programming had been effective. I'd never talked to anyone about this. Never. Not even Isla. She hadn't been born yet, and I hadn't seen a reason to tell her about it when she was old enough to ask questions. "When Dad cheated on Mom, I found her sobbing in the tub with an empty bottle of wine and covered in vomit."

"Jesus, Stetson." She wriggled around to face me. "You were so young."

I swallowed against the surge of memories. "And then she found out he was having a kid with that other woman."

I still heard Mom's crying. The wails. The heart-wrenching pain in the middle of nowhere. I had been young. Those were some of my first memories. I would've done anything to make Mom better.

"I'm not proud," I blurted. I rested my hand on her hip. I hadn't even talked about this with Holden. But the relief was so damn strong, I kept talking. "The way we treat Liam. I wasn't proud as a kid, but I was real fucking mad at Liam. Seeing him destroyed Mom all over again, and he lived in the same fucking town where she'd see him over and over and over. When he started looking like Dad, I worried I'd find her having a breakdown again. And then he was another cousin's best friend, and she said once it was like being repeatedly told she didn't deserve a happy family. And as an adult? Fuck. I understand clearly how awful our behavior is. Dad's a piece of shit for it, but Mom's just as bad. But I was there when she shattered. I've been there as she tries to hold herself together in a life she thought would be a dream come true but is hastily pasted together over a broken foundation. And honestly, that's why I'm not married. I've got the glue and I need to be free to use it when necessary."

My pulse was high, my breathing fast. But once the confession was out, I was light enough to float off the bed. Only, then I'd have to take my hands off Lyric.

She stayed quiet for a moment. Had I said too much? So many people knew the story of Dad's affair and how Liam's mom died in a car accident after a confrontation with Dad when Liam was a baby. Many people knew Dad had practically tried to run Liam out of town. But no one knew what it was like to live with Mom and Dad after it happened. Isla had some concept, but she was born years after the affair.

But Lyric cupped my cheeks, her touch tender. "I stand by what I said earlier. You're the kid in the relationship. You should've never been put in the position of being your parents' moderator or their therapist. You don't have to tell me that Cameron and Naomi Barron would never visit a professional, but that's their issue. It should've never been yours."

As nice as it was to have her support, to have someone confirm that the way I grew up was fucked up and not my fault, I was traveling in deep ruts I couldn't get out of.

"But it is, Lyric." The previous sleepless night slammed

into me all at once. I let out a tired sigh. "It is, and that's what I need the person I'm with to understand."

She curled into me and murmured, "Maybe the person you're with needs to be strong enough to help you enforce new boundaries."

My parents only respected the boundaries they made. I rubbed her back and let my eyelids fall shut. "Maybe" was all I said before I let sleep rescue me from the conversation.

Five

LYRIC

I sank into a chair in the empty break room. My freshly heated meatloaf and baked potato steamed on a plate in front of me, and I held a new thriller I had bought in Bismarck.

I had expected the Bismarck trip to be tense or, at the very least, a solo run for me after the way I refused to let Stetson justify the way his parents put him in a bind. I would never agree with him. I would never accept that what they had done was right. Their actions might be in the past, but the situation wasn't over. I was sure that was how Naomi controlled an almost thirty-four-year-old man.

But we'd awakened, he'd made pancakes while I showered, and then we'd had a fun day in Bismarck. He let his carefree side out, and I didn't think it was a way to deflect his feelings after our conversation. I was one of the few people who got to see the real Stetson Barron. I was too afraid to look into the significance.

The last two nights, we had watched movies and snuggled into bed together. He hadn't made a move on me, and I might've been hurt, but I'd seen the need in his eyes. I'd felt the brush of the erection he tried to hide. I'd been hiding my own need to feel him inside me again. When I disappeared into the bathroom to take a shower, he watched me like a starving hawk watches a chunky mouse.

I caught him looking at me like that a lot. Our relationship had shifted. I was no longer his little sister's best friend. And I wasn't just the girl who was pregnant with his kid. We were something. Neither of us knew what, but that was fine for now.

I just had to be brave enough to try to explore this new aspect of us. It was like wanting to ride the biggest, scariest roller coaster and finally reaching the height requirement only to wonder whether your heart could take the trip or if you'd faint before climbing on.

Emery breezed into the break room just as I opened my book. Her face brightened. "Hey. I've been thinking about you. How are you? How's your mom?"

"She's good. She's moving into the place above the store later today." I planned to stop by after work. Mom and Isla had cleared out all the boxes, making enough space for Mom to sleep. The kitchen had been used as a break room for years. The place was livable and better than staying under the same roof as Naomi and Cameron. "I'm good too. I just had a scratchy throat the day after."

She tossed a freezer meal into the microwave. I set my book down, a nonverbal signal that she could sit with me. Emery was the only one who didn't try to chat with me when I was reading. I loved my coworkers, and I enjoyed talking up patients while drawing their blood, but all the peopling could wear me out. My break was an important mental retreat in the middle of the workday.

But friend time was more desirable right now.

She tapped her fork against her palm. "Just FYI, Holden told me about…" Her gaze drifted to the door. We were alone, but people often barged through the door like a trauma code was happening by the fridge.

"I'm surprised more people don't seem to know. I've been asked about the fire today, but so far nothing about being pregnant." The news would trigger a tsunami of gossip in town, but the earthquake hadn't yet begun. I'd take the reprieve while I could.

"Well, Barrons are good at keeping their business to themselves. Who'd you see when you were in the ER?"

"Dr. Klevin. Meghan was the nurse working. Joan and Arwyn know."

"I don't see them violating confidentiality."

There weren't enough jobs in town to make it worth putting their positions at risk. "It's an unexpected surprise, but kind of nice. Everyone will know soon enough."

"Right." The microwave dinged, and she went to finish preparing her food.

Just as she sat across from me, the break room door opened and Krystal charged in. My heart stammered, then pounded steadily as her direct gaze landed on me. A superficial glint made her eyes shine.

"Lyric. Ohmigod, I heard about the fire."

"Yeah, it was something." I willed her to lose interest in me.

She drifted closer, her gaze as sharp as her ponytail. Her breasts strained against the purple fabric of her snug scrubs. "Are you staying with Isla?"

This was the curse of small towns. Krystal was a nurse in the clinic, but she'd lived here long enough—and worked with me long enough—to know I had lived with Mom and had no one else in town. Krystal was also very aware that I was friends with Isla. And because of it, she treated me better than a lot of others who crossed her path.

"No."

I tried to leave it at that, but she tilted her head. "At the motel?"

There was only one motel in town, and it would be easy enough to verify if I was there. With Krystal's previous obsession over Stetson, I braved the truth. "I'm staying with Stetson, actually. Mom was more comfortable at Naomi and Cameron's."

Krystal blinked with a slight recoil. "You're staying with him? At his house?"

"Yes."

Emery carefully peeled the film the rest of the way off her nuked lasagna, dutifully staying out of the conversation.

"Wha— Why? There's plenty of room at Naomi and Cameron's."

It was none of her business, but Krystal didn't often care about where her business stopped and others' started. "That's just how it played out."

"Are you two..." Disgust twisted her face as her gaze dropped down to the shiny, thick clogs I had just bought. If I was going to be on my feet for most of my shifts while I was pregnant, I wanted to be comfortable. "...seeing each other or something?"

I kept my tone gentle, like I was talking to that unpredictable mare the Barrons used to have. "If we were, it's not something I'd really talk to you about, and not at work."

Her head did that little jerk-back thing, like she smelled something atrocious. "You're way too young for him."

I picked up my book, done with the conversation. I didn't have the boundary problem Stetson did. He thought coming from a family with money and a ton of land gave others access to his personal life. Like he had to justify he'd earned it to make up for being born into it. I had the freedom of growing up broke with a single mom who was stretched too thin. It was either build a dam or get washed away.

Krystal huffed and charged out the door. Had she come in here for food or because I was here and she thought she could get info on Stetson?

"She's going to be a problem," Emery murmured when the door clicked shut.

"I'm not looking forward to it, but I'm not dealing with it at work. I'm not even going to tolerate her outside of work. She doesn't have a right to my personal life just because she's his ex."

"If she causes issues at work, let me know if I can do anything, like be a witness or something."

I wouldn't risk Emery's job. Krystal had left her job suddenly and moved away after her first breakup with Stetson. When he didn't go running after her, she came back, only Emery had her old position. Krystal held a grudge about it, but she'd gotten hired as a fill-in. Someone liked her enough to rehire her, and I didn't want that to affect Emery. "It'll be fine. I can handle her."

Emery dug into her food. "Joan won't let her scare you away."

I hoped I didn't have to count on it, but Joan had my back. I'd need her once Krystal found out I was pregnant with Stetson's kid. For now, I wanted to keep what was growing between me and Stetson as private as our cuddle sessions in the dark. I treasured those moments. Our talks. And once the town found out, people would think they'd have access to them like they did the rest of Stetson's life, and I wasn't sure how Stetson would handle it.

* * *

Stetson

I stopped in to see Mom before I went out to bale what Holden had cut for me. She was finishing her breakfast of a poached egg and an English muffin.

"I'm so glad to have the house to myself again." Mom tapped her fingers along her tightly pulled-back hair. No strand dared stray from its twist. She would be mortified I'd told Lyric about her breakdown. A sense of betrayal burned through me.

I had nothing to worry about. Lyric was private in her own way, and she wouldn't share what I'd said. "It was really nice of you, though. Erin needed the help."

"She shouldn't have gotten herself into a position where she can't afford a few nights at the motel. It's not as if the motel charges much."

"We can't all be born into oil money."

She pursed her lips, and consternation fit her face like a well-molded mask. "Our family worked hard for that money, Stetson."

No, they hadn't. They got lucky in that the land they bought contained oil. Even luckier, they owned the mineral rights, which was much less common now after a few oil booms.

The oil company and the lawyers did the rest. But when I had mentioned that once, I was given a two-hour driving tour of the pastures I had grown up four-wheeling and riding horses in and lectured on the farming and ranching history of my grandparents and their grandparents and how much the family business had grown.

Mom had been raised in Crocus Valley. She'd married into the money.

"So." Mom announced it like she was talking at a city

council meeting and everyone needed to listen. It was just the two of us in the kitchen. Isla usually didn't venture up until Mom left for the day. I braved morning-Mom. Isla chose to be fully awake before facing her. "Now that we can talk freely, what are you going to do about Lyric and that baby?"

That baby. A hot press of anger straddled my tongue. I worked my jaw and swallowed it down. "We're talking it through."

"What's there to talk through until you know if it's yours? Which reminds me." She dug into her large red handbag emblazoned with some designer logo on the front. She carried it around like she was brandishing our family crest. "I did some research on prenatal paternity testing." She pulled out her phone and tapped the screen with a manicured nail.

Uneasiness filled my gut until the scrambled eggs Lyric had made for breakfast threatened to make a reappearance. "You were researching paternity tests?"

She gave me a smile that said I could thank her later. "You'll both need to get your blood drawn. Well, you might just need a cheek swab. I'm not clear on that yet. Maybe it depends on the kit? There's a place in Mandan that deals with prenatal paternity testing. That way you have a neutral third party and it gets done right."

"Mom."

"And tell her not to worry about the cost. I don't want her to think she can use that as an excuse to delay. Of course, we'll pay for it, and you can do it as early as seven weeks. How far is she supposedly along?"

Her tone made me frown. Supposedly? "Lyric isn't Liam's mom."

Mom reared back like I'd taken a swing at her. I instantly regretted my words. If only I could snatch them away from her brain and stuff them back into my mouth. "Stetson Cameron Barron, how dare you?" Her voice wavered with unshed tears. Rage would've been better, but the tears transported me back into the head of that terrified kid who didn't know what to do or what monsters were after his mommy.

"I'm sorry." I went around the island to hug her. "I'm sorry. It's just that I don't distrust Lyric like you do."

"I don't distrust her." Mom pulled away and blinked rapidly. Moisture shone in her eyes. "But women don't behave normally around Barron men. Lyric's been a surprisingly good friend to Isla, but she's not your best friend." Why would Lyric's quality of friendship be a surprise? "We can't have another Krystal situation. Or who was that one girl who pretended to get pregnant?"

"That was Malena, and it was in high school." Our senior year, she'd made a shitty April Fool's Day joke and Mom had almost sued her family. Malena was married with two kids in Nebraska. I doubted she thought about me at all, but I had learned a hard lesson. Always use protection. The lesson had stuck for over fifteen years, until Lyric.

"Exactly. It doesn't matter the age. I'll go ahead and order one."

"Mom. This should be between me and Lyric."

Her gaze grew shrewd. "Has she fought you on it already?"

"What? No. But it's a stressful period regardless, and we have plenty of time." What was growing between me and Lyric seemed too tenuous for me to arrive home and start asking about paternity tests. We had time, dammit, and I wanted to use it.

"Then accept my help. I'll order the test, that way you two don't have to worry about it."

The offer sat on my conscience like an anvil. Lyric didn't

have a home, and Mom was worried about paternity. Other than when I'd first asked Lyric—out of shock, and I'd felt like shit as soon as the words had left my mouth—I hadn't dwelled on it.

Maybe I wasn't ready to acknowledge how I'd feel either way. Mom's reactions were more concerning. How would she feel if the test confirmed what Lyric said?

"Say we do this and the baby's mine. How are you going to handle the news?" I waited, my breath stalling.

She brushed her fingers over her hair again. Her expression turned lofty, making my gut churn. "*Handle* it, Stetson?"

I shrugged. She might not like how I phrased it, but they were her words.

She gave me a look that said I should know better and picked up her red bag. "Your father mentioned helping you hay. Might want to save him a ditch."

I wouldn't save Dad a ditch. He could come ask me. We'd had issues over the years after his dad had died and I'd fully taken over ranching. Mom had pressed Dad to concentrate on his job with the refinery. *It's our stability, our retirement.*

She was correct, and I could see that as an adult. But I didn't think Dad had wanted it as much as she did. He seemed to enjoy the outdoor work of ranching, but I was in charge, and if I started saving him duties, the CEO in him couldn't butt the hell out of other decisions.

"Bye, Mom."

She left, and I stared at the swirling brown pattern in the granite countertop.

Isla appeared around the corner and leaned against the wall, her arms crossed. Her combative expression told me enough.

"You heard all that?"

"I did. A paternity test?"

"It's Mom's idea." Lyric had brought it up too, but I dreaded the idea and didn't know why.

She sighed and marched to the fridge. She pulled out the Simply Orange and slammed the jug on the counter. "Are you going to tell Lyric?"

"Why wouldn't I?"

"Because you didn't tell Mom no." Her eyes narrowed and she leaned over the counter. "Unless you secretly want the test too. This way, you make Mom the bad guy, like usual."

I should want the test. Lyric seemed to think so. Mom did, obviously. But I...didn't. I ignored that part of Isla's statement. "Like usual?"

She rolled her eyes and flipped her long blond hair over her shoulder. "Mom's your out with women. Always has been."

"She's your out with jobs."

Her eyes flared and she straightened, crossing her arms again. "You know exactly how she and Dad are about my work. They think I'll open a business and it'll fail and it'll embarrass them more than...than..." She dropped her voice. "Liam."

"Liam didn't embarrass them. Dad's behavior did. They took it out on him. And they did it because his mom got killed in an accident or they would've socially massacred her." An ominous cloud settled over my head. I had to keep them from treating Lyric like that. I needed all that time I'd thought about earlier.

A pale brow slowly arched up. "I can't believe you said that."

That was twice now in almost as many days I'd spoken the forbidden out loud. "You know it's true." I hoped she did. She was treated like she couldn't string two Cheerios onto a thread, but she was more engaged in her surround-ings than they gave her credit for.

"I know, but I can't believe you said it in the house. I would panic if I said it on the other side of Montana."

I let out a raspy chuckle before reality stole all my humor. "Think Lyric will be pissed? It's just to humor Mom."

"Is it?"

"Jesus, Isla. What do you want me to do? I didn't ask for this. Now it's 'Bam! You're a dad.' Then, 'Maybe you're not.' All I planned to do was put up hay." This was a damned if I do, damned if I don't situation. If the baby wasn't mine, would Lyric pack up and leave? Would she be willing to give me and all my baggage a chance?

And if it was mine?

The answer should be simple, but my parents would only complicate it all. They'd mess it all up. Fucking pater-nity test.

I couldn't stuff down my irritation. Add in that I desired the woman I'd been cuddled next to in bed for the last three nights and I had blue balls that could kill a giant, and irritable was a weak word.

Lyric wasn't pulling the world's most insensitive April Fool's joke. She wasn't trying to control me. But Mom thought so. And Isla thought I was using Mom to push Lyric away.

Yet I was here, wondering if there was something real between me and Lyric and if it was worth tampering with my relationship with Mom. Was it worth interfering with Lyric's friendship with Isla? What would Dad think?

Isla was giving me a steady stare that rivaled Mom's.

"I like her," I finally said.

She didn't speak at first. Moments like these, she took after Mom way too close for my comfort. "You mean it?"

"Yes, Isla. But she's different."

Isla snorted. "No shit." I shot a glare at her, but she remained undaunted. "Lyric won't let you walk all over her. You didn't give her the time of day for years, and she didn't let it stop her from living."

Lyric had said just as much. She might not have settled down with other men, but she also hadn't found the right guy. I'd been her out. A baby wasn't a dudebro with an obnoxious truck.

"I know," I muttered. "We're getting to know each other, you know. The baby..." I lifted a shoulder. "We've gotta figure us out first, and I want time to do that."

"Then maybe try dating her instead of hiding her in your house. And don't let Mom or Dad fuck it up." She wrinkled her nose and looked around like one of our parents had snuck into the house. "Have you seen Dad lately?"

"No. I figured he was avoiding our guests." Dad stepped into enough that wasn't his business, but if it involved Mom and didn't directly involve him, he was fucking gone.

"He was totally doing that. But on Sunday, he napped."

It was my turn to pop my brows. "Dozed in the chair?"

She enunciated each word. "Lay down in bed and napped."

"He okay?" Dad rarely got sick. He'd have to get close to people to catch germs. "Wasn't he catching a cold or something?"

"I don't know. He's just looked haggard lately. That's not Dad."

She sounded worried, but I wasn't. Maybe something was wrong, but Dad could sever a limb and he wouldn't tell us if he didn't want us to know. "Mmm. Maybe he's trying to figure out an early retirement that doesn't involve painting the living room."

The corner of her mouth lifted, but the worry didn't

leave her eyes. "Maybe." She checked her watch. "I've gotta get going."

"To where?" I didn't mean to blurt the question. But what did Isla do all day?

"I'm doing research. I have an idea brewing." A mysterious smile graced her face. "I'll be gone through the weekend."

"Have fun."

"Only if you don't tell Mom."

"She's tracking your car."

"I know," she said on a sigh. "Last month, I parked at the civic center in Bismarck and Ubered all over."

I snickered as she left, but my smile quickly died. She and I had our workarounds for our parents, but I had the feeling those wouldn't last much longer. Just like I had the feeling that we might have made things worse for ourselves in the long run.

Six

LYRIC

Mom bustled around the store while I hung new clothing on hangers she would load onto the sales racks tomorrow. I had stopped by after work to talk about what was going on with the trailer and what her plans were, but I hadn't brought up our living situation. That would mean leaving Stetson's house.

I held up a pink tank top with a unicorn on the front.

"That'd look cute on you," Mom said from where she was organizing shelves of kitchenware.

I studied the shirt. "Where'd you get it?"

Mom got plenty of donations, but not all of it was worthy of selling—or to be bought. She remained aware that Coal Haven was a small town. Not everyone was willing to buy a shirt their neighbor or colleague had donated. Last year she'd started selling stock from consignment and business liquidations, and it had already brought an influx of cash into the store.

It beat the thrift flipping she used to do. She'd combed through deals and yard sales in bigger towns to bring fresh stock into the store.

Those memories were some of my favorites though.

The tank top was a consignment piece. "I think it'd pair well with the black-and-white-plaid skirt I have. The one that won't fit in a few weeks."

Still weird to say. Sometimes the reminder I was pregnant took me by surprise. My boobs hurt, but I was growing used to it. Same with the low-grade nausea. As long as I ate mild food more frequently, my stomach wasn't as upset. I had to go to the bathroom more than usual, but there were still moments I remembered, *I'm pregnant with Stetson's baby.* When my belly was poking out of my clothes, I definitely wouldn't forget.

Mom abandoned the used skillets and crossed to the counter where I was stacking clothing. "Take it. It has a small hole in the seam on the side. An easy mend, or just a hanging-around-the-house shirt." She drummed her fingers on the glass countertop. "Have you given more thought to what you're going to do for a living arrangement?"

I set the top down as the sensation of being suspended over a large hole took over. "You aren't going to use the insurance money to move into a new trailer?" I hadn't thought about what else she would do. The lot was paid for.

Regret shadowed her face and she spoke with hesitancy. "As I've cleaned out the apartment, I've realized it's really cute. And so handy. I'm my own landlord. I'd like to sell the lot...but the apartment is only one bedroom."

She had started removing the floral wallpaper, and she'd gushed about how it brightened the space. *These old buildings have such magnificent windows.* With the apartment, she'd be in the middle of town, close to the diners, and a short walk away from the grocery store. She was friends with

Hattie from the furniture store and could have her over for coffee.

All those benefits would go away and the apartment would go back to being a storeroom if Mom had to make room for me and a baby. We wouldn't be temporary stays, and Mom was telling me she didn't want the apartment to be an in-the-meanwhile thing. I had come back to the nest because Mom needed me. Had she stayed only because she thought I needed her?

I fought off several beats of panic. I was on my own, but I was also an adult. I needed my own place, and Mom wanted hers. It wasn't like Mom was abandoning me because she didn't want me. She wasn't Dad.

"Oh, honey. I know it's so quick after the fire. I don't want you to feel like you have nowhere to go—"

"No. No, it's time for me to be on my own." Alone. With a baby.

My heartburn fired up. Did Mom think I was with Stetson, that we would live happily ever after raising the baby? She didn't know that he and I hadn't even talked about that far down the road. I'd told her we were working through everything, and she hadn't pressed for more. That was Mom. She'd been through her own public drama; she didn't press into anyone else's.

She inspected my expression, worry filling her gaze. "Of course, I'll give you some of the payout. You have all those student loans, and you lost almost all your belongings."

"It wasn't much, and you need that insurance money more than me." My job gave me a retirement plan, and my belongings were easy to replace. I couldn't keep much from my small bedroom. My scrubs would be the most expensive clothing to replace. Funny how clothing meant to get ruined and covered in body fluids cost more and was on sale less often than the regular non-thrift store clothing I bought.

"It was something, and you should get an insurance payout over that something." She pressed her hands on the counter surface. "Are you sure it's okay? I can price new trailer houses and the cost of moving them—"

"No, Mom. You're half moved into the apartment, and you love how it's turning out. Stetson won't kick me out until I have a place."

Her brows pinched. "You don't think you two will stay together?"

"A baby isn't the foundation of a relationship."

Mom winced. Was she recalling her own experience with Dad? I hadn't held them together. I hadn't been enough for him to want to be in my life.

But my parents had had a relationship before Mom got pregnant. "Neither is being into him for years. He's still Stetson. Having known him for so long is making me extra cautious."

"And you have a baby to think about." She tapped her chin, her gaze introspective. "Maybe you should take the apartment. With one bedroom, you and a baby could make do until you can find something bigger."

"You're not giving up your place. I can see what there are for apartments in town." I wasn't sure I could get financing for one of the three twin homes being built by the golf course, but I had relied on the trailer without thinking about the logistics. Our old home had had a bedroom for each of us, but adding a baby would've made the walls close in.

"At least take the shirt. And keep me updated on what you find—and on Stetson. He's a good kid, but I can't imagine what it was like growing up with such hard parents."

"He should be a better dad than his own." I had fantasized about him so much, I couldn't take thinking about him as a great father. But the myriad questions about my future and whether it contained him didn't stop me from wanting to be with him. I took the tank top off the hanger. "I should go. It's my turn to cook."

"He cooks? I thought he went out most nights."

"For a drink or two. He doesn't survive by his grill like Holden, but he's a good cook." He'd actually seemed like more of a homebody the last few days. He was so much more than what the town thought of him. More than what his family thought of him.

"Call me if you need anything."

I gave her a quick kiss on the cheek and took my new tank with me. I didn't think of anyone else when I bought clothes—didn't care about their opinions and didn't want their advice. Would Stetson care if I wore a unicorn on my shirt around town? Would he think it was too kiddish and only highlight our age difference?

Since the fire, I'd worn scrubs, plain shorts and shirts, borrowed clothing—tame stuff from Isla. The real question was, if he said anything negative, would I change myself for him?

No, if he'd been into me before the baby, then how I looked was part of the package. The question was if his parents didn't like my quirks, would he ask me to change? And I feared the answer would be a deal breaker.

Seven

LYRIC

I arrived at Stetson's several minutes later, my belly swirling at the thought of seeing him again. I'd spent time with him this morning over a plate of scrambled eggs before I left for work.

His pickup wasn't parked by the garage yet, but I pulled inside. He'd programmed the opener to my car, and apparently twenty-four was old enough to find that sexy.

Hadn't Krystal bitched because he wouldn't move the Chevy in his garage to make room for her car? Yet he parked his pickup, which cost more than the trailer did when Mom and Dad bought it twenty years ago, outside.

The guy got hotter with every thoughtful gesture.

I put the tank top in the washer, tabling my early worry about Stetson's opinion. I changed into a T-shirt and blue shorts. In the kitchen, I searched his cupboards and the fridge. There was plenty of food to make if I knew what I was in the mood for, preferably anything beef. His freezer was full of a half a cow and there was hamburger in the fridge.

The rumble of his pickup grew louder, then cut off, and a couple of minutes later, he walked through the door. His ball cap was pulled down low, and he adjusted it as his gaze traveled down my bare legs.

The swirl in my stomach was back. "I was trying to figure out what to make for supper. What do you feel like?"

His gaze ate me up, answering my question. The fire building inside my body gave an approving answer. I was growing used to the daily battle of resisting him, but it wasn't easy.

No sex. I'd do whatever Stetson wanted if I succumbed to the way I suspected he was in the bedroom. A quick hookup in a tack room had obliterated my sexual history.

The heat leached out of his gaze as he straightened. "I was thinking...maybe we should go out?"

"Grab some food and bring it back?"

"Eat out."

We hadn't been seen out together. We'd been in the same vehicle passing through town but that was a different type of out.

"I don't eat out a lot." Mom's frugal ways had stayed with me, and admittedly, I didn't have to pay for a lot of my drinks at the bar. I had purposely chosen places and times when I could meet someone. Made socializing cheaper. "I need to save for rent and stuff." My cheeks burned. Stetson had built this house with family money the Barrons had gotten from oil found on their land. But without that money, he'd still be doing well.

His intensity narrowed on me. "My treat. I'm taking you out."

His tone gave me pause. "Like a date?"

He nodded, shifting as if he was nervous. The mighty

Stetson Barron couldn't be nervous asking me out. I brushed a strand of hair behind my ear. I'd left it pulled into a messy bun after work, but the messy part was winning. I adopted a mischievous tone. "I don't know. I mean, I have things going on."

His eyes narrowed, but I caught a glint of humor. "Really busy in those tiny shorts?"

"Really busy." I crossed my arms. I wanted to go out with him. A date was something I would've killed for a few months ago. If Stetson had asked me out, I would've dropped who I was seeing so fast I wouldn't have remembered their name. But as reality loomed over me, things were different. There was more in our future, whether we successfully dated or not. "Seriously, though. You and me on a date? I don't think news of the baby's gotten out, but are we ready for this?"

He scratched the back of his neck and let out a disgusted noise. "I wish it could be different. We could drive to Bismarck or Dickinson to eat, but we shouldn't have to do that. I want to take you out. Let's go out."

"Rattler's?"

He nodded. "The diner is closed, and I'd like more than bar food."

Rattler's with Stetson. We couldn't get much more public. I had the urge to stay home, to preserve what had grown between us since the fire. But hiding wasn't healthy. It wasn't what I wanted in a relationship. I might not know what this was, but I didn't want to be another unspoken regret for a guy.

I made my decision. "Shawn's alfredo is really good."

Satisfaction lit his gaze. "Let's go."

I looked down at myself. I liked dressing up to go out, but I didn't have much to choose from yet. "I should see what else I have to wear."

"I'm a fan of the booty shorts."

"They're just blue shorts." Navy-blue linen shorts that yes, ran on the short side, but as long as they covered my crack, I didn't care. "My shirt—"

"Shows off your tits. I've been looking."

I laughed and tugged down the hem. It was on the snug side, but I liked the way this shirt gave me an hourglass figure. I also chuckled every time I read the "Calm Down and Dilute" wording on the front. Lab humor for the win. But I liked Stetson's reaction even more. "Okay," I said, retwisting my hair into a less messy bun. "I guess I'm ready, then."

"We can take my pickup."

The nerves attacking my gut when he pulled into the crowded parking lot weren't like those that struck earlier when he'd proposed the idea. Arriving alone with Stetson would alert everyone that more was going on between us than me being his sister's friend. Then, when news of the baby hit, they'd either think I lied to him or that he was with me only for the kid.

I could get righteous and give myself an ulcer, or I could ignore them and live my life. I'd chosen the latter all my life, but it seemed easier than what was looming in front of me now. Growing up, I'd heard the whispers about Mom after Dad left.

Once, I'd overheard Naomi on the phone when I was playing with Isla in her toy room.

What did Erin expect? Good things never happen when you have to trick a man to be with him. I just hope her daughter doesn't turn out like her.

If Naomi thought that way, other people did too. And there was nothing I could do but make sure I wasn't giving Stetson an ultimatum. As much as I wanted him to be my dream guy, the love of my life, I wouldn't take him if I was just another obligation.

As we walked in, we didn't hold hands and he didn't have his arm around me, but his hand hovered on the small of my back. The hostess smiled at me, her gaze lighting when she spotted Stetson. She was young, still in high school, and she looked at him like he was a fun old guy who tipped well.

"Hey, Stetson," she said with a chirp. "Normal table?"

"No," I answer quickly. "A booth, please."

"Oh." She glanced at him like she needed his approval. The thought of sitting at the big round table in the back like I was one of his groupies made me want to stomp out and walk the five miles back to his house. She must've gotten the confirmation she was looking for. "Okay. Follow me."

I squared my shoulders and walked past familiar faces. All people I knew, none I was overly friendly with. Stetson rattled off names and greetings behind me. He could be a politician if he was ever willing to deal with conflict outside of his family. When the hostess reached the booth, she set the menus down, smiling at me first. She tried to check with Stetson, as if to make sure the booth was okay, but he was talking to the owner of the downtown tool store, Carlton.

I slid into the booth and watched him work his way toward me. After he told Carlton he was stopping in later this week, he stepped across the aisle to a couple in their eighties. A few laughs and a quick comment on how it was nice not to be affected by drought so badly this year, and he made it to the booth. Then Remington called his name.

Stetson stood at the edge of the seat as Remington approached. The man's black chef's-tie-back-covered hair lighter than his dark scruff, and his gold hoops twinkled under the restaurant lights.

Remington's gaze touched on me, then away, and back again. "Hey, Lyric."

The guy was a flirt, but with me it had never extended beyond the friendliness of business owner to a regular customer. "Hey."

Remington turned his attention back to Stetson. "Not using the table tonight?"

Stetson never planned to host a group when he came here. I'd seen him walk in, sit at the round table for eight, and the table would be almost full within a half hour or so. Stetson's friends, Remington, Holden, and of course, various women, would come and go. I had watched too many women stay, which led to some poor dating decisions on my end. I hadn't wanted to grow mold waiting for Stetson to give me a chance, but I'd met a few duds.

"No, it's just me and Lyric tonight."

"Got it." He clapped Stetson on the shoulder. Remington could read people. I'd seen him work the room enough. "I'll leave you two be, but let me know if you need anything."

Stetson dropped into the booth and scooted to the middle. We faced each other. Maybe the big round table would've been better. It was like we'd been shoved into our seats and ordered to talk.

"So?"

He chuckled. "So. How was work?"

Pleased he actually seemed interested and wasn't searching for empty small talk, I still refrained from a nerd dump of what I actually did. "Good. The afternoon was slow, so I could catch up on some monthly maintenance on the analyzers and finish some continuing ed."

"What do you do in a day?"

The server stopped by, putting a pause on our conversation. Stetson ordered prime rib, and I got the chicken alfredo to change up the protein I was getting while staying with Stetson. When she was gone, he lifted a brow for me to continue.

"Draw blood, test it, get it ready to transport to Bismarck for the tests we can't do. Test urine. We don't do stool testing in the clinic, but we collect it to send to the Bismarck lab. There's maintenance on the analyzers, answering questions from nurses and doctors, handling patients, that kind of stuff. Our lab is too small to do much microbiology, and we can only do limited blood bank stuff. Usually, if a patient is that bad, they have to be transported."

He grunted. "Gimme a cow any day of the week."

"I like it. Some days it's monotonous. Other days I feel like a salty mechanic when the analyzers are acting up, even though those cost more than even your pickup, but I'm learning to be grateful for the slow days. When shit hits, it can be stressful and ugly, which is like working in the hospital every day."

"Yeah?"

I nodded. Most of my dates would've tuned out by now. With Cole, I wouldn't have gotten past the "good." Ugh. Why had I tolerated him that long?

Because Stetson had been with Krystal again.

But those days were over. "Yeah. During my internship, which was basically a year, I liked the fast pace. Then I looked at the older techs. They were all burned out. Some were so bitter I hated working on the bench with them. I didn't want to be like them when I was older."

He seemed to mull over what I said. "And there's nowhere else to work? Just a hospital or a clinic?"

"Not really, not in our small state. There are some private labs in the ag industry and the refinery, but techs stay in those jobs longer. They're hard to find. Our training is so specialized, and our degree isn't considered the same as a nursing degree. There's the state lab. Public health." I shook my head thinking about what I'd heard.

"That bad?"

"The work might be cool, but it doesn't sound like a place where I'd fit in. I might be one of Joan's favorites, but she doesn't mind when I point out issues in our process and procedures or when some staff are treated differently, leaving others with more work. She's not a defensive manager. I dunno. Maybe it's changed there, but I've heard they come down hard on people like me. I'm not a natural ass-kisser."

He snorted. "No. You're not."

"Is that bad?"

"No, Ricky. It's not. You don't blow smoke up anyone's behind, but you're not insulting."

I lifted a shoulder, liking his validation. "Not everyone thinks there's a difference."

A shadow fell over the table, and a cloud of perfume hit me in the face. "You're not at your table, Stetson."

Sienna, one of the women Stetson messed around with regularly, smiled at each of us. I didn't know her well, but as far as his exes went, she could be intimidating with her glossy black hair and radiant smile. Overall, she seemed nice enough.

"Not today. You know Lyric?"

Sienna's grin stayed in place. "Isla's friend. I don't think we've met more than in passing. How are you, Lyric?"

"Good. You?"

"I'm here to meet Holly. I'm going to grab a seat in the bar. You two have a good night." She flashed another smile at both of us and walked away.

Stetson met my gaze, tension ripe in his eyes.

"Are you worried I'm going to throw a jealous fit?"

"Sort of."

"If I have reason to get worked up over an ex of yours,

then I shouldn't be wasting my time with you. I'm not an ass-kisser, and I don't do jealous fits."

His smile was lopsided. "Are you sure you don't want to kiss my ass a little?"

"You'd like it too much."

He laughed, and I let him off the hook with a grin. My bladder started complaining, and I didn't question it. To prove I wasn't going to turn green and hang on him as long as Sienna was under the roof, I scooted to the end of the booth. "I've gotta run to the restroom before our food arrives."

I slid out, weighed down by the stares of everyone else in the restaurant. And I didn't stop to chat with anyone as I went.

* * *

Stetson

I took a swig of my beer, aware of the speculation around me. I wasn't at the table people associated with me. The booth was a powerful sign that I wasn't here for social hour.

Sienna's arrival had speared me with a few minutes of terror. Was the night ruined?

But true to the Lyric I was getting to know, she didn't create drama. She hadn't wanted to be at the table with me, hadn't wanted to be a part of that, and I wouldn't force her. I liked to come and talk with everyone. I liked being around people. But I also enjoyed her company. I liked facing her, not being interrupted, and having her to myself.

She was young, but she was comfortable with herself in a way very few of the women I'd dated were. Was their insecurity what made them attracted to my last name and my reputation around town? I was used to navigating touchy emotions, and I'd done the same with whom I dated. It hadn't helped that I felt like none of them were interested in the real me. They wanted the Stetson who drove a nice pickup and pleased everyone around town to offset how the Barron last name scared respect into others.

I had enough to navigate in life. I wanted to be with someone who could handle her own emotions and didn't pressure me to change just for her.

Lyric had mentioned redefining my relationship with my mother, but I hadn't felt like she was demanding I change my ways, my career, or who I talked to. Still, I preferred to forget about that conversation. No one had been there when I was younger. No one had seen what Mom went through or how hurt she was. No one else but Isla had witnessed the strange relationship between our parents, the sides of them the public and even other family members didn't see.

And I'd protect Lyric from that too. I'd continue to be the buffer between my parents and the world. Tonight would be a good night to bring up the paternity test, but Rattler's wasn't the place, and I didn't want to spoil our first real date with talks of tests and my mother.

Lyric was walking back to the booth. Muscles flexed in her legs, and the loop of hair secured behind her head bobbed. When she'd come home from college, she'd had an undercut I hadn't been able to take my eyes from. It had given her an edge that her longer hair made a person never think might be there.

I knew the edges existed, and I wanted to explore each one.

She was almost to her seat when she looked past me, a smile growing on her face. She bent down, her arms out, and a young boy ran to her, followed by another. Liam's twins.

The nephews I had never talked to. I knew who they were, but they likely didn't know my name, much less how I was related to them. If I were Liam, there wouldn't be a point to introduce me.

"Hey, guys," Lyric said, giving the other boy a hug.

The kids talked over each other, telling Lyric about fishing and their little sister. My heart twisted. I had caught glimpses of Liam and Kennedy's little girl, Ginny.

Liam pulled up alongside the booth, seemingly oblivious to my presence. A baby with burnished brass hair wiggled in the carrier he held. "How's it going, Lyric? Boys, quit hanging on her."

The kids barely backed off, but Lyric didn't look like she minded. "Good." She leaned forward and gently tapped Ginny's chubby hand. "How are my girls doing?"

Kennedy had stopped next to Liam, the group blocking the aisle, not that anyone would try to get around them. Any onlookers were probably frozen, waiting for the frosty fireworks. Liam was within five feet of me.

Fuck, I was tired of the show.

"We're good," Kennedy answered. "I'm getting my classroom ready for the year. Grandma Gin put her foot down about day care."

Liam chuckled. "We didn't want her to feel obligated, so we mentioned we were researching a few places in town for when school starts, but she got first dibs. She demanded it."

Each of Lyric's hands was clung to by a boy, and she grinned at Ginny. "Someone is going to get so spoiled by her grandma."

"So spoiled," Kennedy agreed. "Hey, I'm so sorry about the fire. What can Liam and I do to help you?"

"Everything's getting taken care of," Lyric said, "unless you know of a place that's renting."

What the hell now? Wasn't she moving in with her mom again?

Did she desperately want out of my house?

"I'll ask around," Kennedy said. "Maybe Emery's house is still available?"

Lyric nodded. "I can start there. I should let you guys go eat."

"Do you want to join us?" Liam asked, nodding to the hostess who was at the table where I normally sat. She laid the menus down, apparently giving up on waiting for the group to quit chatting.

"No, I'm here with..." Lyric weakly gestured toward me, and I braced myself for the discomfort about to happen.

Surprise flitted across Kennedy's face. "Oh my gosh, Stetson. I didn't see you there."

"I'm easy to miss," I said in a joking tone.

Kennedy laughed because she was cool like that. Liam's stance was stiffer than when he'd been talking to Lyric.

He gave me a light nod. "Stetson."

I did the same. "Liam."

"Who's that?" Owen, one of the twins, asked, and the dread in Liam's expression went straight to my chest. Resignation that he'd have to answer was next.

Lyric and Kennedy each looked like they were trying to puzzle out exactly how to answer.

"I'm Stetson," I said, trying to rescue us all.

"You're familiar," Eli said, his words less clear than his brother's.

"You've probably seen me around. I'm out and about a lot."

Owen nodded like he'd been known to chat all over town his whole life. "Me too." The corner of my mouth ticked up, then he said, "Do you know my name?"

I took a deep breath and pretended I was thinking really hard. "I think you're Gus and he's Russ."

Owen snickered. "My name's not Gus."

"You must be Owen, then."

Owen's grin could melt an iceberg. Liam cocked his head, studying me like he wasn't sure what I was playing at, and Kennedy blinked. I did my best to ignore their reactions. I refused to look at any of the other customers. Anyone over the age of twenty-five knew the story, and most people younger than that probably knew it and didn't care. I didn't care to see our gathering be a point of conversation.

Eli pushed forward. "Not many people can tell us apart."

"How can they not know you're Russ?"

The kid chortled, showing off two missing front teeth, and damn, it was cute.

Ginny squawked and Liam ushered the kids away. "Come on, guys. Let's leave these two alone so we can eat before Ginny starts hollering."

I didn't know if that was his true motivation, but I wouldn't blame him if it wasn't. Liam didn't need to spare me a second of his time.

Kennedy looked from Lyric to me as she walked away. "Nice to see you again, Stetson." She leaned into Lyric as she passed. "Give me a call. I could use more adult time."

"Will do." Lyric slid into the booth and leveled her gaze on me. "So that was less cringy than I thought it'd be."

Weariness filled me. Maneuvering around my brother for the entirety of his life had gotten old fast. "Thankfully."

"Were you..." She lowered her voice. "Were you guessing about Owen's name?" She shook her head. "Honestly, I wasn't sure you even knew their names. Can you really tell them apart?"

"I know which one's which. Gin's had to shout after

them enough in public for me to know who's who," I said in an easy tone to let her know there was no judgment about kids being kids.

"They're busy boys. Good kids."

"I don't doubt it." Just like I didn't doubt that I wanted to quit talking about how my role as uncle went as far as knowing their names and no more. I wasn't any different to them than a stranger they passed on the street. Just the way my parents had wanted it. Thankfully, I had a valid subject change. "Why are you looking for a place to rent?"

Her lips pressed together like she knew the diversion was deliberate. The server arrived, setting steaming plates in front of us.

When she left, Lyric poked at her pasta. "I guess Mom's planning to move into the apartment above the store. I think she kind of wants a change."

"So she's doing it now?"

"Yeah. With the, uh, you know, space would've been an issue at either place."

The idea of her moving out bugged the shit out of me. She wasn't even moved into my place. The only things of hers at my house were the clothing her mom had rescued from the trailer, the items she'd purchased, and her toiletries. I wasn't ready to be done with her. "I can help you look."

She speared a piece of pasta. "I don't hold out hope for much. Any houses for rent will be like the one Emery rented —old and probably too big for me to afford. Coal Haven's two apartment complexes would be louder than living in the trailer. But it'll be fine. I'm sure I'll find something."

Her tone was light, as if leaving my house didn't bother her. Did she think it was inevitable?

Was it?

"There's no rush," I said, ignoring my prime rib. "It's not like I'm packing your bags while you sleep."

"I know. It's just, we don't know where this is going to go, and I can't find out too late that it isn't going anywhere and have no place of my own."

I cut into my meat. Usually, my mouth watered at the thought of Remington's prime rib. The guy knew what he was doing, right down to the chives in the mashed potatoes. But it all could've been dust on my taste buds.

She didn't know where this was going. Neither did I. We both knew it ended with a baby, yet we each wanted a substantial relationship. Her dad had walked out on her and her mom. My parents hadn't been the epitome of a loving couple.

I wanted it all—and I was growing more convinced that I wanted it all with Lyric.

Which meant I couldn't do what I normally did. Neither could she. This was supposed to be a date. The topic of living together could wait. "What do you usually do on a date?"

She finished chewing and swallowed, her gaze guarded. "I imagine it's what you usually do."

I winced. True. "What would you want to do on a date?"

"Like, what's my ideal date?"

I nodded.

"I don't know." She took another bite. I waited. She took another.

Was she going to ignore me for the rest of the meal? "Like a movie? A romantic picnic? By the lake or the river? Trail riding?" Could she ride a horse while pregnant?

She continued to eat, her expression focused on her pasta. Finally, she laid her fork down. "My answer's the same as the other night, only more mortifying. My ideal date was you, Stetson. That's why I never thought about what I wanted to do. They weren't you. No one had your swagger. No one stopped to talk to *everyone* like you. No one ran a ranch but still had fun like you. No one called me Ricky and made my heart race by just looking at me—by just walking into the same room. So I didn't care about movies or picnics or romantic rides. The guys I dated weren't you, and I eventually lost interest. Or the guy sensed that I wasn't in with both feet and let me go first, like Cole. Most weren't as much of a dick as him, though."

I blew out a long breath. Oh. I'd wanted an answer and I'd gotten it. She'd had the same answer about why she hadn't married, but we were talking about one date. An ideal date. I had to live up to not just myself, but a clueless, shittier version of myself. Past me had tried to ignore Lyric. And she'd still wanted me. "I feel like I should have to do more than just breathe around you."

She laughed. "The bar is low. What can I say?"

I could still try to flex my date muscles. "We can take dessert to go and head to the lake."

"That sounds nice, but I have to work in the morning."

So did I, but I didn't have to clock in at a certain time.

"I'm still good for dessert though," she said. "To go, so I can get my lunch packed for tomorrow."

"Dessert to bring home, pack lunch, and watch the news before bed?" It sounded like the perfect date to me.

The corner of her mouth tipped up. "It's a date. Or a continuation of this date."

"Either works." And I'd never looked forward to being with a girl more.

Eight

LYRIC

Isla peered into the cupboards one by one. She had come with me to look at the first apartment I'd heard back from. I had just closed the lab, but I found a change of clothes in my car—a spare pair of black shorts and an athletic tee for the times I went running after work.

I'd been too tired to go for a walk or a run, but I wanted to start again after my living situation was figured out. I loved being outside. Maybe I could walk at Stetson's before I moved out. The land around his place was gorgeous, and without the buzz of traffic, I could hear the meadowlarks and cows.

I hadn't seen Isla much, so when the landlord of this complex had returned my call, I'd asked her to go with me. Thinking about looking through places with Stetson that weren't his house left me empty. I couldn't bring myself to actually do it. And it wasn't like we could discuss baby topics around a landlord I didn't really know but who probably knew all about the Barrons. Like Hank.

Hank, the landlord, wandered through the living room with his hands in the pockets of his cargo shorts. He was in his fifties, and while he didn't scream perv, he didn't exactly fill me with confidence that he wasn't a tad creepy.

"Hmm." Isla bent and looked through the cupboards under the counter. "Mm-hmm."

Isla was a lot of things, but duplicitous wasn't one of them. She couldn't say one thing and mean another. Her expression gave her away, like it did now. Which was why she was hiding her face in an old cupboard with peel-and-stick lining on the bottom.

I shared her worry. It wasn't the outdated pattern on the lining. Half of the shelf protector was missing, most so worn in places, it'd become one with the wood. I wasn't relining shelves while pregnant and working full-time. In the grand scheme of living conditions, I couldn't care less about what lined my cupboards as long as it could be cleaned.

My main concern was how my eyes watered from the heavy fragrance hanging in the air. The perfume had seeped into the walls and the carpet. What would it be like to live in this space? Would all my belongings smell like I'd laundered them in a perfume vat?

Hank pushed up his wire-rimmed glasses. "The carpet's been shampooed, and it's all clean. I'd just need the deposit, first and last month's rent, and you can move in." His gaze lingered on Isla's jean-shorts-clad ass. We were easily half his age.

"I'll let you know what I decide." I hoped I didn't have to talk to him again. The apartment was a corner unit on the second of three floors. It was adequate, but not what I wanted to call home.

A dog barked from directly above the unit. Hank lifted

his gaze to the ceiling. "Better than a crying baby, am I right?"

Well. The irony almost made me giggle.

Isla straightened, her gaze shooting to me. I exchanged a look with her. Hank wouldn't be able to tell what my face said, but Isla pressed her lips together like she was holding back a nervous laugh.

"Thanks," I said to Hank, willing him not to glance at Isla again. "I'll be in touch if I decide to go with it."

"You'll want to move fast. You're the third person today I've shown it to."

Isla shut the cupboard doors and crossed to me. She flipped her pale hair over her shoulder. "How long has it been open?"

Annoyance flickered through his expression but not enough to keep him from ogling her long legs. "Not long."

She smiled sweetly but with an edge reminiscent of her mother. "How long is 'not long,' Hank?"

"A few days." He cleared his throat. "A week."

"*One* week?" she asked.

"Three, uh, months," he said gruffly and scooted to the door. "But like I said, you're the third person I've shown it to today, so I'd move fast."

"Sure." I forced a friendly smile. What if this was my best option? I wanted to go back to Stetson's house and resume what had quickly become our routine over the last week.

He'd get home in time to cook dinner or hang with me while I cooked. He'd have a beer on the porch, and I'd have lemonade, then we'd talk about our days. He'd tell me who he'd talked to if he'd run errands in town, and I'd say what I could about the mundane and cool cases I had from work.

Before Isla and I reached my car where we could talk about how I didn't want to live in a middle unit with Hank as my landlord, Stetson parked behind my car by the curb and got out.

"Are you looking at places already?" He glanced between me and his sister.

"I thought I'd get some friend time."

His jaw tightened, and he nodded. Had I hurt his feelings?

We'd been growing closer. Sleeping together, but nothing more than kissing. We hadn't even made out, and I couldn't bring myself to do what I wanted to with him yet.

Stetson scared me. The man I'd wanted for so long was within my reach, but I knew him; that was the first problem. He was a good guy; that was the second. I needed to be certain he was with me for me. Not out of obligation. Not because he was trying to be the peacekeeper.

Despite all that, we'd formed an intimate friendship of sorts, and I'd blocked him out of something he'd asked to help with. Guilt reignited the heartburn that had finally died down.

Isla frowned. "How did you find us?" She rolled her eyes at his guilty expression. "The tracker. Never mind."

Stetson did mental and verbal gymnastics around his parents. Isla physically evaded them rather than speaking out about the way they monitored her. I hoped she only needed time to get her feet under her, to save enough money to pay for her own phone and car so her parents couldn't justify their controlling behavior.

He adjusted the brim of his hat. His clothes were still dusty from working outside all day. I liked him dressed up, but this was the Stetson I'd fallen for. "How was this place?"

"I feel like I'd have to look for hidden cameras in the bathroom," I said, "and there's an issue Hank doesn't want to talk about since it's been open for so long."

He looked around. "Isn't this where the old school librarian died, and no one found her right away?"

"What?" I faintly recalled overhearing the nurses discuss a similar story. There'd be no end to morning sickness today.

"Yeah. Mrs. Miller. She worked at the school when Dad went there. She passed away and no one knew. The neighbors were complaining about the smell when they finally found her. Poor thing."

Definitely poor thing. The next apartment had to be a winner. I didn't want to start my single life in a place where a lonely woman died.

Isla blanched. "I remember, but I thought it was a town house."

He shook his head. "Carlton said it was the westmost apartment complex."

My phone rang. A message confirming I could look at another place flashed across the screen. "There's another apartment close to downtown I can look at. It's a house that's been turned into a triplex. Want to go with us?" I asked Stetson. I wanted him with me, but I also liked hanging out with Isla. The three of us roaming town wouldn't be a new thing, but since Isla and I had graduated, Stetson hadn't needed to run us around.

"I don't want to intrude on girl time." His expression was earnest, like he absolutely wanted to intrude.

Isla held her hands up. "I can't say it's still not weird for me, but I don't mind if Lyric doesn't mind."

"It's that place a couple blocks behind the hardware store and Hattie's furniture store." I'd be close to Mom instead of on the edge of town.

"I know the one. I'll meet you there."

He got back into his pickup and drove away. A few minutes later, we pulled up to the big farmhouse that had been converted into apartments. I'd been driving past this place my whole life. The entrance to one unit was in the front of the building, which said to me that the second and third apartments must be accessed from the rear. The detached garage had only two bays.

The landlord came out of the front door. Zelda, a stout woman in her sixties with curly dark hair, owned the complex and lived in the main unit. She grinned. "Oh, we have a group."

"Hi, Zelda. I hope you don't mind, but I brought more opinions." I had gotten used to making small talk with people by working in the clinic. It was a long shift if I didn't chat with patients. It hadn't come naturally at first, but I had emulated Stetson. Stuck to safe subjects like weather, and if not successful, used a little humor.

She chuckled and waved for us to follow her. Isla went first, and Stetson fell into step next to me, his elbow brushing my arm. It'd be so easy to curl myself into him, but we were almost to the stairs, and I wouldn't want to extract myself if I did.

My stomach sank when she led us up the back stairs to the second-floor unit. Exterior stairs in winter with a baby wouldn't be fun. Stetson's slight frown said the same thing.

The apartment was cute, though. We piled into the little entryway, and the arched ceiling was immediately visible.

"Nice," I said, admiring the hardwood and matching ceiling beams. The kitchen was farther in, but the floor plan was open. Matching wood on the kitchen cabinets seamed the whole look together.

"I must admit that I baby this apartment a little. It's my favorite. I'd move in if it wasn't for my knees. But you're young." She flashed a smile, giving off vibes a world apart from Hank. "I want you guys to talk freely. Go ahead and look around. I'll be out in the garage."

"Does one of the stalls come with the unit?" I asked.

"Yes, I save the garage for the tenants. The stall on the right would be yours. I'll be back in a few minutes." She scurried out.

"My vote is this place," Isla said as soon as the screen door closed.

"I know, right? A garage. I've never had a garage." I took Isla and dragged her to the closest bedroom. "Oh, this is gorgeous."

The ceiling was sloped and the room was empty, but the layout of a nursery formed in my mind. Three-foot bookshelves on the outer wall where the ceiling dropped the lowest. A crib and a changing table against the far wall. Maybe even a rocking chair by the rectangular window that overlooked the driveway and garage.

"Can you imagine?" Isla gushed, peering out the window.

"I can." I spun to check out the other bedroom. Stetson blocked the doorway, his expression disgruntled. The sloped ceilings would make the bedrooms uncomfortable for him. He'd be able to stand on only one side of the room. He'd have to stoop to reach into the crib. "You don't like it?"

Isla gave me a half hug and pushed past her brother. "I'm going to walk to the clinic to get my car and get going."

"Are you sure? I can take you." Did I do something to drive her away or was she giving us alone time? The one time we finally took my vehicle, and she needed hers.

Stetson handed his keys to her. "Go ahead and drive to your car. Lyric can give me a ride when we're done."

I followed Isla to the door. Stetson stayed behind.

"Hey, is everything okay?" I asked.

She glanced behind me. "I feel like you two need to talk about this. He's clearly not happy about something."

"He doesn't need to drive you away." I was still protective of my friendship.

She grinned. "I love that you'd rather hang out with me instead of Mr. Popularity, but I was going to go to Bismarck tonight anyway."

"Another brewery?"

"Don't tell anyone," she whispered and jogged down the stairs.

I walked to the first bedroom, but it was empty. The light at the end of the hall was on. Stetson stood on the side of the room, under the highest peak of the ceiling, spinning in a slow circle, a frown on his face.

The room was as cute as the one I would make the nursery. I could picture a bed—maybe even a queen-size bed—against the wall. This room was so much bigger than the one I'd had in the trailer. I couldn't see what was causing Stetson's expression. "This place is nice."

"Those stairs are going to be hell with a baby carrier. What's going to happen when it snows? Or when you have groceries to carry in?"

Defensiveness rose as he pointed out the same worries I'd had. This place had a nicer landlord, and as far as I knew, the last tenant hadn't died in it. "I'll shovel and make two trips. Carefully."

"These bedrooms aren't very large."

"Compared to your place."

"My place is nicer."

"But it's not my home."

"And why the hell not?" He whipped his cap off and pushed a hand through his dirty-blond locks. "I want you there, Lyric. I don't want you fucking here."

"But it's *your* house." I didn't want to be here either. I wanted to be at his place. With him. Yet, I wasn't going to be a squatter because I was afraid to be on my own.

He stuffed his cap back on and stalked toward me. I

backed to the wall, surprised by his intensity—and maybe a little turned on.

"Do whatever you want to it, Ricky." He towered over me, and it propelled me right back to our first time together. "Fill it with pictures of chickens or doilies or whatever the fuck, I don't care."

My breath was coming in pants. He was so close. But I couldn't resist testing him. "I saw a spoon holder with a chicken on it the other day."

"I'll buy it for you. Will that make you stay?"

"We haven't even—"

"Fucked? Lyric, I've been around you for over a week, and I only want to be around you more. We've only had sex once, and believe me, I want more, but I just want to be with you."

I fisted his shirt at the waist. He hadn't tucked it in. I was so close to touching abs I'd been able to only look at. I liked everything he said, but I couldn't give in, and I didn't know why other than it was something I wanted so badly and I was scared. "This place is nice, though."

"My place is nicer." He claimed my mouth, pressing my back against the wall. I opened immediately for him, and our tongues clashed, moving against each other like we were dancing.

I let go of his shirt and wrapped my arms around his neck. He picked me up, and I hooked my legs around his hips. *Finally.* That was the only word ricocheting around in my head.

Finally. Finally. Finally.

He ground against me, and the erection I'd gotten to experience only once answered the throb between my legs.

I could scale this man like a mountain, putting every ounce of my effort into conquering the pleasure he could give.

The squeak of the screen door broke through my haze. I jerked my head back, hitting the wall. "Shit," I whispered.

He set me down and adjusted himself, turning his back to the door.

I stole two seconds to straighten my clothing before I stepped into the hallway. Zelda was by the door.

"Sorry," I said. "Isla left, and Stetson and I were talking about how this would work out, and I think…" Was I really going to do this? Was the length of holding out only going to be a minute? We'd been taking baby steps, but this was a giant leap into a future I didn't want to slip out of my reach. "I think I'm going to stay where I'm at."

Disappointment crossed Zelda's face. "I understand."

"I would've taken this in a heartbeat. It's really beautiful."

"No worries. I'll lock up behind you."

I walked out with Stetson. What next? We go back to his place and do what we'd been doing? We were jumping around all the stages of a romantic relationship when usually I went from dating to breaking up. We'd gone from baby making to moving in to barely dating and now we were living together. Was that a good thing?

At the bottom of the stairs, he slipped his arm around my waist as if the same uncertainties hadn't crossed his mind. "Want to grab a bite to eat first? When we get home, you won't make it far before you're naked."

The questions vacated my brain. We were back in dating territory. Sort of. I could work with that.

* * *

Stetson

· · ·

Rattler's was full, so Lyric and I sat in the bar. I would've rather stopped at the diner, but they were closed already, and I couldn't remember which bar downtown I'd been to last. I didn't care to remember, and I wasn't in the mood to worry whether my visits were unbalanced.

Polly leaned over the bar. "Usual, Stetson?" She was as old as Mom and had been working here since the place opened.

"Not tonight. I'll have a Coke and the Rem burger with fries."

"Same," Lyric said.

Polly pushed away with a nod. Nothing fazed the woman. I preferred when she was working over the other bar staff. I didn't feel like Polly was helping start shit by spreading around what she heard.

Lyric swirled on her stool to face me and used the footrest close to the bottom. I didn't need it. My legs were too long.

The drinks were slid in front of us. She took a sip. "Come here often?"

I bit back a smile and answered honestly. "Too often, but not lately."

She tipped her head and tongued her straw in a way that went straight to my dick.

I groaned. "You're gonna kill me, Ricky."

She leaned her chin on her hand. "You only call me Ricky when it comes to sex."

"We haven't had sex for almost two months, and I've called you that since then."

She rolled her eyes, but a blush stained her cheeks. "When we're being more intimate, then."

"I used to call you that to remind myself you were my sister's best friend."

"I'm still your sister's best friend. I can be something to more than one person."

"It's not Isla I'm worried about." That wasn't true, and I didn't feel like hiding it from Lyric. "Well, maybe a little."

"Why?" she asked like the thought hadn't occurred to her.

"She doesn't have many people. She's kind of a loner."

She averted her gaze and took a long pull through her straw. What wasn't she telling me?

"She's not a loner?" I asked. The second-biggest hang-up about being with Lyric, behind my parents, was that the success or failure of our relationship would affect her friendship. Isla had too few people in her life for that to sit well with me.

"Outside of Coal Haven, she makes friends easily. She's not the wallflower everyone in Coal Haven thinks she is, but that's all they'll see."

"Because of our parents. And that's why I had to remind myself that you're my little sister's best friend."

"They don't have the power over me they have over you two."

"I know." I was processing what I learned about Isla, but hearing that Lyric was confident my sister could take care of herself eased my concern. I leaned into her. "Maybe that's why I find you so damn sexy."

The *tink* of plates being set in front of us kept me from kissing her in public. Was she ready for that?

I was.

We inhaled our food, sharing the ketchup. There was no awkward conversation. We'd been together for a week, but I hadn't attained this level of comfort with anyone else before.

Lyric finished her last fry and stole one of mine. I pushed my plate closer to her as I ate the last of my burger. I took a couple twenties out of my wallet and set them by my plate.

Polly swung by and didn't bother to ask if I needed change. I never did.

I diligently refrained from thinking about what was going to happen when I got Lyric home. I'd almost embarrassed myself at the apartment; I wasn't doing the same at Rattler's.

We turned off our barstools at the same time, coming face-to-face with Krystal.

Shit.

"I knew you were a cheater." Accusation shook Krystal's voice, her gaze jumping to Lyric and back. "You were with her when we were together."

My relationship with Lyric had been going stronger than I thought was possible in the short time since the fire, but then it'd been just us. Mom and Dad hadn't approached me since I'd told Mom, and Isla had accepted us quicker than I could've hoped. But a loud confrontation in the middle of Rattler's would upset me and Lyric and migrate to the rest of the Barrons. Shit.

"I'm not doing this with you again." I couldn't get past her without shouldering her out of the way. I wasn't pushing Lyric aside to run from my ex.

Lyric had no issues. She tugged me sideways with her, but her movement drew Krystal's laser gaze. "Does he know you're pregnant?" Her voice rang through the bar.

I held in a groan. I wanted to tell her to stop, but Krystal was highly reactive when she was pissed. Several customers I recognized stopped their conversations to stare. Remington was at a table in his black chef's coat, chatting with a couple, but he straightened, a brow cocked.

I snaked my fingers through Lyric's. The move hooked

Krystal's gaze. Her jaw went rigid, and she flipped her hair back.

"He does know, Krystal," Lyric said and cocked her head. "But I'm wondering how you do."

Krystal opened her mouth and closed it like a fish being held above the water. She lifted her chin, her gaze defiant. "Dr. Klevin."

He'd been the doctor on call when Lyric had gone to the ER. Had he really told others?

Lyric's expression said she didn't think so. "Hmm. Are you sure? If IT did an audit, would they find that you'd gone into my medical records for no good reason?" Krystal's nostrils flared, but Lyric leaned in. "Our baby isn't your business."

Krystal's gaze shot to mine. "It's yours?" Moisture glittered in her eyes. "You two are having a baby?"

I didn't have to answer her. Lyric was walking away, and I gratefully followed, still holding her hand. I'd always tried to reason with Krystal, but Lyric must have known that was impossible.

"I'd make sure it's yours if I were you, Stetson," she called after us.

I slid my arm around Lyric's waist, and we walked out as a unit.

Once the warm air hit my face, I kept Lyric by my side. "That could've been worse."

Lyric snorted. "Work is going to be fun."

"Are you going to talk to your boss?" I wouldn't put it past Krystal to have looked at Lyric's medical records.

"No. I'm not diving into that fire. She'll get herself in trouble if she keeps digging into records she has nothing to do with."

"The news is out." I opened the driver's door for her.

She had to drop me off at the clinic where Isla had parked my pickup.

"The news is so out."

We had each known it was coming, but we'd thought it'd be a gradual spread of speculation. The town gossip would be factual after tonight. Part of me was relieved. The other part was worried about Lyric. I was used to ignoring rumors about my family.

I stopped her before she got in and captured her mouth. She was sweet from the pop and salty from the fries. I couldn't wait to devour her—but she had to relax first. Krystal shouldn't have said any of that. Lyric seemed unbothered, but she was as stiff as a plank of wood.

"Are you okay?" I murmured against her lips.

"No? Yes? I want to vibrate out of my skin right now, and I'm dreading work on Monday."

"Let's get home." I wasn't trying to get her to my place so I could sex her problems away. Krystal was an issue. A frustrating one. I had people closer to me making this thing between Lyric and me flounder. I didn't need an enraged, jealous ex to add to it.

When Lyric dropped me off at my pickup, I unfolded myself from her car and leaned in through the open door. "You gonna come straight home?"

"I can't exactly stop at an off-sale store and grab some beer." She scowled. Lyric wasn't an angry drinker. She was a light social drinker like Isla. "Could you imagine if I was seen going into a place that sold only alcohol right now? It wouldn't matter if I was just buying tonic water."

"How about ice cream? I'll stop and grab some." I didn't know what would relax her, but I didn't want Krystal between us when our clothes came off. And if we didn't have sex tonight, I still wanted to cheer Lyric up.

She rubbed her belly. "I'm full, and I don't have the metabolism of a six-foot-four rancher."

But she was growing that rancher's baby. "You can watch me eat it."

She laughed, a carefree sound that made me want to slap my ball cap against my thigh and whoop. "Cookie dough."

"Got it." Grateful I'd taken her mind off what happened in Rattler's, if just for a few minutes, I said, "See you at home."

I liked the sound of that.

I stopped at the gas station instead of the grocery store so I could get in and out faster. They had pints of Ben & Jerry's. I paid quickly and walked out.

The owner of the grocery store was in line in front of me, buying a Powerball ticket. She turned, smiling when she saw it was me, then her gaze dropped to my armload.

Dammit.

"Did you know we're running a sale on ice cream?"

"It was just a quick stop." Nothing more. It was never anything more with me. Why couldn't business owners in town see that? I wasn't Dad. I wasn't boycotting the grocery store to get fucking Ben & Jerry's for my pregnant girl-friend. The gas station was on the way out of town.

Her smile was pleasant enough as she turned away, but I made a mental note to hit up her ice cream sale.

Then I was on my way home. The thought of being with Lyric attenuated my disgruntlement, and I cared a little less where I bought my damn ice cream. I just wanted to be home with my girlfriend.

Why did this time with a girl feel so real? It didn't have anything to do with the baby, but with Lyric.

When I entered the house, she was already curled up in what I now thought of as her corner of the couch with her feet tucked under her. I toed my boots off, grabbed two spoons from the kitchen on my way through, and plopped down next to her.

She accepted the spoon I handed to her and eyed the pint of ice cream. "Saves on dishes?"

"I'm resourceful. What are we watching?"

"I put on the news. Rain's moving in."

I nodded and took a scoop of ice cream. I had seen the forecast and looked forward to a cleansing rain that didn't involve high winds or hail. A little mud was worth it if there wasn't devastation to clean up.

By the time the news was finished, so was the ice cream. The container and spoons were on the coffee table. She'd had a few bites, but she'd stayed quiet, a comfortable silence. Sunlight had faded and clouds covered the sky. A slow patter started on the roof and hit the windows.

"It's raining," she murmured.

"We need it. Should probably turn on a light." The glow from the TV made the living room cozy.

She tossed off the blanket and flipped until she straddled me. Stunned, I kept my hands off her, unsure of what she was doing.

She set her ass on my thighs, and my dick woke the hell up. "Are you bothered by what she said?"

"What who said?" I couldn't tell her my name right now, much less figure out what she was asking.

"Krystal."

"Fuck Krystal."

With a small smile, she took my ball cap off and pushed her fingers through my hair. "Other people are going to be thinking the same thing."

The paternity comment. Krystal knew how to make words cut like a scalpel. And then there was my mother and her offer to pay for testing. But Lyric was on my lap where I'd wanted her for so very long, and I didn't want to think about anyone else. Not my family. Definitely not exes. And not the rest of the town. I rubbed my hands up and down her legs, her silky skin teasing my palms.

"I'm going to be honest, Ricky. All I care about is getting back inside you." I pressed her down on me as I rocked my hips up. "I wasn't going to pressure you after Rattler's."

"She got me down, but she's not ruining my night with you. You called me Ricky again." A sly smile spread across her face. "Stoney. Hmm, I don't know if I can taunt you with that anymore."

"I'm all stone right now, baby."

Her soft chuckle wafted over my skin. She tugged my shirt up, exposing my abs. "I've been wanting you to myself for so long, I want to play."

Hell, yes. "How do you want to play?" I shifted forward, giving her room to remove my shirt. She tossed it into the corner where she'd been sitting.

She trailed her fingers over my pecs, and my abs tightened. "You have such a nice body."

"How?" I had muscles, but I wasn't ready for a firefighters poster. I had a big frame and a physically demanding job. But I also liked beer.

She squeezed my biceps and groaned. "These. Flex."

I didn't move my arms as I tightened my biceps.

"Yes," she hissed, and my ego shot through the roof. Then she tapped a pec. "You know, the way your shirts hang off your chest and then pool at your waist." She danced her fingers down my stomach. I didn't intend to tighten my gut, but her touch was making it hard to stay still and let her have her fill. I wanted to flip her onto her back and plow into her—if I could undo the zipper that was wedged into my raging erection. "Your thighs are massive."

"Wanna take my pants off and see them up close?"

The heat in her eyes was enough of an answer. I died and went to heaven right then. "I'm going to take your pants off."

"Only if you take yours off too."

She slipped off me before I could catch her and hug her to me. The way she jerked her shirt off and flung her bra onto the couch next to it mesmerized me. Pale tits with peaked, rosy-pink nipples were in my line of sight, and I saw nothing else. Until she shimmied out of her shorts and underwear.

A small tattoo above her hip bone riveted me. I sat up, ignoring the excruciating pinch of my dick by my jeans. A dandelion gone to seed. Simple, but elegant, done with such fine detail I wanted to find the artist and give them a tip. "How didn't I know you had a tattoo here?"

She outlined the art with her fingers. "I got it last summer. Mom and I used to collect dandelions and blow them all over on our walks around the trailer park until the manager lost his shit because we were spreading weed seed."

"Puff all the damn dandelions you want out here." I gripped her hips and placed a kiss on the ink like I'd been wanting to do since I saw her in that red bikini. Heaven.

I would've kept going, but she pushed me back and dropped to her knees between my legs. If I was dreaming, waking me up would be cruel and unusual. The sultry look in her eyes. The way I was about to jackknife off the couch when she touched me. I knew I could've dreamed of this.

I hissed when her fingers landed on my waistband. I almost trembled as she unzipped and unbuttoned my jeans. But when she wrapped her warm hand around my erection and freed it—god*damn*.

"All you have to do is hold it, Ricky, and I'll do the rest."

"I wasn't thinking about using my hand."

And I watched, too scared I was in an alternate reality and I'd wake to find out I'd drifted off during the news.

She scooted closer. My jeans were only opened and hindering her efforts, but she didn't let them stop her.

Her lips closed around my cock, and an exhale exploded out of me. Hot, wet heat and Lyric kneeling in front of me. I hadn't dared to dream this.

She took as much of me as she could and pumped the base, then released me from the heaven of her mouth to lick the tip. Cool air caressed where her lips had been, and my cock twitched. This was as exquisite as it was torturous. I wanted to plow into her, but fuck...*Just keep exploring!*

Another pump, and her mouth was back on me. I anchored my hands in the cushions to keep from fisting her hair. I was able to take another minute, energy coiling inside me, ready to explode, before I said, "Fuck, Lyric."

She smacked her lips and pumped her hand. "Can I climb on?"

"Hell yes."

She climbed onto my lap. I stroked her hips, up her torso, and thumbed her nipples. She moaned and hovered over the glistening tip of my cock.

She licked her lower lip and looked down at the point where we weren't yet connected. "Stetson?"

"Yeah?"

"Does this feel...momentous or something?" She rolled her eyes and increased the distance between us.

I cupped my hands around her boobs. *Momentous* was a good word for the feelings raging inside me. "Yes. You're special to me. You're..." I dropped my hands down to her hips again. "You're—*we're*—going to have a baby." I couldn't bring myself to touch her stomach, to spread my hand out over her belly and think she was growing our baby. Not yet. Not while she was poised and ready to be impaled by me. "I've known you for a long time, and we're both going into this thinking of the future. I've never done that before. I don't want to fuck this up, Lyric."

"I don't either. But I can't escape the feeling that if we don't do this, there's nothing to ruin."

"Doing it the first time finally brought us together. And what happened from that?" I grazed her stomach with my thumbs. "It finally got me over myself. I won't ever regret it."

I must've said the right thing, but I wasn't telling her whatever would get me inside her faster. I meant what I said. And when she sank her wet heat onto me, my groan said it all.

"You feel fucking amazing." We hadn't talked about protection—again. It seemed pointless with the pregnancy and our abstinence since, but it signaled a bigger commitment, one that I was ready for even if we didn't say the words.

Any more thought was wiped away as she took me deeper, not stopping until she was fully seated.

"Fuck, Lyric," I said on a whisper, unable to be any more eloquent.

Wrapping my hand around her neck, I drew her head to mine, catching her mouth and licking my tongue inside.

She rode me, tentatively at first. I hadn't prepared her like the first time, but she also didn't need it. Still, I let her set the pace, rocking up and down, when I really wanted to bury myself deep inside her and release while still claiming her mouth until she was filled with nothing but me.

I wasn't usually a territorial prick, but I wanted her to be mine. Only mine. Forever mine. And I wanted her belly to grow big and show everyone she was mine. That this slightly nerdy girl with an intoxicating edge was having my kid, she was coming home to me, and everyone could leave us the fuck alone.

When she was almost to her climax, she clamped around me, her body tight. I brushed my thumb across her clit. She let out a cry into my mouth.

"Be loud, Ricky." The last time I rubbed her off had kept me hard both day and night. Lovely torture. My days had been filled trying to forget how quickly she'd come for me. Each time I'd thought of her while in the tractor I contemplated driving to the house to take care of my own business.

"Stetson." Her breath heated my ear as she ground onto my cock.

"Louder." I added pressure and thrust my hips up as she was coming down.

"Stetson!"

"Let me feel you come." I finally let my restraint go. My free hand dug into her ass cheek, and I pumped into her as hard as I could while seated.

My name echoed through the living room until it became a wail as heat flooded between us. Sweet, hot, and wet.

An unseen vise squeezed my balls until I roared louder than I ever had, coming long and hard. Stars exploded behind my eyes, and for a few heartbeats, I couldn't breathe. When I came back to myself, she was tucked against my chest, her head buried by my neck.

A tremor traveled through her body when I took my thumb off her clit. I put that hand on the other side of her ass where it belonged. "You don't work this weekend, right?"

She shook her head.

"Good. 'Cause I ain't done with you yet."

Nine

LYRIC

Of all the ways I'd imagined sex would be with Stetson, fun didn't enter my mind.

"Stop it." My giggles were coming too fast.

"What?" he asked innocently, as if he hadn't just discovered I was ticklish when he grazed my armpits.

"I'm not going to let you touch me again."

"Aw, Ricky. You've had me now. You're not going to want anything else." He rose to his hands and rocked in and out.

Pleasure made my eyelids flutter, but we were both desensitized. This was our third round, and I'd lost count of how many times I'd come. I wasn't sure I could do it again, but being filled with him was still too good to pass up.

"Throw your toys away, 'cause you got this now."

I laughed and lightly scratched my nails down his sides. "I'd have to buy more. I can't put scorched dildos in my body."

He stopped, gazing down at me. Interest brightened his expression. "What are you going to buy?"

I wiggled under him, but he didn't move. I widened my knees and stuck my heels in his butt; he refused to thrust.

If he wanted an answer, I'd give him one. "A giant pink vibrator with a tip that's flared like a cowboy hat. And I'll call it Stoney."

That got him to kick his hips. "What if I help you use it?"

This time I was the one who stopped. Weren't guys touchy about them? I'd mentioned it once to a date after college, and he turned red and sputtered. I hadn't broached the subject since. "You don't mind toys in bed?"

"Why would I?"

"I dunno. Insecure?" He had zero to be insecure about. Stetson could use his impressive cock size to be a selfish jerk. But he knew how to use it—and he knew what to do when he wasn't using it.

"Have I seemed insecure in bed?" He punched his pelvis forward in the angle he knew would earn him a moan.

"No, but we haven't used toys."

"Toys are tools." He lowered himself to his forearms and set a steady pace. "And I happen to be good with tools."

Another groan left me. Energy burned hotter. I was on a journey to another climax. "Is there anything you're bad at?"

I'd watched him for enough years to know he was a gifted bastard most people would hate, but he was the type of nice guy that made him hard to dislike.

"I can't knit," he murmured against my neck, sending shivers down my spine.

"You haven't even tried."

"Not true." He nibbled up my neck to my ear. The man was hitting all my erogenous zones. "When I was a kid, I made a scarf that had a ninety-degree angle in the middle."

"Sounds like maybe you aren't good with your hands."

He cocked a brow before pushing one of his hands between us to strum my clit.

I moaned as I bucked against him. "I'm still not convinced."

Minutes later, I exploded, my body wringing me of the last of my energy as he came inside me.

I'd never get tired of that. There was nothing between us. I wanted it to stay that way, inside and out of the bedroom.

He rolled to his side and flung the comforter over us. My eyelids were heavy as I curled into him, but I wasn't ready to sleep. "Okay. I believe that you're good with your hands."

His chuckle vibrated through my cheek. "Isla tried to get me to knit. And our grandma wanted us both to learn how to crochet, but my big hands kept fumbling the hooks."

"I can knit, but I prefer to crochet. Mom cross-stitches. Mostly, we need something to do with our hands while we're watching TV at night."

"I'll give you something to do with your hands."

I bit back a smile. "Oh? What's that?"

"This place gets dusty."

I laughed and rolled so my back was to him. "I'm surprised you don't hire a housekeeper."

"I did once. Remember Mrs. Thatcher?"

The name was familiar. "Who?"

"The lunch lady? She probably retired before you got to school. Anyway, she took on part-time housekeeping after she retired until her arthritis got so bad. I didn't really care how good of a job she did, but she cared and quit. Mom and Dad hated that I had a housekeeper."

"They don't trust easily. Why do you think that is? Your family has been here for generations, but your parents act like they're living in the middle of a metropolis and they're surrounded by muggers and people trying to get state secrets."

He answered readily, and I liked that he talked so freely with me. "Dad was treated like a prince in that he would rule one day. Grandpa fostered competition between the brothers. 'Keep 'em strong' kind of thing."

My dad was Cameron's age, and they were nothing alike, but there were similar threads of selfishness in their behavior. Each was an apex, and their needs came first. "What about your mom? She wasn't raised like that, was she?"

"I think it was the affair." His voice rang with regret for an act he had nothing to do with. "I think it was living with Dad. Dealing with my grandparents. I don't remember everything, but she was alone through a lot of that. Her identity had become Mrs. Cameron Barron, and it wasn't like she could walk away. The house was his. The money. Everything."

Would that have been my mom if my dad hadn't left? Beaten down and bitter? The difference was that my mom would've sheltered me from it. Naomi had armed Stetson to fight her battles. "I'll be empathetic when dealing with them, but, Stetson, I'm not going to let them treat me or this kid poorly. They've been cordial to me, and that's all I'll expect." Anything more would set me up for disappointment.

"Just talk to me, okay? Don't get upset at something either one said and then expect me to read your mind."

"Have you had problems with that?" I didn't want to think about Stetson and his exes, but they were a part of his past that formed his future. If I wanted to be in his future,

I'd have to learn from them. I couldn't twirl through the pastures, proclaiming I was different and special. He'd said I was, but at one time, those girls thought they were.

Isla had mentioned her parents had scared away more than a couple of his girlfriends. Of course they had. It was what they did to people. I'd slipped through because Isla and I had been so young when we'd become friends. I hadn't been a threat then. Would I be now?

"Mom and Dad say things, and people expect the worst," he said. "Mom can tell someone 'nice dress' and they'd think she was insinuating something or that she hated the dress. So, just talk to me. Okay?"

"Okay."

He tightened his hold around me. "Want to go to the cabin Sunday? We can see if Isla can come. Maybe Holden and Emery and the kids? Nora."

I got along with Holden's sister just as well as the rest of them. "Like last time?"

"If you wear that bikini again, yes."

"I didn't wear the bikini last time. I thought the red made me look washed out, so I cleaned it and put it for sale at the thrift store."

"Damn." He shifted his arm, his hand landing by my abdomen, and he slid it to rest on my hip. He'd been grazing my stomach. A light brush here and there, but he otherwise avoided my abdomen. He might not know I could tell. It was early yet. I barely knew what to do with myself; I couldn't expect him to know. I wasn't showing yet. I was just crossing the two-month mark, and I might not show for months yet. But I longed to feel his warm hand on my belly. To see the warmth and excitement in his eyes when he looked at the baby bump.

And if he didn't act like that? I would worry about it then.

* * *

Stetson

Carlton looked over his glasses as he tapped into the cash register. His shock of white hair might make someone think he wasn't as spry as he used to be, but just a few minutes ago, he'd practically shoved me away from the ladder to get a box of screws from the top shelf. And since the hardware store was in an old downtown building, the shelving went to the ceiling and the ladder was on wheels that slid up and down the aisle.

But he'd informed me, for liability reasons, he was the only one allowed to use the ladder. I thought he also liked to have a reason to climb it.

He rattled the price off, and I handed him my card. "What's in store for today?" The same question he asked every time I was in.

"Cutting silage. A lot of my summer is getting winter food ready for the cattle."

He grinned, his dark skin creasing at the corners of his eyes and across his forehead. "Let me know if you need anything else."

"Thanks, Carlton."

"You betcha. Tell your dad I said hi." Carlton also said that each time I was in, and he was the only one who ever sent well-wishes with me for Dad. But Carlton hadn't grown up in Coal Haven. The fear of the Barrons wasn't bred into him like the rest of the town. Dad was just another good customer, and if he shopped elsewhere, Carlton figured he had a reason. This place would do fine without our business, like most other stores. But if I could buy something in Carlton's hardware store that I could get at the farm supply store, I'd make an extra trip.

"Will do." Outside, I got into my pickup. The casserole dish Mom wanted me to take back to Aunt Willow's was on the passenger seat along with a box of special cookies from a shop in Bismarck. There was a second box for me. Mom hadn't included Lyric when she said she'd gotten them for me, but I planned to share them with Lyric—naked.

I drove through town to the side opposite from where I lived and took the highway that'd lead to Uncle Bruce's place. A couple miles out of town, a pickup was parked half on the road and half off. The ditch was too steep to move over any farther.

My stomach sank when I recognized Liam's pickup. Two little heads bobbed in the back window while Liam strained against the lug nuts of one of the back tires.

When he spotted my vehicle, he stopped what he was doing and slipped behind his pickup to keep off the road. Did he recognize my truck? He wasn't watching me, but he was saying something to the kids.

I made a split-second decision. He wouldn't want my help. He might ignore me, maybe even tell me to fuck off, but that didn't seem like Liam, not that I knew him that well. But if the tire was easy to change, Liam probably would've been done by now. He'd grown up farming and ranching. Guys like us could win tire-changing competitions. He wasn't far from his house, but he had his kids with him. Was the baby in there too?

Hitting the brakes, I couldn't stop until I'd passed him. I pulled over as far as possible, killed the engine, and hopped out. He'd have any tools I needed if he didn't ask me to get in my truck and leave.

One of the boys poked his head out the window. "Which one am I?"

I gave Eli a wink. "What's up, Russ?"

He giggled and ducked back into the pickup. Liam's forehead stayed scrunched as he met my gaze. "Stetson."

"Liam. What's the issue with the tire?"

He took a moment to answer as if he was reading into my tone. Finally, he rubbed the back of his neck and eyeballed the ornery flat. "I got two of the nuts off, but I can't make the rest budge. Kenny's supposed to be resting with Ginny. I was trying not to wake her."

"Care if I give it a shot?" I'd helped plenty of stranded motorists. Blown tires, broken belts, transmissions that took a crap. I acted the same now as I had then. Liam was just a guy who needed a hand.

He evaluated me for a heartbeat before nodding. "Go ahead."

I was bracing myself to pull on the wrench he'd left on the nut when one of the pickup doors opened behind me. I kept going, a passive audience to how Liam interacted with his kids.

"Get back inside, Eli. We're on the highway."

"But we want to watch."

"It's cooler in the cab."

"But—"

"Fine. But don't get out this side." His tone was slightly exasperated, but his temper was in place. I hadn't ever challenged Dad like the boys did Liam, but Dad would've issued an order and expected me to comply. And I would've. Liam had all the patience Dad didn't.

The door shut. "Go out the ditch side, but be really careful," Liam said. "That's where it dips down." He passed me to stand by the bed of the pickup. "Get up in there."

In a minute, two boys were peering over the side of the pickup. I wasn't having any more luck than Liam, but not every flat was as easy to fix as YouTube would like us to believe.

"It's stuck?" Owen asked.

"Yep," I said. "Think I should jump on it?"

"I'll do it." Liam stepped in to take over. "If something busts, I want it on me."

He put a boot on the long arm of the wrench and slowly added his weight. Nothing.

"I'm heavier. I'll try." I could pay him for anything I broke. My savings was full of money he hadn't gotten but should've.

He relented, and I did the same thing. My size had to do the trick. I was optimistic until Owen said, "Are you my dad's brother?"

The wrench gave, and I slipped off. I caught myself on the side of the pickup. Liam moved like he was going to catch me.

When I steadied myself, he averted his gaze. "Guys, we discussed this already."

"But he's our uncle."

Liam assessed my reaction before saying flatly, "Not really, no."

The truth of his comment burned into my skin like a brand.

Eli propped his little elbows on the frame. "Kenny said not all family gets along."

I ducked my head. Would I have to explain to my kid one day why they couldn't talk to Liam? Would I have to keep them from playing or associating with Eli, Owen, and Ginny?

What a dick move. I couldn't imagine sitting a kid down and telling them not to talk to decent people they were related to. I'd had the lecture. Isla. Holden. Probably Nora. Uncle Bruce's sons, Evander and Derek, had probably gotten the same lecture, but Derek had been braver than all of us. He'd been Liam's best friend.

Liam's wife was Derek's widow. When Liam and Kennedy got together after Derek's death, I thought Dad would go nuclear. He'd tried to interfere, but Liam had the same stubbornness the rest of us were all born with, plus more from the grandparents who'd raised him. But Bruce had changed after my cousin's death, and he'd told Dad to back off once Liam and Kennedy were married. Things were tense between my uncle and my dad. I was tired of all the strain.

"I'd like to change that." I said it to all of them, but I wanted Liam to know it wasn't just to defuse an uncomfortable situation.

"Boys, why don't you hop back in the cab of the pickup?"

"But, Dad—"

Liam cut them a warning look, the same as the one I'd gotten from our dad while growing up. Liam had Dad's eyes. I had to glance away.

"Go on," he said to them. "I've got to talk to Stetson."

Dramatic sighs were carried away on the breeze as the kids climbed down the tailgate and got into the back seat of the pickup.

Liam kept his back to the window. "Did you mean it?"

He hadn't shut me down. A good sign. "Yes, but if you want to tell me to fuck off, I get it. I deserve it."

He gazed down the highway behind me. "You've been civil, Stetson. That was more than I got from your parents. But I'm not letting my kids endure what I had to, and that includes not sitting aside while you ignore them when Cameron or Naomi's around. Or your aunt Kira."

Holden's mom was as rude as my dad. Uncle Bruce had been the same once upon a time, but losing a son and nearly severing his relationship with Kennedy, the former daughter-in-law who was like a daughter to him, had changed things.

"They're kids," Liam continued. "They adore Holden, and they're going to lump you in with him. They only know you're their uncle. You hurt their feelings, and it'll cut a lot deeper than it ever did me. Because I knew where I stood."

He'd been on the outside since he was born. And he'd never been invited in. Things wouldn't change with my kid if I didn't take the helm. "I'll handle my parents."

He searched my expression. "You might think that, but you haven't seen the ugly side of Cameron I have. You're his golden child. He belittles Bruce because the guy has the audacity to be a good neighbor to me."

I knew all about Dad's ugly side. I'd spent a lot of my adult life making up for it. "Dad would belittle Bruce anyway." It was how he was raised. Bruce was a younger brother and needed guidance. I wasn't using the same justification. "And Mom...is Mom. I can handle her."

"Don't jerk my family around." His warning was clear. He'd cut me out of his life, and he wouldn't have to dig very deep. He studied the highway again. The distant sound of an engine reached me.

"Lyric's pregnant," I said in a rush to let him know this wasn't just about him and me. His kids and my kids deserved better than the cards forced into our hands.

His brows rose. "Yours?"

I nodded. Mom's paternity test discussion banged around my head. She wouldn't forget about it. I'd have to talk to Lyric.

"Cameron and Naomi must've died on the spot."

A laugh sputtered out of me but cut off quickly. Dad hadn't talked to me yet. We'd been communicating via text messages about what was going on with the ranch. Nothing more. "Something like that. I told you in case you're wondering about my change of heart. It's making me rethink some things I should've put more effort into earlier."

"Lyric doing okay? She's gotten pretty close with Kenny and Laney, but they haven't said anything."

Laney's husband, Archer, was another cousin I wanted to get to know better but had been warned away from by my parents. Family members who didn't bend to their will were seen as threats to their assets. Like Liam had said, I was the golden child. I had to be different. "She's good. The news is out now. We kept it to ourselves as long as we could while we were figuring it out."

We were still figuring it out.

The approaching vehicle was almost on us. I looked over my shoulder to see Uncle Bruce slowing down. His stunned expression paired well with his jaw hanging open. "Everything okay here?"

His shock vanished, and he grinned at the boys wildly waving at him.

"It's fine," Liam answered. He was the one Bruce was probably checking on anyway. "Stetson stopped to help me with some cranky lug nuts."

"Need a hand?"

"Naw," I said. "I think my big ass jumping on the tire iron will get the others loose."

He nodded, taking in the whole scene once more. "Call if you need anything."

"I'll be by to drop off Aunt Willow's casserole dish." I could hand it off, but I wanted to say hi to her. She flitted around the kitchen at family get-togethers instead of sitting with the group. Almost forty years married into the family, and they still intimidated her.

"See you in a bit." He drove off.

I wrestled the last of the lug nuts off with Liam, and from there, it took only minutes for us to change the tire and lift the flat into the back of the pickup.

I wasn't sure how to leave. My congenial nature failed me when it was someone I needed to make a good impression on for myself and not for the sake of redeeming the Barron name. "I, uh, have some cookies. Can the boys have some?"

"They'll strip you down faster than a big-city mugging."

Laughing, I retrieved the cookies and passed one to each of the kids. Liam leaned against the pickup, his arms crossed. Wary, like he still wasn't sure what to expect.

"See you around."

He nodded, and I walked to my pickup. I'd had my first real conversation with my brother.

Ten

STETSON

I parked in front of Bruce's farmhouse. It was an older place they'd remodeled over the last ten or twenty years. My great-grandfather had purchased this land to add to our family's growing accumulation. The oil wells were on our side of town, most of them scattered over land that would've been my uncle Allen's had he stayed in Coal Haven.

Bruce's truck was by the shop, but I ran the casserole dish into the house first. Willow was just putting another casserole in the oven. One time, I'd been looking for a potholder and opened a cupboard that housed at least thirty different types and sizes of baking dishes.

"Hey, Aunt Willow."

She shut the oven and spun, a bright smile on her face. Her gray-blond hair was pin straight, and even though I doubted she'd left the house all day, she wore gray slacks and a pink blouse under her apron. "Stetson. What a nice surprise."

She said that to everyone, but each time I grinned like I was a kid again. "Mom sent this with me to return."

"Perfect." She took the glass dish and set it by the sink. "How is she?"

"Good." The years might change but the script stayed the same.

"And you?" Her expression was different. Not aloof, expecting me to answer with *fine*. "How are you doing? And Lyric?"

I hadn't told her or Bruce about Lyric or the baby, but it was an unspoken rule that family would always be informed before gossip hammered at us like a cold spring rain. Mom or Dad had likely told them. "She's well. She'll be staying with me for a while."

I stuck my hand in my back pocket, standing off-kilter like I had when Aunt Willow had caught me and her oldest son, Evander, digging for dinosaur bones in her treasured rose bushes when we were eight.

"How's she feeling? Any morning sickness?"

"A little, but not too bad."

Willow's smile was relieved. "That's good. I got so sick with each boy. It was bad with Evander, but with Derek, I had an older boy to run after and Bruce was in the field." She patted my shoulder. "But I know you'll take good care of Lyric. Want a cookie?"

"Absolutely." Mom's cookies would keep. Aunt Willow's baking was responsible for half my height. She had loved feeding me, and I'd loved eating her food.

Several times over the years I'd wished Mom was more like Willow. I'd never tell her, of course. I'd never tell anyone. Evander had felt smothered by each parent, by being a Barron, and he'd ditched Coal Haven to rarely return over the last fifteen years. But I soaked up Aunt Willow's nurturing when she was around.

I took a handful of chocolate chip cookies. I gave Willow a quick hug and went outside to find Bruce. Typically, I'd find him to talk shop. This time, I wanted to see what he had to say about what he'd seen.

Bruce was in the shop, bending over and inspecting underneath his John Deere 4020.

"Got a leak?"

"Damn hydraulics." He straightened and lifted a silver thermos that had been set in the giant wheel well of the tractor. It was coffee. Bruce drank the same thermos of coffee throughout the day, from hot to cold, topped off only once when he had lunch with his wife.

"Want help?"

"Archer's on his way, but you can stay if you want." He took a steady sip from his thermos while he inspected my reaction.

A family gathering I wasn't normally a part of. My world tipped as if it could get flipped upside down. There was no reason this had to be awkward. "I could stay for a bit."

He nodded. If he was surprised I was willing to hang out with Archer when my dad wouldn't approve, he didn't show it. "Did you get Liam all straightened out?"

"He should be home by now."

"Nice of you to stop."

"Yeah." I shoved a cookie into my mouth. Willow made some of the best cookies in the county, but it was dust on my tongue.

"You know, Stetson." Bruce dipped his head and fiddled with the lid of his thermos. "I think I was a little like you." He let out a humorless laugh. "A lot like you, actually."

"How so?" I asked around my mouthful. Another sign I was more comfortable around my aunt and uncle than my parents. Mom would've chided me, and it wouldn't have mattered if we were the only two people in a hundred-yard radius.

"I bought into it. Because they told me to."

I regretted taking extra treats. The first cookie landed like wet mud in my gut.

"Cameron's the boss. He's the oldest son. The one in charge." He set his thermos on the shop counter. "I grew up being told to shut up and do what he said. But all it did was rob me of a relationship that could've been really rewarding. That attitude stole some of the precious time I had with Derek."

Derek and Liam had been best friends. As close as brothers. Liam had been a point of contention between Derek and his dad. Between Derek and the whole family. But Derek had done what the rest of us couldn't. He hadn't cared what my parents said.

"I almost lost what relationship I had with Kennedy because of that stupid attitude." He made a disgusted noise. "That kid is my nephew. Just as much as you are. It's not his fault. And no matter what my brother says, Liam's a good guy. A goddamn good father too."

"I know," I said quietly.

He took a cleansing breath. "But we were in a hard place. You still are, I guess."

"Yeah, I am. I'll deal with it."

"I know you mean well, Stetson. But if Naomi hears about you going out of your way to help Liam? You might not be the one to suffer."

I would. But not as bad as she'd amp up her shunning of Liam and his family. I'd hold my ground. She'd have to back off or take her anger out on me. Or Dad. Liam didn't deserve it.

The noise of an engine reached us. Probably Archer.

Bruce was about to walk past me to greet Archer, but he stopped. "Just know, they ain't hearing nothing from me."

He didn't catch my quick smile. For the best. My uncle was hiding that I helped Liam. My brother, who was stranded on the side of the highway with two kids. It wouldn't have mattered how close Liam was to his house. I would've been expected to drive on by.

Archer jumped from the cab of his pickup. "Bruce." His expression flickered when it landed on me, but he smiled. "Stetson."

"Hey, Archer." We didn't cross paths that often. Holden kept his friendship with Archer and Liam separate from me. Best to avoid the drama. "Helping Bruce with the 4020?"

He grabbed a pair of work gloves out of the passenger seat. "And here I thought y'all had it taken care of and I'd just get to sneak cookies."

Bruce snickered. "She made a double batch. I think you're getting some sent home."

"That's good. Delaney sent more eggs." He was the only one who called his wife Laney by her first name, and I had to remind myself who Delaney was each time.

"Good," Bruce said. "We were out, and I can't have scrambled eggs from the store-bought kind once I had hers." Archer chuckled. Bruce shuffled back into the shop, waving Archer after him. "But I want cookies too, so let's get this leak fixed."

Archer swaggered in behind him, and I was left outside the shop, a rare feeling trailing through me. I was out of place.

Coal Haven was my home. My family had helped to found the town. Bruce was my uncle. Archer my cousin. But watching those two together revealed a history I wasn't part of. Bruce had alluded to getting to know Liam. The three of them and their families—all members of my family—lived on the other side of town from me. Away from my side. Away from hurt and control and resentment. And they were thriving. Bruce was already laughing from something Archer had said.

The yawning emptiness inside me ached like I was being pulled apart. I fisted my hands to focus on something else. The cookies ground together in my palm.

Shit. I had to get out of here. "Hey, uh, I just remembered I told Lyric I'd bring dinner home."

Archer popped his head up from where he was going over the game plan with Bruce. "See ya, Stetson. Tell Lyric hi from me and Delaney."

Bruce gave me a nod and went back to chatting with Archer. I was dismissed.

Long strides carried me to my pickup. I tossed the cookie remnants into the roses I had once dug in.

As I drove away, the hole inside me began to mend, but it was like it couldn't go together as solidly as before.

I'd told Bruce I'd deal with my parents, but having just had a taste of being on the outside, I was no longer so confident as to what I'd do if they shut me out.

* * *

Lyric

The sun beat down on the four of us. Soft waves lapped at the shore several yards away from where I was sitting in the green grass behind Stetson's small cabin. Boats zoomed across the lake with a few bobbing in place while the occupants fished.

Holden and Emery had come by themselves. The kids were spending the afternoon helping Emery's mom garden.

My sunglasses helped to hide how my gaze kept straying to Emery's belly. She was a couple of months further along than me, but her belly was rounded. She'd started wearing maternity tops at work.

Her swimsuit was a tankini and as cute as ever with her stomach sticking out. I wasn't the only one who thought so. Holden would swoop by every so often to bring her a water, more sunscreen, or a snack. And each time, he'd either touch or kiss her belly.

Maternity clothes and public affection highlighted the pregnancy. Would Stetson and I reach that point? He was hesitant around my stomach, and the public already commented on my clothing. Maternity clothes would be like a personal invitation. I wanted Stetson to be free enough to act like Holden when it came to the baby, but he hadn't touched me since the others had arrived.

I swallowed my longing with the lemonade Isla had brought. I'd needed the liquid for Nora's oatmeal cookies. I had nearly pissed myself coughing when I bit into one and hit a raisin I thought was a chocolate chip.

"Are you nervous about work tomorrow?" Emery asked. "After Friday?"

Isla crossed one leg over the other. "I heard about that." She pursed her lips. "Mom heard about that."

At some point I'd have to deal with Naomi and Cameron. Stetson couldn't be a barrier forever. But today wasn't that day. "I would bet half my paycheck Krystal looked at the notes from my ER visit. She was in the wrong, and she knows it. She'll lie low for a while."

"Would they actually fire her, though?" Emery's question wasn't rhetorical. She'd been in Coal Haven and at the clinic for just a year. Some places enforced the rules only on certain people, and since Krystal had been hired back after she'd quit in a tizzy over Stetson breaking up with her, someone at the clinic liked her.

"I don't know. I've heard of people at the hospital getting fired for going into records they shouldn't. I don't know if our clinic's admin would do it, but it won't come from me. She can work at the nursing home or even the refinery. My options are more limited, and I want to stay on my coworkers' good sides."

"It's not right."

"Joan's got my back. The other techs. X-ray. You. I'm not worried about Krystal making work hell. She'll just be a little more annoying."

Isla rolled her head where it rested on the seat back to look at me. "At the grocery store, I was asked three times if I'm looking forward to my new niece or nephew."

Nora laughed. "Same. But Holden and Emery's baby isn't as scandalous."

"That's fine with me," Emery said and nudged me. "I can spread a rumor about myself and take the focus off you."

"Just wait," I said, laying my head against the lawn chair and stretching my legs out. Closing my eyes, I soaked up the warmth of the sun. "Someone will start one for you."

A shadow fell over me. "I don't know who's starting what, but I'm starting the hamburgers and hot dogs. Who wants what? And don't say Holden's lettuce. Leafy greens don't belong on the grill."

Emery groaned. "It's good though."

"You're partial," Stetson grumbled. "Holden could grill dirt and you'd be first in line. What are your orders, ladies?"

He loomed over me as he mentally noted what everyone wanted. Blocking the sun, he didn't touch the chair. Or me. Considering where we'd started as a couple, we'd made progress, but that didn't stop disappointment from filtering through me.

We were here as a couple. Everyone knew it, but we weren't acting any differently than before. Was that a bad thing?

"Nora, no vegan burger?" he asked.

She pushed her sunglasses up. "I've had to clean a lot of things out of my diet, Stetson, but beef wasn't one of them. Just don't put anything extra like oatmeal or crackers in my patty, please."

"That would be meatloaf." He stepped away, but not before grazing his fingertips over my shoulder, leaving electrical pulses where he touched.

I couldn't stop my little smile, and Isla and Nora noticed. They exchanged amused looks.

"It's hard to get used to," Isla confessed to Nora.

"I wondered how weird it'd be." Nora set her sunglasses back on her nose. "But it's no different from before. I don't know what I expected. It's not like our family is super touchy-feely."

"Neither am I," I said. I'd like to show him affection around people, but I was taking my cues from him. Was he taking his from me? This was new to both of us.

"Not unless it's in the back of Holden's barn." Isla snort-laughed.

"Isla!" Fire burned into my cheeks. I turned my wide gaze to Emery.

She was fighting her grin and failing. "Is that where the magic happened? Do we need to get a plaque made?"

"What would it say?" Nora's impish grin was what the rest of the town didn't see when they looked at her innocent, big, blue eyes. She had a wicked streak a mile wide that she hid well. "The Banging Tack Room."

"You'll need to put a sign up by the riding helmets

Holden hung up for the kids." Isla's smile turned syrupy sweet. "Always wear protection." She snorted harder. Nora's cackle mixed with Emery's giggle.

"You guys suck. All of you." I coolly inspected my short nails. "The sign should read Ride Hard."

Isla's laughter ended in a sigh. "Seriously, though. I'm happy for you guys."

"There's going to be a lot of little Barrons running around," Nora said. "Emery and Holden. Liam's kids. Now yours. I wouldn't be surprised if Archer and Laney planned to try for a baby soon."

A lot of little Barrons. "What if..." I clamped my lips shut. How could I think of saying my thought out loud?

"What if what?" Isla asked. All the other women's eyes were on me.

I sat up and gripped the arms of the lawn chair. "I lost what I was going to say, sorry. That's a lot of cousins."

Nora nodded, back to the sweetly innocent girl. The opposite of her mother.

"Ugh, I've gotta use the bathroom again. I'll be back." I rushed to the cabin, hoping that my departure looked more natural than it felt. I had to get away from the conversation.

Inside, I used the toilet. After I washed my hands, I splashed water on my cheeks. *A lot of little Barrons.*

There were other Finnegans running around. My half-sibs. They might know my first name, and they probably thought Mom had forbidden my dad from seeing me. Or that I had. Maybe I was the bad kid in their minds. The girl who didn't love her father, and he had no choice but to go on without her. Poor guy.

Some days, I hated that I had his last name. The same one as his other family. The ones who were good enough for him. But Mom had kept her married name, and I felt a little better because of it. We were the Finnegans no one wanted.

I wouldn't let my kid feel that way. If Naomi and Cameron wanted to treat the baby like they had treated Liam, would I let the kid walk around with the last name of a family who wanted nothing to do with it?

I left the bathroom and stopped in the little kitchen. I wasn't ready to go outside, and there was nowhere else to linger. The cabin had only one bedroom. It was small but nice. Stetson's dad had a bigger place on more land. I'd been there a few times with Isla, but I'd always preferred Stetson's homier cabin.

Grabbing a mineral water from the fridge, I stayed in the kitchen. The screen door creaked open, and Isla entered.

"I'm after a water too." She crossed through the square living area and got a strawberry-flavored mineral water. She cracked the can and leaned against the counter. "Gonna tell me what's wrong?"

I winced. "Was it obvious?"

She shrugged and took a drink. "Probably not to the others."

I wasn't going to bullshit Isla. One of the biggest fears of things going wrong or right with Stetson was losing her. "When Nora said 'a lot of little Barrons,' it just..."

She took another drink and set her can down. The need to understand was in her eyes, but she didn't know what I meant. I'd have to spell it out.

"What if this baby is a little Finnegan?"

Her eyes flared. "Oh."

Yeah. Her flat tone that couldn't disguise her astonishment and disappointment was exactly why I had shut my mouth when the thought occurred to me. "I'm still in my first trimester, but that only leaves like six months before the baby's born. I don't feel the need to be married before it arrives, but what if..." Marriage seemed so far away from where we were.

"But what if you two don't marry? Or what if you do, but it's Baby Finnegan until then?"

I nodded, relieved at the lack of judgment in her voice. "I haven't thought that far ahead. But I know it's not going to be Baby Barron just because that's what's expected."

Her lips formed a wry twist. "That's what everyone expects, so it definitely won't be Baby Barron."

"My toxic trait."

"I'd like to be able to give you advice, but I know nothing about babies. And I think this is most definitely a conversation you need to have with Stetson. It's really no one else's business."

We shared a knowing look. We both knew that certain people would insist the baby's name was their business.

"I'll worry about it when I get there," I said, shrugging off the concern for another day.

"Don't be afraid to talk to me, okay?" Her tone was earnest, her gaze searching. "I'm one of them, but nothing has changed. I'm still the dorky Isla you know and love."

I chuckled, but my relief was undeniable. Isla wasn't going to side with whatever her parents wanted instead of me. She'd be in my corner. My champion. Whatever my decision, I just hoped she wasn't alone in that corner. "Thanks."

Stetson pushed through the door. "There you two are. Food's done. Holden's taken my grill hostage for his lettuce." He paused and took in how close Isla was standing to me. We were tucked into the wedge of the cabinets and had been speaking quietly. "Everything okay?"

I fiddled with the ends of my hair. "I'm thinking of going blue." I pushed off the counter. He'd brought the smell of the grill in with him. My stomach growled. Slowly, my morning sickness had made way for more of an appetite. "I need to eat."

As I walked out, his hand landed on the small of my back and chased away the stress of the last name issue looming in our future. He followed me, so close the heat of his body rivaled the air temperature. And he didn't leave my side as we loaded our plates with the food he and Holden had lined up on the picnic table.

On the way to my lawn chair, I paused. "You need a chair."

The guys had been messing around with the grill and setting up the meal.

"You can sit on my lap." He dropped into my chair and held his plate to the side. His lap was wide open. At my hesitation, he said, "I can get my own chair."

"No. This is fine. It's just different."

"They'll get used to it."

I settled on his lap, sitting at the edge of his knees so we each had room to eat. This shouldn't have been such a big milestone, but it was. Hanging out with friends and family as an obvious couple was a huge step. But we had a long journey to make together.

STETSON

I stood in my guest room, looking from the generic comforter on the bed to the plain walls. Instead of the bed, I pictured a crib. On the walls, some horse pictures. Or dogs. What did babies like? A changing table in the corner. A small dresser that would hold even smaller clothing. A rocker.

This morning, while Lyric slept next to me, I had researched baby rooms, looking at pictures and reading blogs. When was the last time I read something online that didn't have to do with cattle or the weather?

I couldn't shake the unbalanced sensation in my chest. Like I was breathing too deeply but couldn't pull in enough air. The day at the cabin last weekend had been almost perfect. I didn't have many guests at my house, but I loved having groups at the cabin. There was a freedom there I hadn't grown up with, and I didn't have to worry about the peace I'd found in my home being disrupted. The only thing that had haunted me at the cabin was Lyric when she had been there.

Lyric in her bikini. Lyric as Isla's friend. Lyric the untouchable.

I hadn't been sure how to act with her around friends and family. How comfortable was she with public displays of affection? They weren't something I'd ever given a second thought to. I hadn't cared whether the world knew I was dating someone.

But I'd wanted to touch Lyric. I'd wanted the world to know she was mine. And then she'd sat on my lap while we both ate. We couldn't be any closer, but it had been casual. Relaxed. Us.

We were on the right track. And for the last week, I'd been coming home, knowing she was still in my house and I'd get to be in bed with her each night.

The apple blossom scent of Lyric's shampoo wrapped around me when she stepped into the room next to me. Her damp hair hung in waves, the purple ends clumped together. She wasn't going to dye it blue until her first trimester was over. *Just to be safe and shut people up before they can start.*

I didn't know what people she was worried about, but I doubted there was a person in Coal Haven who'd tracked her hair colors as closely as I had.

She leaned against the doorframe and crossed her arms. She didn't say anything, as if she knew something significant was on my mind.

"I thought this would make the best room for a nursery."

Surprise flickered in her eyes as she looked around the room. "I agree."

"When do you think we should get stuff? Cribs and shit."

She chuckled. "The insurance payout is supposed to arrive this week, and the lot is up for sale. Mom's insisting on giving me some of that sale too."

"You don't want it?"

She shook her head. "I'd rather she put everything into savings or retirement. She supported me long enough. I'll be fine."

I could afford to outfit a thousand nurseries, maybe more. The oil trust money my cousins and I had received from our grandparents had more than paid for the house. Evander hadn't touched his from what Bruce had said. He'd joined the military and forgotten everything and everyone at home, and as far as we all knew, he was still in the Army. His brother, Derek, had died before he'd been able to get his, and I didn't know what Uncle Bruce had done with it.

Holden had built his house and socked the rest away. Same with me. Archer and his brother had been cut off along with their dad. Isla and Nora were too young to receive their payouts yet.

Lyric wouldn't care if I paid for hundreds of cribs, but she wouldn't be comfortable if I paid for everything.

Our nursery. "There's no rush," I said.

She rested her head against the doorframe. "It's early yet."

I'd lost count of how many times we'd said that since we'd discovered she was pregnant. The unbalanced sensation was returning. It was like a warning. *It's early yet*. There was more to do before there'd be even more to do.

"How would you decorate it?" she asked.

Did she have an idea? She'd tell me if she did, right? Lyric didn't hold back. I'd built the house with family in mind, and yeah, I'd had an image of a nursery that had started to seem unnecessary the older I got. "Horses. Maybe some tractors." I dug at the hardwood floor with my toe.

The guest room, the room I knew I could convert to a kid's room, had thick carpet that would go with any style. "Agriculture, you know, kinda like I had."

"Didn't you have a giant combine painted on your wall?"

She'd have seen it the many times she and Isla tried to sneak into my room when they were in elementary school. When I built the house, Mom had taken pictures for me but had put Dad to work painting over the artwork so she could convert the room into an office. "A combine in a sunflower field. I had a mobile with horses too. I think Mom saved it for me. We could do something like that. Horses. Tractors."

Floof twined around my ankles, then did the same to Lyric. She picked her cat up and nuzzled him. She was dressed in her shorts with skulls and a loose white shirt that showed the pink sports bra she usually wore underneath.

"What are you going to do today?"

"Help Mom with the store. She has to pick up a shipment from Bismarck. I was thinking about going with her. Do you need me around for anything?"

I had to work on equipment repairs in the shop, but her trip brought up another issue that had been weighing on my mind and churning the acid in my stomach. "Remington messaged me. He wants to know if I can come in tonight. Hang out. He asked Colt. Messaged Holden too." Holden wasn't dropping by Rattler's anymore, and neither was I. Without us, I doubt Colt stopped in. "I think he misses us."

"Okay. Have fun."

I monitored her reaction. She was cool with it? "You sure? I might be out kinda late." Rattler's closed at eleven, but sometimes the guys would move to one of the downtown bars that was open until one—if we didn't have anyone to go home with. That part wouldn't be the case tonight, but I'd like to catch up with the guys even if it meant staying out late.

"Why wouldn't I be?"

"I'd be sitting at the big table. People would be dropping by. We might go to one of the bars after Rattler's closes." I had to be sure, or I wouldn't go. Rattler's had been a contentious issue with past girls, but none of them had been Lyric.

She gave me a sidelong look and crossed one curvy leg behind the other, as if she was pressing forward without actually doing it. "Can I trust you, Stetson?"

"Of course." Without a doubt. I'd never cheated, and I never would. I liked to think I would be like that even without my dad's history to learn from. "But I'd be going out without you, and I'd be out late." A lot of women I'd dated didn't like that combination.

"If I can't trust you, then I have no business being with you."

"You can trust me, Lyric." I'd never meant anything more in my life. "But I don't want you to think I don't respect your feelings."

She worried her lower lip for a few moments. "I think being so infatuated with you so long made me set limits that maybe I wouldn't have had before. You'd think it would've made me a doormat when it came to you. If the guys I dated did something I didn't like, I was gone, and it's carried over to now. With you. But I didn't settle with them, and I'm not settling with you. If you want to go out and you say I can trust you, I'll trust you. If I can't, then I'm gone. If you start going out to avoid me, then we have deeper issues to work on, and we either fix them or we're done. I'm not in this halfway, Stetson."

Sweet relief poured through me. "Me neither. It's just different. You aren't reacting like I'm used to."

"I can drive by your exes' places, glare at them in the stores, and sit on your lap at the bar."

"Could you? Drive real slow while pretending you're not paying attention."

She tipped her head. "That's very high school. How 'bout I show up at a family function I wasn't invited to and look into their confidential medical records?"

My lips twitched. "Deal."

"But if we want to go both ways, then you have to mock me for the skulls on my shorts and my tattoo choices and tell your buddies that I just 'work in a lab or something' while pretending that what you do contributes to the essence of life itself."

Anger at her exes sparked inside me. She wasn't just referencing Cole, but the guy dug under my skin. Lyric had her own mind, but my shitty decisions with women had driven her to him. I wished I could tell him off for her, but they were all said and done. Thank fuck.

To keep this light, I pretended to think. "Only if I can start gelling my hair and wearing jeans with crystals on the pockets."

"I believe they're rhinestones, Stetson, and all the hardcore blue-collar bros wear them. Points if you have a wife and kid in another town. Seriously, though, the jeans would look good on you; they just aren't you."

Just like a business suit wasn't her. "I have to be honest, I have no idea what the hell you do in the lab."

"No one does. It's magic."

"It's not magic. You're smart as fuck."

She tried to play my comment off as casual, but she couldn't extinguish the pride fast enough. She didn't get much credit for what she did or for what an amazing person she was. I grabbed her hand and tugged her to me. "Have fun with your mom."

"Don't drink and drive."

"I used to crash at Remington's if I had too much, but if you're at home waiting for me, that's not going to happen. I'll have one beer and switch to Coke."

"Mm. I might be naked too. You never know."

Desire punched me in the gut. "I'll be back by nine."

"I'm not like Cinderella. I'm not suddenly going to get dressed at midnight and disappear."

"Promise?" I lifted her, and she giggled as she wrapped her legs around me. The fence repairs could wait.

* * *

Lyric

"I hope you don't mind I saved this for you." Mom held up a onesie that read *What happens at Nana's stays at Nana's.*

"It's fine." It'd be the first baby item I received. This was getting real. "I just don't have anywhere to put it."

She folded the onesie and watched me. "Oh?"

I knew that tone. It was the *Tell me more because something in what you're saying is off* tone. "We talked about turning the guest room into the nursery."

"Mm." She picked up a pair of tiny brown pants with a cream top and set it with the onesie.

"Mom, did you save a bunch of baby clothes?"

She gave me a guilty smile. "I did. Sorry. There were so many cute clothes, and I didn't know if you and Stetson planned to find out the gender. I got a little of everything."

"I haven't even had my first prenatal appointment yet, and Emery said they won't do much other than review the due date and do some lab work."

"But you and Stetson are going to make a nursery. In his house?"

His house. It wasn't mine, but I was living there. I was starting to get mail at his address, and I had picked up groceries after work earlier this week. But I couldn't shake the freeloading feeling.

I'd come home after college and parked myself with Mom, thinking she needed me. Assuming she did. She hadn't. And when that place was gone, Stetson had taken me in and I hadn't left.

Stetson and I were weaving all over the typical dating time line. We'd barely dated, but I was moved in and we were having a baby together. What happened if we didn't work out? I couldn't crash with Isla.

I'd be on my own. For the first time ever. It'd been scary before, but each day brought me closer to baby time.

Before Mom caught a hint of my worries, I answered. "Yes, we talked about making his guest room into a nursery. I guess the question is when, and we don't seem to be in a rush."

"Seem to? Haven't you talked about it?" she asked as if we were avoiding the topic.

"It's early yet." The more I said it, the more it felt like an excuse and not an explanation.

"I understand. But you'll both need to be on the same page to deal with his parents."

I was surprised his mother hadn't elbowed between us saying I shouldn't stay with Stetson until the child's bloodlines were confirmed like a foal from a prized stud. But I wasn't going to question it. She'd be an issue soon enough. I wanted the time to work on me and Stetson.

"Then it's probably a good thing I passed on the crib and matching changing table," she said.

"Mom." The floor and shelves in the store were full. She

kept as much stock out as possible, rearranging it periodically to display the merchandise differently. Her apartment was even smaller, and she still stored some stock in there. A crib and a changing table would take up prime floor space.

"I like to prepare."

"You're excited."

She walked around the table for the new children's items for back-to-school sales and faced me. "You're not?"

"I'm...ambivalent?" I'd be nervous if I let myself dwell on it. A doomsday pessimism was hanging in my mind like an intimidating cloud. So I hadn't been thinking about it.

"Are you scared?"

It was her quiet mom tone that did me in. I pushed some clothing aside and lifted myself onto the table. My legs swung. "Yes, maybe a little. I mean, it's the baby. It's Stetson. It's his family. It's where I'm living. His house isn't mine. We've known for a few weeks, and it hasn't sunk in, and I'm afraid when it does, all hell will break loose. But it's going really well."

"Things are allowed to go well and not go to hell."

I chewed my lower lip. "I know."

"Is it your dad?"

"Doesn't help," I mumbled. Stetson wouldn't leave like my dad. His roots were buried so far in Coal Haven, he couldn't find the ends. But he could abandon me nonetheless, and I didn't want to be taken by surprise. Unprepared like Mom had been.

Mom took the piles of youth pants that I'd moved and neatly restacked them. "There were a lot of red flags I ignored."

"Like what?" I'd talked about my dad with Mom. We discussed the divorce and why my dad didn't want to see me. He hated being reminded of his responsibilities. Receiving child support had been an ongoing struggle, and once I was old enough, he'd cut off all ties. Having an ex who knew what a slimy bastard he was and a daughter who could attest to what a shitty father he was could be bad for the image he'd built for himself as a real estate agent in South Dakota. A family man, with a doctor for a wife, and two kids who went to private school.

Mom didn't shy away from the topic of my dad, but we hadn't discussed their relationship beyond the logistics. She had glossed over her feelings and what she'd thought of him. She didn't trash Dad, but she didn't sugarcoat his behavior.

She sucked in a long breath. "I got pregnant, and he felt pressured to marry me." She put her hand on my arm. "I wasn't like you. You're a strong girl. Independent. And I didn't have a mom who assured me everything would be okay. I thought I'd be on the streets if I had a baby alone."

Her clarification helped, but it also poked that part of me that wondered if Stetson was into me for me. Or if he felt responsible. I had studied Stetson for so much of my life. I knew him, and that was the problem. He'd been the loyal son to a fault.

Mom continued. "He had one foot out the door even when we were dating. He always talked about moving, about getting out of Coal Haven. He hated the Barrons, but I can see now that it's because he wanted their lives."

"He got it." And so would I if things worked out between me and Stetson. I worried my lower lip again. I made decent money, but people would think everything I owned had come from Barron money.

What others thought shouldn't bother me.

It didn't.

It wouldn't. I knew who I was, and I wasn't a user.

"Then there was his wandering eye. The way he discredited every point I tried to make—especially if he was wrong.

And all his problems were everyone else's fault. Ultimately, those traits were the flags."

The tension in my shoulders eased. Stetson was the opposite. He took responsibility when he shouldn't. It wasn't a red flag, but it could be an issue. He didn't have a wandering eye, and he respected what I said.

So that left the other insecurity about getting pregnant before we could really solidify a relationship, but we were both working on it.

"I wonder what it would've been like if we'd started dating before..." I looked down at my belly.

"That happened because you two weren't dating each other when you wanted to. It's a moot point, so don't dwell on the what-ifs. You're both adults. You're both good people. And I think you each see what's going on a lot better than I ever did. Than his parents do. You've never cared what anyone thought because you have faith in yourself. Hold on to that."

I gave her a small smile. This was the Mom talk I'd needed.

My phone buzzed. I looked at the caller. "It's Isla. I'll be right back." I answered as I wandered away from the table to stare out the window to the street. "Hi."

"Do you have plans with my brother tonight that would make me vomit?"

"That was earlier."

She made a heaving sound. "Ugh, I don't even know if you're joking. Can I pretend you got pregnant by being on opposite sides of the county?"

Giggling, I said, "The Barrons never believed in AI."

She mimicked her dad's deep voice. "'We breed bulls as valuable as our land.' Anyway, I had a shitty day at the farmers' market and could use a pity party with a sympathetic ear."

"I'm game. Just not Rattler's. Stetson's out with friends, and I don't want to look like I'm checking up on him." When her silence stretched too long, I let my rising defensiveness out. "I'm not bothered by him being at Rattler's without me."

"I know, I know. I should know better, but I guess I expected you to get a little uptight about him. But you're still you."

"That's your mom's main complaint."

Isla snickered. "Want to go to Crocus Valley?"

"It's a date. I can pick you up in a couple of hours when I'm done at the store."

"See ya, babe."

"Bye."

I returned to the table. Mom had it all set up and was arranging the sales signs. "How's Isla?"

"Good. We're going out after this. Only this time, I don't have to worry about waking you when I get home."

"I'm a mom. I'll always worry, but it's nice that your relationship with Stetson didn't affect your friendship."

If the last week had been a view into my future with Stetson, I couldn't be more delighted. My dreams come to life. But it was early yet.

Twelve

LYRIC

I stretched deliciously sore muscles and rolled over. Stetson was at the football game for the kids he coached. I had helped yesterday morning, hanging outside and driving around in the tractor with him.

Over the last month, we'd settled into our new routine. Nothing had changed. He went to his parents' house to check in and work in the pastures around their place. His parents hadn't come over. I hadn't run across them in town.

Things were in stasis between us and them.

I was a couple weeks out of my first trimester. My first prenatal appointment was next week.

Today, I'd dye my hair. A task that would take my mind off the simmering excitement. Would they do an ultrasound? Would we hear the heartbeat? Either way, a change was coming. I couldn't explain why the doctor's appointment was the turning point. Perhaps because a professional would know and confirm. It'd be on paper.

I dressed in the unicorn shirt to color my hair. The nice clothes I had were for public, and the shirt with the hole was perfectly oversized for private. Leaving my bra off, I stepped into a pair of shorts that weren't as long as the shirt. I had no one to impress.

I might as well enjoy the relaxing morning in a big house. Once the baby arrived, things would be different.

Nerves fluttered through my belly. Once the baby arrived.

I was growing more excited and anxious each day.

The coloring proved to be the distraction I wanted. I didn't turn my whole head blue. Pulling off an ombre style with the color wasn't easy, especially with my own hair, but I'd done this enough to get the effect I wanted. I was pleased with the results, enjoying the normalcy dyeing my hair brought.

When I was done and my hair was drying after washing the dye out, my stomach growled. Stetson had mentioned stopping home for lunch. I could make something for myself that'd keep for when he got back.

Ruffling my hands through my hair to help it air dry, I went to the kitchen. What did we have in the fridge? I planned to get groceries today—

Naomi walked in through the mudroom door, her jeweled sunglasses pushed to the top of her head. She was dressed down for Naomi Barron in denim capris, a black refinery T-shirt, and pristine athletic shoes. "Oh. Lyric."

The subtle downturn of her lips said it all. Not quite a frown. Not an expression of pure distaste. Just enough to indicate something was lacking and it was me.

Of course his parents had a key. I'd never thought to ask. Could I tell him to get it back since I was now here too? "Hey, Naomi. Stetson's still at football."

Naomi brandished the box she was holding in her

hands. Her lips pressed in a tighter line when she looked at my legs. Did she think it was the middle of the day and I was only in a shirt?

And what would be the problem if I was?

"I wanted to drop this off." At my bewildered expression, she cocked her head. "The paternity test."

What? I had told Stetson I was willing to take one early on. Did he know his mother had purchased one? If he did, why hadn't he told me? I was the one who brought it up first.

She waved her hand as if all this was inconsequential, as if her dropping by to question the validity of Stetson's paternity was a daily part of her business. "They're expensive, so I thought I'd help."

"Is that why you did it?" My tone was flat. I wasn't able to be nonchalant about her arrival, and I might experience the backlash. But weeks of anticipation and dread had built up. If this was the explosion with his mom, I wanted it done.

She lifted her chin. "I'd like to help, but you're a smart girl, Lyric. You know we're going to have questions. We're his parents."

I crossed my arms, my heart sinking as I remembered I wasn't wearing a bra. This was looking better and better for me. "He's in his thirties. It's our business."

"It's our family. And you were just seeing some man from the coal mine before you and Stetson..." She pursed her lips as if she couldn't bring herself to say S-E-X.

I wasn't as shy. "And I had my period right after we broke up. Which put me at my most fertile when I had sex with Stetson."

She grimaced as if I was reciting smut. "It's still good to verify."

"Are you checking with all his exes to see if they also had unprotected sex with him and when their cycles were?"

"Don't be crude, Lyric."

"You're the one who walked into this house without knocking and insulted me."

Her sharp inhale resonated in the quiet kitchen. Sun flooded the space, so cheerful when my day had considerably darkened. "This is my son's home."

"You might not like it, but it's mine too," I said with conviction I didn't feel.

"Well, that remains to be seen." She turned to go, her hand on the doorknob.

"Why don't you like me?" She paused, and I pressed. "I'm serious, Naomi. You only tolerated me as Isla's friend, and you clearly don't like the idea of me and Stetson. You've known me my whole life. What is the reason?" Why wasn't I good enough? My best friend's parents should at least like me better than the dad who left me. They didn't.

She kept her hand on the knob. Her expression wasn't lofty or arrogant. She stared at me as if I should prepare for a metric ton of truth getting dropped on my head. "Isla didn't have any other friends. I kept hoping she'd make some with ambition and drive, but you at least didn't seem to be using her for our money."

Isla and I had an equal friendship. We paid for each other's drinks or our own. I rode with her a lot, but I also had her over for dinner. When we were kids, she'd always slept over at my house where we could curl up in front of the TV with pillows and blankets all night and watch movies. At her place, we'd have to wake up for chores and it was lights out by ten.

"You haven't been a negative influence." She said it as if it was a huge concession. The closest to a compliment I'd get from her.

Tension crept along my shoulders as I waited for her *but*.

"But you're not exactly helping her do the best in life she can. Going to the bar to pick up God knows what kind of man while she fiddles around with the farmers' market?" Naomi stiffened as if she was physically holding back a stronger opinion. "She needs more powerful people in her life, and you're not it, Lyric. It's not inherently a bad thing; you're just not what she needs."

Hurt burned in my gut. "And you've talked to her about all this?"

Her features tightened. We both knew the answer. "As for Stetson—"

"A guy who also frequents the same bar and was known to pick up women like the men you think were so horrible for us? Do you hear yourself?"

Annoyance flashed across her face. "I can see you're not even trying to understand and I'm wasting your time."

She opened the door. A startled Stetson was on the other side. His eyes were already wide. Naomi's Range Rover would be parked in the drive.

"Mom." His wary gaze toggled to me, then back to her. "What's up?"

I answered before she could spin the story to suit her, sarcasm dripping from my voice. "She was so kind to bring us a paternity test."

He winced, but there was no surprise in his reaction.

He'd known she was going to buy one? That part didn't hurt. I was surprised she hadn't presented a test earlier. That she hadn't shown up, tossed a hood over my head, and pushed me into her car to drive to a center to draw my blood. It was that he hadn't talked to me.

My stomach twisted, and my appetite vanished. "I can't believe this."

Tears seared my eyes as I stomped out of the kitchen. I didn't want them to see me crying. Damn these hormones. I also didn't want to hear whatever accusations Naomi flung around. She'd been saved from having to justify why I wasn't good enough for her son. She'd been spared from hearing how ridiculous her excuses sounded.

Their voices faded behind me. I entered Stetson's bedroom and closed the door. I didn't slam it. I could be the mature, rational one, dammit.

This is my son's home.

Her words stung. I paced the bedroom, wishing I knew what Stetson was saying to his mother, scared it would only disappoint me, and regretting that I had walked away.

A strong urge to leave hounded me. I wanted to storm to the closet and pack my scrubs. Grab my underwear from the dresser and gather the toiletry items from the bathroom. I couldn't leave—wouldn't—until I knew how he'd handled the situation.

I was in danger of wearing a path in the lush carpet Stetson had put in all the bedrooms when the door opened.

He didn't come all the way in. "I should've talked to you, but I didn't think she'd go through with it."

I gave him a *You know better* look. "She was waiting for me to be far enough along to test so there wouldn't be any doubts."

He let out a sigh, stuffed his hands into his front pockets, and walked farther in but stopped before he approached me, like he wasn't sure I wouldn't spin him around and push him right back out. Even though this was his house.

"I know." His jaw was tight. "She left."

"What'd you say to her?"

"That it was between you and me to discuss."

I didn't know what I expected him to say. That was the

gist of it. Part of me wanted him to tell his mom to fuck off. The other part of me knew that was unfair to ask. And a huge part of me dwelled on what she'd implied. "She said this is your house and acted like I'd be out on my ass if the baby isn't yours."

His brow furrowed. "This is your home too."

"It doesn't feel like it." The paternity test didn't piss me off. It was part and parcel for the Barrons. As soon as I saw that extra pink line, I knew I'd have to prove the baby I was carrying was Stetson's. I'd accepted it, and I wasn't angry. Yes, I wanted to be trusted, but I had a career in science. Nothing was one hundred percent, and seemingly impossible occurrences happened.

The living arrangement bothered me.

He drew closer, concern etched into his face. "What do you mean?"

"What if I wanted to paint the ceiling in here blue and put a mural on the wall?" I squinted at the walls. "Like...a carnival mural?"

His expression stayed carefully neutral. "Is that what you really want?"

I liked his bedroom. It was spacious and tastefully done. Simple and refined. Not my personal style but the calm my brain craved. "Maybe for the nursery. Instead of horses and tractors, I'd like more animals. Lions, tigers, and bears. Balloons." If I gave myself a chance to think about what I wanted for a nursery, I'd pick something other than the neutral tones Stetson had chosen for the rest of the house. "Not...tractors."

I hadn't given much thought to how I'd decorate my kid's room. My walls had been bare until I was old enough to tape pictures up. A room was a room. I wanted it functional, and I'd add the flourishes later. Kind of like my own look.

"Not tractors, then." He sounded tired. "Or sunflower fields."

Why were things so easy between the two of us? Then the outside world entered and tangled up our emotions. "I kind of like those."

"Sunflowers and lions?"

A soft chuckle left me. "Sunflowers and bumblebees?"

"Sunflowers and bumblebees." The humor drained from his eyes. "What do you want to do about that kit?"

If Naomi paid for a paternity test, then she'd get a paternity test.

* * *

Stetson

I expected a huge blowup. Yelling. Stomping. I thought I'd walk into the bedroom and see her packing, and I wouldn't blame her. Mom had a way of driving people off, and Dad had a way of keeping them gone.

But she was still here.

"Let me read the instructions." She didn't make a move for the kitchen where the white box sat on the counter. "I've drawn blood for a few special testing kits at the clinic for patients, but I'll see what the directions say." Her expression grew guarded. "If there's going to be a legal battle over the results, there might be a slightly different process."

"No legal issues, Lyric," I said softly. The question of paternity had its own shadow, one that was amplified by my family. Dad might be staying out of the discussion, but he supported Mom. He always did, but in this case, he would've insisted if Mom hadn't.

"We can do it on Monday." She ran a hand through the

ends of her hair, concentrating on the new color. It started gradually a few inches off her scalp, deepening to a darker blue at the ends.

I liked it, but she could add anything to her hair, and I'd be all about it.

"I can take the kit to work. If we need to get blood from you, you can stop in. If it's a cheek swab, I can collect it here and take it to work." She hugged herself. "Unless you want to come to work and make sure it's packaged all at once."

It took a moment to muddle through her tone. "By packaged all at once, you mean make sure you aren't sneaking to the coal mine to swab what's his name's cheek so it looks like mine? Do you think I'm worried you'd do something like that?" I wanted her to trust me, but she needed to know I trusted her.

"Sort of, yeah. I don't want you to question the results."

I wouldn't. She didn't need a baby to trap me. I'd willingly walk in. "No."

"You probably should so no one else will question it."

"I trust you, Lyric." I closed the distance between us. "And you don't even have to—"

She put her fingers on my lips. "You know we have to. Otherwise, the topic will keep getting kicked up like a dust storm in July."

"Not by me."

Her gaze softened, but half a heartbeat later her eyes filled with concern. "You've been cool about the test, but what about the results?"

The baby was mine. "I don't care, Lyric."

She pulled back, inspecting my face like she needed to know I was serious. "You don't? I'm sure it's yours, but in science it's kind of never say never say never, so there's always a freak chance—"

"It's mine. You're mine." I'd never been so sure in my

life. And maybe I'd been sitting on this question, afraid to answer, worried I'd disappoint myself in addition to her. But nothing compared to the fear that had sliced through my spine when I walked in and saw the way she and Mom were facing off. I didn't want to lose her. Genetically mine or not, the baby had become a part of my life.

I cupped her cheek with a hand. "Even if I'm not the kid's biological dad, it's going to be stuck with me. I want to make sure you don't feel stuck with me. Or stuck here."

She gripped my wrist and turned her face into my hand. Closing her eyes, she took a measured breath. "I wasn't scared, but I guess there was a part of me that wondered how you'd react."

"I'm not gonna lie. There was an annoying voice in my head telling me the minute possibility I wasn't the dad meant there was still a possibility and that could mean you and I might be doing this just for the baby." I lifted a shoulder. "When I saw that kit, I had to figure out how I felt really fast. And it was easy. This thing between us is real."

"The baby forced you to get over yourself?" She said it with a wry smile, but I had to stress how serious I was.

"I'd like to think that I would've come around eventually. Being with you rocked my damn world down to the foundation and then bulldozed it in. It was taking me a minute to get over it, but then you happened again. And I'll be forever grateful to this kid for doing that."

She rose onto her tiptoes and smashed a hard kiss against my lips. I was ready to tip us back onto the bed when her stomach growled.

She smiled against my mouth. "Shit, sorry. I was going to make lunch before your mom walked in."

I grabbed her hand and pulled her toward the kitchen. She needed to eat or her morning sickness would get worse. "What do you want?"

"Food. But don't you have to meet Holden?"

"We're not meeting Uncle Bruce for an hour." I let her go to comb through the fridge. When I pulled out with my arms full of sandwich material, she was looking out the window.

"It looks gorgeous out."

"It is." September didn't feel like it should be part of summer, but the pleasantly high temperatures delayed the bitter months to come. "Want to eat on the deck?"

Her face lit up. "Yes. I'll go wipe the table and chairs down."

The drawback of country living. Everything outside—and inside—got dustier quicker. She took a rag from the drawer and rushed out. I tore my gaze away from watching her ass sway as she moved the chairs. I normally loved the view from my deck, but having Lyric on it was next level.

I put together four ham sandwiches, loading them with lettuce and cucumber like Lyric preferred. If she didn't want seconds, I'd take her other sandwich with me for an afternoon snack in case I didn't get back until late.

I never knew anymore when I was working with Uncle Bruce. He used to work from dawn to dusk—all outside, all the time. But he'd slowed down the last couple of years. Holden and I were pitching in a little more with working cattle, and Holden had said Archer and Laney had helped Bruce a lot with calving season.

Uncle Bruce wasn't going downhill, but he'd changed. He didn't have the stamina he used to, and he had quit saying he thought Evander was coming home. When I'd asked a few months ago, he'd confided that Evander had reenlisted for a few more years.

Damn.

Lyric popped inside to grab our drinks. I followed her back out to the deck, loving the way her shirt covered her shorts until it looked like she wore nothing else. My mom probably hated it. At the very least, she would've despised the lack of a bra.

I fucking loved it, and the illusion that I could slide Lyric's shirt up and sink inside her wasn't one I'd quickly trade.

She sat in the chair next to mine at the little round table in the corner of my deck. When the world hammered at my door, I relaxed out here and listened to nothing but the wind and the cows. Sharing it with Lyric was special.

Would we sit out here on mellow summer days with our kids in our laps as we talked about life?

Damn, I hoped so. I could do this for the rest of my life.

We munched on our food. She stretched her legs out under the table. Her feet were still bare.

All I'd planned to do was come home and eat, enjoy Lyric's company, and then go back to work. A perfect damn day. Instead, I'd walked in on a brewing storm. It had dissipated, but I couldn't escape the feeling that clouds were gathering in the distance. There'd be another storm, and I would drive right into it without knowing.

Lyric and I had talked. The longer she was here, all the touches she added to the house to make it feel like hers, the less she'd feel like an impostor. I wanted her to put down roots. With me. With our kid.

I wanted to marry this girl.

Thankfully, I had just polished off the sandwich. My throat was closing up. I took a long pull off my Coke. Another from my glass of water.

I'd never thought about getting married. No, I'd thought about it, but there'd never been a face attached. I had no history of looking for rings, no history of considering ring shopping. If a girlfriend started dropping hints, I'd formed my exit plan.

I'd always wanted to get married. To have a family. To grow old with that one special girl. I had a good job. A lot of familial support. A little money. I wanted what I didn't see growing up. A close, caring relationship where both sides respected each other out of love and trust and not fear. No fear of abandonment or embarrassment. No fear of being alone. None.

"The last time I tried to sit out here, I got sandblasted by the wind." Lyric got up and walked to the railing. She leaned against it, her ass sticking out, revealing the tiny shorts she wore. "It's just right today. Keeps the sun from getting the deck too hot, but strong enough to keep the bugs away."

I couldn't rush out to buy a ring. Not yet. That damn paternity test hung over us. Not the results, but my parents' reaction either way. Having to manage them. Would they accept Lyric once they saw how I handled the answer?

I didn't want to referee Lyric and my parents for the rest of my life. Nor did I want to cut either party from my life.

I'd figure it out.

But I knew what I wanted right now.

I rose and walked behind her. Palming her ass, I stroked my thumb down the line of stitching that ran between her ass cheeks.

She peered at me over her shoulder. "Don't you have to get back to work?"

"If you hadn't noticed by now, work can wait for certain things."

She wiggled her butt. "Am I one of those things?"

To answer her, I slipped my thumb along her skin and under the shorts and underwear.

Fuck it. I yanked her shorts and underwear down until they pooled around her feet. Her butt flexed as she stepped out of them. I could come from that view alone.

I slid my hand down her ass until my fingers brushed her

folds. She rocked into my touch. I slipped a finger along her seam until I hit her clit.

She moaned, her hands braced on the railing, not caring we were outside. The way she stood, ready for me? I struggled to control myself from going too fast. This was a moment to savor.

I anchored my free hand next to her, ignoring the throb of my erection as I bent. I circled her clit. "That blue hair drives me fucking crazy." So did her tattoos. I couldn't see them now, but I'd traced that damn mariner's compass more than a few times since she'd been under my roof. "And this shirt shows your tight little nipples when you're standing still."

"I didn't think you'd like my pink unicorn shirt."

"I like what's under it more."

Her slickness coated my fingers. I wanted to sink into her, but not yet. She was my treat, but I wanted to be even better for her.

I leaned farther over her until I could murmur in her ear. "Before it gets cold, I'm going to fuck you everywhere on my land." She moaned, and my hand was soaked. "I'm taking you in *my* barn, goddammit. The tractor. Your car." I didn't care about the logistics of fitting us together in her tiny sedan. I'd fuck her on the hood and pound the dent out later. "The shop. Out in the open fucking field."

Her body spoke her approval. She was putty in my hand, so damn close to climaxing.

I could finally let go of my restraint. I pushed off the railing and ripped my zipper down, freeing myself. Placing my cock at her hot, wet entrance, I growled, "Hang on tight."

Her knuckles turned white, but she bowed her back, giving me all the access I needed.

I shoved inside. The ruffle of the breeze was a gentle

contrast to the inferno I sank into. For several moments, I didn't move. My world was fracturing while the birds merrily chirped. She was contracting around me, ready to explode, but I kept us at the boiling point. Once I started moving, I was going to go fast. The roller coaster of emotions I'd been riding since I'd walked in the door for lunch needed an outlet.

With a groan, I backed out and started thrusting. She was with me the entire way, meeting my drives into her body with a force of her own. Our height difference worked itself out as I anchored my feet against the floorboards and she rose to her tiptoes when I punched into her.

"Yes, Stetson!" was carried on the wind to get lost on the rest of my land. I was taking my woman in the great outdoors. My home. This was mine. She was mine, and soon enough, everyone would know it.

Everyone.

The stress of that statement threatened to intrude on my looming orgasm. I refused to dwell on it and instead concentrated on the tight hold she had on me. The heat firing between us. The way she was clamping harder on my cock.

I knew I was going to be done soon, and my fingers dug into her hips, but when she reached between her legs to touch herself, I detonated.

"Fuck! Lyric!" How could a simple move blow my damn mind? Wave after wave of ecstasy slammed into me, and her body tightened around me. She was coming too. My name on her lips rang in my ears and over the yard, but I didn't stop thrusting until I was empty.

She sagged over the railing, breathing hard. I wasn't ready to disconnect from her, so I curled over her like her own personal shelter.

I wasn't ready to marry her, not until the fucking test was done and my family was mollified. I wouldn't ask her to say vows in that mess, but I could tell her everything with just a few words. Words I had never said to anyone. "I love you."

She turned her face toward mine, our position putting us at an odd angle. "I love you too, Stetson."

Thirteen

LYRIC

I love you.

How was I supposed to work when I wanted to grin and relive that moment during deck sex?

Stetson hadn't told me I was the first woman he'd said that to, but I suspected I was. And it was the same for me.

The analyzer kicked the vial of blood out. I put the tube in the fridge and logged on to a computer to report the results. I had a couple more tests running and then I could shut down the lab.

It was almost closing time, and we had our typical end-of-day rush of patients. The doctors were finishing their day and sending patients to the lab so we could all attempt to get home on time. Joan had stayed late to help with blood draws so we could get the testing done and reported and I wouldn't have to risk overtime.

Joan walked out of the office. "Need anything else before I go?"

I thought about the kit in my tote bag. "Would you mind helping me with one last draw?"

On the way to her office, I shrugged out of my lab coat and grabbed a handful of sanitizer. My hands were dry before I reached for my tote.

By the time I had gotten to work, another tech and the phlebotomist had also been here. I could've asked them to draw the sample, but it was Monday. The busiest day of the week. There was no rush, but I wanted the test finished and in the mail before I went home. I didn't want to have to justify why I waited. Over the lunch lull, I'd stopped at the admin desk and had them put in orders for the blood draw. I'd bent the rules for the pregnancy test and was busted. This task would be by the book.

Joan waited in the doorway.

"So, this is the paternity kit." She raised a brow, and I shrugged. "I was going to do one anyway, but his mom expedited it. Stetson only needs a cheek swab, but I need a blood sample." He was meeting me after work. He'd swab himself, put his sample in the kit, and seal the kit. We'd drive together to mail it.

Not that I was paranoid. But I'd grown up around Naomi and Cameron. I wasn't taking any chances.

"Sure."

I handed her the instructions. I could tell her what was required, but techs were uptight like that, especially managers.

I settled into the drawing chair and crossed my legs. She scanned the instructions, nodding. "Simple enough. The results come pretty quick, huh?"

"Yeah. It's a relief." In two weeks, I should have Naomi's answer. I could create an account and have them sooner, but I wanted hard evidence. And I wanted to make Naomi wait.

As Joan was pulling out gauze and getting the bandage ready, Krystal breezed into the lab.

Shit.

Her features pinched when she saw us. "I thought you couldn't run tests on yourself?"

"We're not." I left it at that.

Joan ignored the comment. "Can I help you with something, Krystal?"

Nurses didn't usually linger in the lab unless it was slow and we were chatting. They dropped off samples, asked questions, or stocked up on specimen cups for small in-office biopsies.

She flung a biohazard collection bag onto the counter. "A guy dropped off a post vas."

Joan's mouth flattened into a line.

I would be getting overtime after all. Post vasectomy semen samples were time critical and couldn't be rushed. I wasn't going to be responsible for any surprise babies other than mine.

The patients were usually instructed to drop off their samples before three o'clock, but they didn't always follow directions. And Krystal probably didn't pass along those specific instructions.

"Got it," I said as Joan tied the tourniquet around my arm.

As I was poked, Krystal drifted closer.

"Need anything else?" Joan asked in a tone that said she knew Krystal was being nosy and that we all knew this wasn't her business.

Krystal ignored her. "What are you drawing?"

"Blood," I said flatly. "Have a good night."

Annoyance crossed her face right before determination set in. She picked up the sheet of instructions and smirked as soon as she read the title. "You know you have to check in and get charged for the draw."

Had she ever learned about privacy? "I did." My words were succinct, and I might regret what I was going to say next, but I let my tongue flap. "The results are getting mailed, not sent to the clinic. You know, in case you go looking again."

Joan pursed her lips as she finished the blood draw. I hadn't told her about Krystal's outburst in Rattler's.

Krystal rolled her eyes as if she didn't care. Yet she was still here. "It's not going to matter. You know that, right?" Her tone had an unexpected kindness to it, and her gaze wasn't hiding an edge. "His priority is his family, and whatever's best for them he'll do, even if it doesn't include you."

Her parting smile was almost sympathetic as she went out the door she'd entered through. Her lack of cattiness left a lump in my throat. She had a knack for targeting people's weak spots. That was why she'd said what she did. She didn't care about me; she only wanted to get to me.

Joan tapped the tube lightly on the counter, snapping me out of my head. "Did she really look at your chart?"

"I don't know. I wouldn't be surprised if she did. She knew I was pregnant, but it's Coal Haven and it's Stetson."

Her displeased demeanor didn't dissipate, but she handed the vial over. "I'll check with the front to see if the clinic is ready to close. You start on the post vas, and I'll shut down the analyzers."

"Thank you."

I folded the instructions as I went to the office. I slipped the blood into the specimen envelope in the kit. Joan did as she said and took off while I was at the microscope looking for sperm in the sample.

I finished the post vas report and prepped all the blood

and specimen samples the courier would pick up to take to the Bismarck lab for the testing this lab couldn't do. After tossing my lab coat on a hook and washing my hands, I grabbed my things and found Stetson's pickup in the parking lot. The stress from Krystal's quick visit hadn't completely diminished. Her words ricocheted through my head.

I climbed in, admiring his relaxed, long-legged sitting position. "Ready to swab?"

"Can you do it? I don't want to mess it up." He flipped his ball cap backward and leaned over the console between us.

Pleased he trusted me to get the sample, I brandished the swab. "Open up."

He smirked before he did as I asked. I followed the directions and packaged his sample with mine. Sealing up the kit on which I had already printed his address, I said, "Ready?"

He was still leaning over the console. "Can I kiss you now?"

Pressing my lips to his, I allowed the rest of the knot inside me to loosen.

He pulled away. "I'd rather have your tongue in my mouth than that swab. But"—he kicked the truck into gear—"off to the post office we go."

As he was turning out of the lot, Krystal walked out of the employee door of the clinic. She cocked a brow at me as if to say *You know I'm right.*

I averted my gaze, not wanting a stare down, not wanting to be lured into thinking she meant well. But the farther Stetson got from her, the more the knot inside me tightened.

* * *

Stetson

. . .

Holden threw his arm across the back of the diner booth. Jocelyn picked up our plates without even asking if we were done. Since she'd served me countless times in this cracked plastic booth over the last three decades of my life, she knew damn well when I'd finished my food.

"Thanks, Jocelyn." I tossed a few twenties on the table. She wouldn't take the money until we were done.

"You beat me to it," Holden said.

"Yeah," I said with a dry tone. "You were really rushing to get to your wallet."

He smirked and scooted out of the booth. "Thanks, man. I'll get it next time."

It was Saturday, and we'd met after the kids' football game we'd just got done coaching. Emery had taken the kids to the house to give me and Holden time to organize how we were going to work cattle—mine and his. Colt would lend a hand, and we'd do the same for Aunt Kira. Uncle Bruce needed help. Normally, we had a system for whose cattle we worked when. Who pitched in. But things had changed. Archer and Liam would help Bruce, but Holden would stop out, and I planned to as well. My dad no longer lent a hand since Uncle Bruce had mended fences with Liam and gleefully accepted Archer into the family.

I slid out and followed Holden to the sidewalk.

"So, two weeks?" he asked before we broke apart.

"Two weeks for the cattle, but I'll see you Tuesday for practice."

"Landon won't let me forget." His grin was wide.

Last year, I'd had to cajole him into coaching with me, but this year before the season started, he'd approached me about helping again. Now his second-oldest stepdaughter had his tutelage in her sights. "Heard Afton's bugging you to teach fast-pitch."

"I'm going to have to hire some help so I can be free to coach all these activities."

I chuckled. "Pretty soon, you're going to have your own team."

A familiar pickup parked next to Holden. Liam hopped out and nodded at both of us. My trained reaction to walk in a different direction almost made me turn, but I kept my feet rooted to the sidewalk. His boys spilled out of the back and beat their dad to our little group.

"How's it going?" Holden said.

"Uncle Stetson, guess what?" Eli said with a slight lisp of my name.

Holden jerked his gaze to me. Liam did the same. We were in downtown Coal Haven where anyone could've seen or heard.

"What?" I asked Eli as if it was an everyday occurrence.

"Dad said he'd think about letting us play football when we're in third grade."

I exchanged a glance with Liam. His gaze was cautious, his jaw tense. Telling him I wouldn't shit on his kids when we were in private was different from accepting them and coaching them with no issues for the whole town to see.

"You're in second grade now?" Both kids vigorously nodded. "Then I'll be waiting for you on the field. If it's okay with your dad."

They directed their attention to Liam. He held his hands up to quiet them. "We have a year to decide. I'm not making any promises."

"You promised we could have a milkshake," Owen said, grinding the heel of his little cowboy boot into the sidewalk.

"About football," he clarified. "I can see Jocelyn making your shakes."

Movement a couple businesses down attracted our attention and we all turned our heads toward it. The door to the law office opened and Dad stepped out. Tension rippled over our group, almost a visible blanket descending upon us. Dread clawed at my stomach, and for a heartbeat, I regretted not walking away when Liam arrived. But, I resolved, as long as I took the brunt of Dad's attention, not Liam or his kids.

He squinted against the sun and glanced over. Doing a double take, the muscles in his jaw jumped. He pinned me with the tractor beam of his hard stare and walked to us. "Is something wrong, Stetson?"

He made it sound like I was on the brink of being jumped. Eli and Owen stilled, as if they had been programmed to be inconspicuous around Dad.

"No. We're just talking football." I broke away from the group. The farther away I got Dad from Liam and the twins, the better. "If I'd known you were in town, you could've grabbed a bite with me and Holden."

His lips were downturned, but the way he looked at me was like he didn't know me. And he didn't really.

"Catch you later, Stetson," Holden said, probably to give Liam an opening to leave.

"Go on into the café," Liam told his kids behind me.

In unison, the boys called, "Bye, Uncle Stetson."

Dad flinched like the words had shoved him with both hands.

I forced a smile and waved. "See you, guys."

Liam rushed them in as if he didn't want to experience the fallout of Dad hearing what they'd said.

When I turned back, Dad's steady gaze was on me. "Uncle?" Astonishment rang in that one word.

I liked being called uncle and I wasn't making excuses for it. "I'm getting to know them."

"Stetson." He'd never sounded so disappointed.

What could I say that he didn't already know? It wasn't their fault? It wasn't Liam's? I was their uncle; why not get to know them? I shrugged.

"Have you told your mother?" he asked.

If I'd told her I'd shared the gifted cookies with Eli and Owen, I might've returned to find her sobbing on the bathroom floor again. "No, it's not necessary."

"It'd be better for her to hear what's been going on from you."

What's been going on. As if I was fifteen years younger and he'd found out I'd been cheating on tests or drinking. "I'll think about it. They are my nephews, though."

Dad assessed me, his hazel gaze full of warning. "How far are you going with this?"

"What do you mean?" I knew exactly what he meant. Would I dare refer to Liam as my brother?

"We had our limits set in place."

Irritation made me speak when I'd typically use this as an out to move along and hope he forgot the whole thing. "Maybe as an adult, those limits don't make sense."

Dad stepped closer, his calm exterior unable to fully mask his determination. "Then you'll need to figure it out. You've always done your own thing, but you can't on this, dammit. Everything's finally settling back down after..." His glare touched on the café. "After him and Kennedy. Then Archer."

By everything settling back down, he meant he didn't feel like his history was being dredged up. He wasn't being painted as the bad guy but as the refinery CEO and prominent landowner. He wasn't the bird shit on the family name, and Mom wasn't making him repeatedly clean the windshield.

I understood. I didn't agree, but I understood. "It'll be fine, Dad. I've got it handled."

He watched Holden pull away from the curb and drive down Main Street. He avoided looking at the café. "You need to make sure you do."

His tone rubbed like a wire brush. "Heading home?"

"No. Isla has the farmers' market tonight. I'm going to stop and check on her."

I couldn't tell if Dad liked to witness Isla in her element, if it was a way to participate in something other than being a Barron in town, or if he thought Isla needed the help.

It didn't matter. Isla felt undermined, and Dad either didn't care or was oblivious to it and Isla would never tell him.

Dad got into his truck. I was parked where Holden had been. I backtracked to the front of the café. A knock on the window caught my attention.

Owen and Eli were both waving. Two kids who were so willing to accept me just because I was a relative. The opposite of how my family worked. I didn't look hard enough to see Liam's expression. I gave them a smile and a wave. As I turned to get into my ride, Dad drove by. A foreboding cloud gathered over my head. He'd seen. My luck wasn't going in the right direction for him not to have.

I'd made it through the revelation that I was talking to Liam and his kids. Even worse, that I tolerated being called uncle. I could admit I liked the ring *Uncle Stetson* had to it. I didn't know when Isla was going to have kids, but I'd become Uncle Stetson much earlier than I had anticipated. I liked it.

But I wasn't doing exactly what my parents wanted, and there was one universal truth in town—no one got away with that behavior. And for a few moments, I'd forgotten I wasn't any different.

Fourteen

LYRIC

I stuffed my fingers into my mouth and blew out a whistle. Landon jumped around the end zone, the ball forgotten at his feet as his teammates cheered. Stetson and Holden grinned at each other. It'd been a week since Stetson had run into his dad outside the café, and we hadn't heard from his parents. He hadn't talked to his mom like his dad had asked him to.

Stetson had said he was used to the conflict. But he didn't admit this was different. He was going against his dad's wishes about Liam. I was proud of him. His reaction gave me hope for our future. As a team, we could work through the family drama so our kids and Liam's kids and any other little Barrons wouldn't have to deal with it.

"That was a close one," Emery's oldest daughter, Avery, said.

Emery put her hand on her chest. "I don't think I'll ever

get used to watching him get chased by a bunch of other kids.”

“If he keeps out of their reach like that, you shouldn't have to worry.” I helped her gather all the items she'd brought for the kids. Sippy cups. Snack bags. Blankets.

How much of this was the future for me and Stetson? Would I be on the sidelines with our kid watching Stetson coach? Would we have a boy who'd play? A girl? Did Stetson want to find out their sex? Did I?

It was early yet, but more excitement built each time I had these thoughts.

The morning was cool, with a brisk wind that warned of the steady drop in temperature in the days to come. This afternoon would be a completely different day. The high was supposed to be in the midsixties. Not bad for an early fall day.

I followed Emery, her girls, and her mom down the bleachers. We were the only people making our way onto the field instead of out to the parking lot. Stetson and Holden, both dressed in Coal Haven Drillers hoodies that proclaimed “Coach” on the back, were bumping fists and high-fiving the kids as they ran to meet their families.

Their energy was contagious. The games weren't something Isla had attended; therefore, I'd had no reason to attend. *I just want to watch the coach* hadn't been a valid excuse. *I'm the girlfriend of the coach* worked now.

Holden swooped his youngest stepkid, Riley, up to his shoulders. She giggled and kicked, but he kept a firm hold on her legs. “Want to come over?” he asked me and Stetson. “I have some chicken thighs to grill.”

Stetson and I exchanged looks, but he left the answer up to me. I nodded. I never turned down Holden's grilled food.

Stetson and I stopped at the grocery store. Inside he picked out a chopped salad. “Holden can't grill this.”

"He'd try if he heard you."

"Hey, Stetson, nice to see you." The owner of the implement dealer on the edge of town lingered by the display of ready-made sandwiches.

"How's it going, Joss? Enjoying the nice weather?"

"It's great, especially when we know what's around the corner."

"Snow and wind," Stetson agreed. He gave a little nod and put his hand behind my back.

That was the signal for me to move. I sidestepped to get around Joss.

Joss's gaze brushed across me and bounced back to Stetson. "Haven't seen you in a while. Everything okay?"

I didn't know how I kept my eyes from rolling, but I achieved it. The Barrons' accounts were coveted all over town. Cameron wanted it that way; he'd curated the idea. He thrived on the competition for his money. Bruce and Kira did their business where he told them to. If Joss ignored Naomi when she walked past him on the sidewalk? Then Cameron made sure the new combine he purchased in Dickinson rolled past the dealer on its way to the ranch.

Stetson's smile was winning enough to bypass the irritation I let through in my expression. Joss was fishing for a sale, be it a snowblower or a harvester. "Good. It isn't time for an upgrade, or I'd stop in."

Joss's bright-white veneers flashed. "No upgrades? Did you add another to your fleet?"

"What do you mean?"

I crossed my arms, anxious to get on with our day. Joss was being unduly nosy, but Stetson wouldn't call him out.

"I saw the new forage harvester parked by your shop yesterday."

"My shop?" Stetson's mouth formed a troubled line. "You mean my dad's."

"Yeah." As if they were the same thing, and they were, in a way. The shop at Stetson's was the ranch's. Not his. Cameron had built it before Stetson built his house. A subtle but effective way to keep Stetson on Barron land instead of striking out on his own where he wouldn't have to occasionally battle his dad. It'd be too hard for Cameron to control his son without the land.

"I haven't talked to Dad in a couple of days, so I'm not sure."

If Joss sensed Stetson's impatience, he ignored it. "Well, keep us in mind next time. We have our certified techs in town that can run right out when you have problems. They live right in Coal Haven. With their families."

"I went to school with Damon, Joss." Stetson kept his tone wry, but I heard the exasperation. "I've coached his boys in football."

Joss bobbed his head. "Then you know what the steady work means to him."

Frustrated, I blurted, "Stetson didn't buy the equipment, okay? If you have a problem, maybe you should be asking Cameron." There was no way Joss would confront Cameron.

Joss blinked, and it was like he noticed me for the first time. "O-okay. I'm sorry. I didn't mean to sound like there was an issue."

This time I did roll my eyes. He'd absolutely meant it. He might've used Damon for an example, but Joss had a habit of drinking too much and blowing hundreds to thousands on the poker machines in the bar. He wanted Barron money to pad his own pockets.

"Don't worry about it." Stetson's strong jaw worked through his smile. "I've gotta get going, but hey, I'll talk to Dad."

"Appreciate it."

Stetson towed me away.

"I overstepped, didn't I?" I muttered.

"I don't know, but I'm sick of the way he corners me in public so others can hear." Affection softened his features. "So I'll give you a pass this time."

I would press him about his dad buying equipment without talking to him, but we were in public. Stetson had pissed off Cameron about Liam. The purchase was nothing but Cameron flexing, showing his son who was still in charge.

Pulling Stetson to a stop at the brownie display, I was tempted to grab all that would fit into my arms and have him take the rest. "Think we should bring dessert?"

"Are you asking or telling?"

I selected two kinds. A tray of blondie brownies and a tray of regular. "I should bake a few dozen and freeze them for times like this. Then we won't have to run around and buy stuff. We'll have it on hand."

"Be careful, or we're going to turn into an old married farmer couple," he whispered in my ear. "Including the part where you yell at people on my behalf."

"I didn't yell."

He cocked a brow. "That's not what the rest of the town will hear. Maybe I'll be left alone more."

Good thing I didn't care if someone thought I'd yelled at Joss. It wasn't far from the truth. He'd overstepped.

Smiling and joking, we finished our shopping without any more interruptions. At Holden and Emery's place, the kids ran out to meet us.

Emery was at the front door when we approached. "Mind if we go in the back?"

"Not at all. It's too nice to be inside." I held up the grocery bags with brownies and salad. "We couldn't come empty-handed."

She took our contributions. "Perfect. I made cookies, but I think Holden put a bigger dent in them than the kids."

"Football works up an appetite."

"That's exactly what Holden said." She grinned and waved for us to follow her. "Grab a drink on your way out. We stocked some extra juice and mineral water in the fridge for those of us who can't enjoy a beer for a while."

I stopped to grab a water for me and a beer for Stetson.

Holden and Emery reclined on the chairs in the back. The kids ran around with the dog, Sally, and Tabby, the recently retired mouser, was also outside to play.

This would be us soon. Floof wasn't allowed outside. He'd been an indoor cat too long to rely on his survival instinct. But Stetson's dogs were too old to act like Sally, jumping and licking every chance she got. They preferred the barn when Stetson wasn't working.

Stetson settled on the wooden bench built between short stone pillars. I sat next to him.

He spoke to Holden. "Hey, uh, did Bruce say anything about my dad buying a harvester?"

Holden frowned. He didn't have to think about his answer. "No. You don't just go out and grab one while you're in town."

"He must've done just that, but he didn't get it from Joss."

Holden's brows popped. "Is he pissed at you or Joss?"

"I dunno. Both maybe?"

"Because of Liam?"

"Yep."

Holden's expression turned equal parts incredulous and impressed. "Did he forbid you to talk to him and you told him no?"

"Pretty much."

Pretty much meant Stetson had tried placating his dad

like he always did, but Cameron had seen it as a rebellion. His hold was slipping. Stetson was thinking for himself, and that was something Cameron didn't like his siblings or his children to do.

Stetson took a swig from his bottle. "He wants me to talk to Mom about how things are changing."

Holden's face went solemn. "She's going to—" He glanced around. The kids were playing several yards away. "She's going to shit when she hears Eli and Owen call you uncle."

"I am their uncle."

Holden's *Are you really?* look was exactly how I felt. Emery crossed her feet at the ankles, staying out of it like me.

"I can't make up for the past, but I can do better going forward. I can be better." Stetson set his beer on the pillar next to him with a *thunk*. "I'll go slow with Mom. Make some small comments and let her get used to the idea."

It sounded like a good plan, but this was Naomi. Stetson wanted to think the best of his mother when he of all people should've known better. Holden's dubious expression suggested he felt the same way I did. Emery was too new to town, but she knew what Holden's mom was like. Kira and Naomi were only sisters-in-law, but they had a lot of the same hard edges.

None of us thought Naomi would relent. Liam had just celebrated his thirtieth birthday, so she'd held her ground for three decades. I shuddered to think what her breaking point would be. I couldn't begin to comprehend what it might mean for me and Stetson and our own little nuclear unit.

Sally ran through the group, breaking our spell and prompting the guys to talk shop.

The afternoon stretched into evening. Nora arrived and was tackled with hugs. Her giggles carried across the backyard.

"Aunt Nora, look what I can do." Afton cartwheeled across the yard.

"Nora!" Riley did the same, putting her hands on the ground and kicking one leg up.

"Look at you! You've both gotten so good." She jogged toward us. "Did I miss the food?"

"The thighs are all gone, but I'm going to start on some steak soon," Holden said.

Delight crossed her face. "That sounds yummy."

Emery rose. "I have some potatoes we can fry up. And fresh fruit in the fridge to go with it."

"You're my favorite sister." Nora followed her into the house.

Holden tipped his head back to call, "Avery!"

Emery's oldest girl popped around the corner. "Yeah?"

"Want to help me get some steaks from the freezer in the shop?"

"We're grilling again? Can I do it?"

Landon tripped over his feet but recovered before he slammed into the ground. "I wanna try too."

Avery let out a long-suffering sigh. I'd never experienced the annoyance of a little sibling, but Stetson had reacted the same as Avery did around Isla until he hit his twenties.

"We have a lot of steak to cook." Holden spoke as if he'd had this argument before. "But we have to thaw it first. First one to the freezer gets to pick what we're eating."

Landon and Avery raced away, yelling at each other about what cuts they'd pick. The other two kids followed them.

"I gotta go referee. Go ahead and call Isla to come over." Holden disappeared after the noise. Stetson and I were left alone on the patio.

"And to think he's going to have five." Stetson's chuckle died. He tangled his fingers in mine. "I'm happy for him.

And for us. Our kid is going to be running with the pack one day."

A desire to see that so badly sent a shiver through me. I was an only kid. I hadn't had a big friend group growing up. Isla had been just as isolated as me, but she'd had Stetson and their cousins. And now they'd be my child's family. Like Stetson had said, no matter what. I hoped we wouldn't have to test those boundaries.

* * *

Stetson

The days were growing shorter, and the temperature dropped with the sun. I dug a sweatshirt out of my pickup for Lyric. The amount of pleasure I got from seeing her tucked into my clothing was absurd.

She'd let her fading blue hair down to ward off the chill and it swirled around her face as she laughed with Isla, Nora, and Emery. Avery huddled in a hat and coat next to them, thrilled to be included in the big girls' club.

Colt swaggered around the corner of the house, his cowboy hat tucked low. He usually wore either a beat-up cowboy hat or a greasy trucker's hat. The guy never quit working. If Kira didn't have anything for him to do, he roamed the countryside like an old-time cowboy.

None of us knew Colt's real age. He'd joke and ask how old we thought he was. He could be a mature-looking twenty-eight-year-old or a young forty-five. He wouldn't tell anyone when his birthday was. Aunt Kira would know. She was his employer, but she talked less about Colt than he did about himself.

When she'd first brought him home and announced he

was the new ranch help, I'd assumed he was her toy of the month. She'd moved him into the one-room apartment in one of her shops. Kira dated a lot, but very few of her relationships had gotten serious. As months passed, Kira was as aloof with Colt as she was with her kids. She and Colt weren't messing around, but it wasn't like she was a mother figure or a surrogate aunt. She was his employer. Nothing more.

Holden and I had gotten to know the guy, but he was a vacuum of information. The perfect employee for a Barron.

Holden grinned. "You decided to make it."

"Got nothing better to do," Colt said as he leaned on a stone pillar. The cold had to seep through his jeans, but that type of nuisance never bothered Colt. His deep-brown gaze speared Nora. "Figured she'd need a ride."

Nora made a frustrated noise. "I've had two drinks."

"Not 'cause you been drinking. Because of that piece-of-shit car that burns oil like it's the one with a drinking problem."

Nora's brow furrowed. "It doesn't burn oil."

"Have you checked it lately?"

"Why would I?"

His stony look was enough to make us all think we should run to our vehicles and check their oil levels. "It's been burning oil for months. When's the last time you had it changed?"

"Fifteen hundred miles ago." She crossed one black yoga-pants-clad leg over the other and bobbed her foot. The reflective panels on her athletic shoes glinted in the porch light. "It's not time for a service."

"Might not be time, but it needs it."

She sucked her tongue against her teeth. "Just in case you're driving, you'd better stick to mineral water."

I held back a laugh. Nora knew exactly how to poke the bear.

Colt's granite expression cracked. "I'd rather suck yellow snow through a straw than drink that fizzy shit."

Holden chortled. "Give it a month or two and we can make that happen."

Colt's eyes crinkled in the corners. His version of a smile. He glanced at me. "You increasing your silage stores?"

Even with the drought last year, the ranch had what it needed to feed the cattle. We didn't need to grow more silage. Unlike my dad, I liked what downtime my career gave me. I didn't feel like adding more work unnecessarily.

Dad couldn't walk away from decisions that weren't his to make. He'd been trying to make mine since I was born. He thought I could go to college, get a business or engineering degree, and follow in his footsteps.

There had never been a time I wanted to be like my dad. My grandpa, maybe. Until I'd gotten older and realized his undaunted pride was actually a controlling personality.

I was the ranch manager, but there was still only one of me. We'd occasionally hire part-time help, but in the end, it was my decision.

But the land I worked on was still his. The cattle. Everything but the house I lived in and the two acres that included it. I was surrounded by what an entire county considered mine but legally was not.

And sometimes Dad had to remind me. "Maybe Dad is planting an extra field in the spring. Who the fuck knows?"

Colt crossed his arms the way his ankles were crossed. He had on his usual long-sleeved plaid shirt, but he wouldn't wear a coat until most people were burrowed deep in parkas. "He drove that new tractor around like he was in a parade."

"Parade of one, and I don't know what he's cele-brating."

"Pissed Joss off. I don't think Kira's quit laughing." Colt seemed to understand our family dynamic better than we did some days. He knew that Dad made impulsive, expensive decisions and I was left to answer for them without explanations.

Landon ran up to the newcomer. "Colt! Can I show you the saddle Holden got me?"

He dragged Colt to the barn, and Holden bugged Nora about what could be wrong with her car. She insisted the sounds it randomly made were nothing.

When the sun sank below the horizon, I led Lyric to the pickup.

"Hey, can I drive?"

I tossed her the keys. I hadn't had a drink in a couple of hours, but I wasn't precious about my pickup. The drive to my place took only minutes. Lyric pulled close to the mailbox on the main road past my house. I leaned out the window and grabbed the mail.

Sifting through it as she drove, I stopped on an envelope. The name of the company on the paternity test kit we'd used was stamped in the corner. A chill washed through my veins. Not because of the results, but how others would react.

I held up the envelope and said, "It's here," before any sort of emotion set in. I'd dropped it in the mail and done my best to forget about it.

"Oh." The carefree fun from the evening vanished. "And now we deal with your parents."

"I don't need to see what it says."

She coasted down the driveway, coming to a stop in front of the garage. She killed the engine. "Yes, you do."

She snapped it out of my hands and ripped it open. I

jumped out and hip checked the door shut, my emotions clogging my throat and undulating beneath my skin. Was the whirlwind in my head due to what my reaction might be? Maybe I wasn't as ambivalent about the results as I claimed? Or was it because this was it with Mom and Dad? They'd have their answer and they'd act, no matter what the results were.

She opened her door and called, "Hey, bio dad. You wanna see?"

A grin stretched across my face. Elation whipped through my blood until I could've floated away.

I raced to her and yanked her into my arms. I was thrilled either way, but that nugget in her belly was half-mine.

She giggled and buried her face in my neck. "Are you relieved?"

Yes, but it didn't make sense. I set her down and gazed at the way her blue eyes glowed under the house light. Why did I want to twirl her around my yard? My answer came quicker than I thought. "It's one less obstacle to maneuver. I didn't like Cole, but I wouldn't want to exclude him from the baby's life. But if the shit he said to you was how he treats those close to him..."

"It is a giant relief, isn't it? I can't imagine having to deal with Cole for the next eighteen-plus years. It's bad enough thinking I'll run into him at Rattler's again."

I dropped to my knees, the pavement cold through the denim. I lifted her shirt and placed a kiss on her rounded abdomen. "Hello, little Barron."

Her stomach tightened. Was it something I said? I looked up.

Lyric opened her mouth, then hesitated before she spoke. "I just can't believe we have an answer so fast."

I stroked her warm skin with my fingertips. It wasn't like

her to hold back. "You're still worried about my parents. It'll be fine. I hate to think how they would've acted otherwise, but one less thing to worry about, right?"

Her nod was shaky. "Right. Your parents. Why am I suddenly exhausted?"

"Come on. Let's get you inside." After we told my parents, we could discard this drama behind us. None of it was mine or Lyric's. The baby was welcome, and it was mine. That envelope didn't change things.

I'd deal with them and then I'd propose to the love of my life.

Fifteen

STETSON

I parked in front of my parents' house. Lyric and I stared at the place that loomed over us. The house that clocked us like a predator. Like a silent owl in the middle of the night. Only, the sun was up, the wind was brisk, and we weren't prey.

Lyric twisted her hands together in her lap. "I warned Isla, and she said she would vanish for the day." She'd tied her hair back, tucking the bluest portions under the browner strands. This was the first time she'd done something to appease my parents. The way she favored bright hair, loud clothing, and inked skin gave Mom more reasons to dislike her, to think that Lyric would never fit into the family.

I appreciated the effort, but I hated to see her hide herself. "You don't have to change your appearance."

She touched her knot of hair. "Just this once. To make it easier on me. But...thanks."

"Come on. It'll be fine." We slid out, each shutting our doors like we didn't want to wake bad energy.

I stuffed down my anger and frustration. This shouldn't be such an issue. Telling my parents I was the biological father shouldn't need to be an announcement.

It shouldn't be their business.

But Dad hadn't been raised that way. Technically, neither had I. But I'd had more time on my hands. I hadn't had three younger siblings to order around, and that had given me more time to reflect while he was at work all day and Mom was at city council meetings. People spoke more freely around me, perhaps hoping their opinions would travel to my parents via me. I processed it all, and I had decided I would be different.

It hadn't been easy, and sometimes, I hadn't felt like I was the better man.

When we walked through the sliding glass door I usually came through, Mom was at the counter, a steaming coffee mug in front of her. She wore thin silver readers, and a tablet that probably had the morning paper pulled up was by the mug.

Her lips pursed when her gaze landed on Lyric. She took her glasses off and set them by her tablet. "Stetson. Lyric. Good morning."

"Hey, Mom. Dad around?"

Her gaze turned appraising. "You have the results, I take it?" I nodded, and she pushed away from the island. She gathered her tablet and glasses. "I'll be right back. Have a seat."

She called for Dad. The bedroom door opened and closed. He wouldn't come out here in his silk pajama pants, but I was surprised he was still in the bedroom. Isla had mentioned he'd been tired lately.

I sat on a stool with Lyric next to me. She pressed a hand

to her stomach. "It's like my morning sickness has come back with a grudge."

"It'll be fine. We're going to tell them and then go to town for breakfast. It'll be fine." If I kept telling myself that, would it be true?

I had broached the breakfast idea when the thought of putting something in my stomach before this task was completed had sat like lead in my gut. Food would be worse. Lyric had agreed.

Mom tightened her cashmere cardigan around herself as she reentered the kitchen. Dad was right behind her. His hair was barely more than finger-combed, and he wore an old green college sweatshirt with work jeans.

My worry increased, but it had nothing to do with the baby. Since I had taken over, Dad had worked the ranch on the weekends to give me some breathing room. It gave him something to do that wasn't Mom's side projects and lightened my load. I didn't mind; there was always work to do, and I stopped by anyway. Since I had learned Lyric was pregnant, I hadn't helped as much. Was the extra work getting to him?

Mom took her post on the other side of the island. She folded her hands on the surface. "So?"

I kept my tone even. "I'm the biological father."

I wasn't sure what reaction I was expecting, but her slow nod wasn't it. She exchanged a charged glance with Dad. "Now what?"

"Nothing's changed," I said carefully. Shit. This was like sitting in the middle of the road with a semi bearing down on us.

Mom assessed us, her face the same mask I had witnessed during city council meetings. "Lyric, can you give us some privacy?"

Lyric cut her gaze to me.

Frowning, I put a hand on her forearm even though she hadn't moved to leave. "We're in this together."

"You two are having a baby together," Dad said. "But it's still our family."

I brushed my thumb on her skin. I wanted her to be part of my family, but this wasn't the place for a declaration. "She's with me."

Mom made an exasperated noise and pinned Lyric with her stare. "You got what you wanted."

"What do you mean?" The indignation in Lyric's tone fueled my increasing outrage.

"Mom, what's this about? What's happened between Lyric and me is new. She's been Isla's friend for twenty years."

"Her mom cornered her dad into marrying her. Now she's doing the same to you. It's been tried on this family before. I didn't tolerate it then; I'm not tolerating it now."

Silence descended. Shock robbed any reply from my tongue. What the *hell*? Why would she wield Lyric's family history against her like that?

Lyric's jaw was tight, but she didn't respond. Her arm vibrated under my hand.

I needed to gauge how bad their reactions were, and we'd seen only Mom's. "Dad?"

Dad tipped his chin down and propped his hands on his hips. He led with silence when it came to his infidelity, but this time the subject was about me. "What do you want me to say, Stetson?" The rigid authority usually in his tone was gone. He was letting Mom lead this battle. "You know how it looks, and your mother's explained how it feels."

My mind buzzed. This didn't make sense. I'd thought Mom would be satisfied.

The knuckles on Mom's clasped hands whitened. "Naturally, we've had a prenup prepared for years for when you were ready to marry, but you can't fall for this."

My temples throbbed. A prenup? "Fall for what, Mom? What are you afraid of? This isn't about you. Lyric and I are partners, and we're going to be parents."

"Stetson, you need to slow down and think. You've been so careful, don't let one accident—"

"I've had enough." Lyric pushed away, nearly tipping over the wooden stool next to her. I stood, but her angry gaze was on Mom and Dad. "I've had to watch Isla and Stetson put up with you since I've known them. I don't have to."

Mom scoffed. "If Isla could make one single friend who wasn't you, believe me, I would've warned her long ago. I saw what your mother did. Women like you and her seem to grow on trees in Coal Haven."

"Mom!"

"Don't you dare"—Lyric stabbed a finger toward my mother—"insult my mother. She hasn't deserved your derision at any point in her life. Not then, not now. And neither do I."

Mom's face remained placid, as if she thought she had the high ground. "You aren't going to run us out of this child's life like your mother was able to do with your dad's side of the family."

No. She couldn't talk to Lyric like that. "Holy shit, Mom. You know nothing about that. Show some respect."

Mom jerked as if I'd slapped her.

Fury raged over Lyric's face. "You point fingers at my mom. At Liam's mom. At me. You blame us for your own insecurities. There's one righteous you and so many of us gold diggers. Have you ever thought the problem might actually be you?"

Mom gasped, a hand flying to her chest. She looked at me, her gaze pleading. "And you're okay with her talking to me like this?"

"You asked for it." At Mom's gasp, I put my hands up like it was enough to stop the argument. "Listen—"

"Stetson!" Mom's chest heaved, on the verge of a panic attack.

Dad cast a worried glance toward her. Her hazel eyes glittered, and color was draining from her face. She was going to cry. Then she'd sob. A collapse might come after.

"Perhaps Lyric should leave while we discuss this," he said.

"The only reason Lyric should leave is because she doesn't need to be insulted." My tone was hot. Lyric wasn't a user. "Neither does her mother."

"I don't want to be here. I can't believe the two of you produced two decent kids." She did a double take toward Dad and clenched her jaw.

The reason dawned on me, and I wanted to groan. Dad had produced *three* decent kids.

Mom's sharp inhale could've just as well been a shout. Lyric straightened, but regret was in her eyes. She probably hadn't meant to shine a spotlight on my parents' festering wound, but maybe this house needed to quit tiptoeing around the unspoken.

"I'll be in the pickup." Lyric stormed out the door before I could decide whether asking her to stay was the right thing to do. She didn't deserve the hurt being caused today.

I eyed my parents. Mom had sagged since Lyric had left. Dad's expression was full of worry and regret. "What the hell, guys?"

"Don't swear at me, Stetson." Mom hugged herself and turned somewhat away from Dad.

"That could've gone better," Dad muttered as he leaned against the counter. Dark circles rimmed his eyes. "Do you really love her, Stetson?"

"That's how they work," Mom hissed before I could answer.

"Mom, she's not like Liam's mom—" Warning glares from both parents shut my mouth.

Dad pinched the bridge of his nose. "We've known Lyric her whole life, but your mom has a point. That girl knows better than anyone what you have and how you are. If anyone knew how to get close to you, it would be her."

She hadn't tried. She hadn't pursued me. I'd been clueless about her infatuation. I'd gone on with my life, and I'd seethed for the last few years as she'd gone on with hers. I couldn't implant those feelings and memories in my parents' heads. But how could I get them to understand?

"If money was what she was after, she could've stayed with her ex or some other plant or oil field worker. A guy with no attachments who doesn't care how she spends his money while he's gone." As long as she didn't ask questions and he came home to a piece of ass. I'd known a few of those guys over the years. They were magnets for women like Mom was talking about—or insecure women were a magnet for them. Either way, that wasn't Lyric. "Lyric has a good job. She put herself through school. She's not using me."

"Her mother—"

"Had a shitty husband," I said, exasperated and more than a little angry. "And he was a shitty father."

Mom's scowl deepened. "Stetson—"

"I know, language. But he's the user, not her."

"He's still a role model for her, Stetson." Mom feathered her trembling hand over her hair. "You should be thinking less about a relationship and more about custody. You should be documenting how much you're supporting her now."

Nothing I said was getting through to her. I hooked a hand on my hip and turned to Dad. "And you agree?" I knew the answer. I needed to hear him say it.

His brow furrowed, and his glance at Mom was guarded. "I think you and Lyric are rushing into things."

"The baby's going to be here in a little over five months," I said.

"Exactly why you should slow down." His expression was strained, like the past was ramming at his brain. "Is she pressuring you?"

"Of course not."

"Good. That's good." Dad traded another loaded look with Mom. "I think you need to remember what's on the line. We can't risk our assets."

"A woman tried to split this family once." Mom's voice shook, her body as taut as a guitar string.

Lyric wasn't just any woman. She was her own person, and that was one of my many favorite things about her. But I wasn't going to change their minds overnight. They needed time to process reality. Their initial reaction was always heavy handed. I had to believe they wouldn't drive away someone so important to me.

"Look, I know this whole situation has been a turn from what's been going on in my life." Which had been a whole lot of nothing. "And even though you knew it was coming, today has been a shock for you. We can discuss this more later. I just wanted to let you know what the results were since you paid for it." The words were sour on my tongue. Too close to thanking Mom for interfering when we didn't need or want her to. "Lyric's waiting. I should get going." I didn't wait for their response and walked to the door, an even pace to keep from letting them know how upset I was.

Dad followed me. "You need time to think; I understand that. But realize we have your best interests at heart."

I met his gaze before going out the door. "Are you sure about that?" And I left. Lyric needed me.

* * *

Lyric

When Stetson slammed into the pickup and drove away, he didn't say a word and I didn't pressure him. Green pastures dotted with black and reddish-brown cows rolled past the window until he turned into his driveway and parked in front of the garage.

"Did they threaten me?" I finally asked. I fought the urge to cringe against the door of the pickup like his confirmation was going to strike me down.

"No. they told me to think about it. I think they need the time."

A tiny spark of disappointment flared in my chest. Typical Stetson. "Think about what? It's not like they can go from hating me to 'eh, she's not so bad' in a few days."

His weary expression was aimed my way. "They don't hate you, Lyric."

They didn't like me, and they weren't ambivalent about me. What was left? "They're living in a different reality, Stetson. You're going to be the one to have to decide if you want to stay there with them." And if he did, what would I do?

"They're scared."

Naomi and Cameron Barron scared? Of what? They had everything.

Stetson must've read my expression correctly. "Things

are changing, and they've been in charge for so long. But they're aging. I didn't become the CEO rancher Dad wanted me to be. I'm not on any city boards or councils or whatever the fuck Grandpa used to be on. I'm not a major figure in Coal Haven beyond being their son. Isla's still living at home, and some days she acts scared of her shadow."

"The shadows are them."

He shrugged, a sense of helplessness I'd never seen settling into his features. "Isla has her reasons. If she wanted to challenge my parents, she would."

I opened my mouth but stopped before speaking. He was correct. Isla used her parents as excuses. Did she know why she did it? She hadn't shared with me, so probably not. And Stetson's problems were becoming my problems. My shoulders weren't big enough for hers too.

Would I be around to listen when she needed to talk?

After the way I was treated in that house, I would only go as close as Stetson's place.

How would my living arrangements change if Stetson's parents didn't come around? "So you give them time to think. Then what?"

He scrubbed a hand down his face. "Then we talk."

"It's not going to be a talk, Stetson. They order. People obey. If they don't, they face the consequences."

"I'm their son."

"You're also your own adult, in your thirties, and I'm still sitting here with you wondering why the hell it seems like they have such a say in our relationship." I willed him to accept the reality of his parents. If he didn't, then I wasn't sure how we were going to work. My heart ached. No. We'd make it.

"They don't have a say, Lyric. They're my parents. They're a part of my life. I love them, and I'm in love with you. I don't want those two parts of my life separate forever."

Neither did I. For his sake more than for us.

We hadn't left the pickup. The wind was picking up outside, and puffy white clouds raced across the horizon. The sunny, mellow morning was going to turn gusty and the temperature would drop. Fitting.

"Telling them to think for a minute isn't going to cut it," I said, knowing he'd still hold out hope.

"I'll handle it, Lyric. I've always handled them."

"Is that what you tell them? You'll handle me?"

"No." His brows drew together, but confidence was lacking in his voice. "What do you want me to say? What do you want me to do?"

I didn't have an answer.

He twisted toward me and draped an arm over the steering wheel. "She shouldn't have insulted your mom like that. She shouldn't have insulted you. But if I push too hard..."

There he was. The scared boy who thought he was losing his mom and everything he knew in the world, who'd turned into a parent-pleasing man who was still afraid he would lose everything. I wanted to reassure him, but he wasn't a kid anymore.

Neither was I. "What your mom said didn't bother me as much as why she said it. She can think what she wants about Mom, but I know the truth. My dad left us because he wanted more. He saw me and Mom as nothing but an anchor on a sailboat going nowhere."

"Is that why you got a mariner's compass on your back?"

I swallowed and dropped my gaze to my lap. "It was the first tattoo I got. I heard him say that phrase, you know. 'Erin, you're an anchor. You're a luxury liner that's happy to stay in port. And I'm a sailboat. I want to go where the wind takes me. And I won't be able to go anywhere in life with you.'" I batted tears away. The abandoned little girl was still inside me.

He brushed a thumb along my cheek. "Using all those metaphors when leaving your family is a mega douche move."

I let out a soft chuckle. "I thought it was so poetic that he must be right." I twined my fingers together. "When I saw this compass after I'd gotten a few paychecks in college, I knew it was what I wanted."

"To remind yourself you can sail in any direction?"

I chewed the inside of my lip as I thought. I hadn't considered the compass for more than a couple minutes before I made my appointment and slapped the picture down. "No. I knew I was coming back home to be with Mom, but I wanted to remind myself that I could go anywhere if I wanted to. That wherever I landed was by choice and not because someone was my anchor."

He grabbed my hands in one of his big ones. "You're not my anchor."

Emotion swelled inside me until my skin cinched too tight. No wonder Naomi's words had stuck with me. Fear that Stetson would believe her and leave me had been a constant companion. But he was here. With me. "I guess the one thing Dad left me with other than a sense of abandonment was shitty clichés."

"You and I are in this for the long haul." He leaned over and tipped my face toward him. "Love conquers all. You had me at hello."

I suppressed a giggle. Our impending fight dissipated. I'd expected him to behave one way because of my past, but he was behaving another way because of his. "I guess we need to let it run its course, so shut up and kiss me."

"Oof, baby. Those were two good ones right there." He claimed my mouth, and it took only seconds before I was climbing onto his lap as he moved his seat as far back as it'd go.

We could go inside, but this moment in the cab was about us and only us. The world outside could wait.

Sixteen

STETSON

I hunched like a hulking lumberjack in the clinic's small waiting room chairs. Lyric had one leg crossed over the other. Her leggings had comic book panels on them. She wore an old Coal Haven Drillers shirt of mine, knotted at the waist, and her black Converse sneakers.

Emery poked her head through the doors to the rest of the clinic and smiled at us. "Come on back."

The three of us crowded into a small exam room. Why did these rooms become tinier as I got older?

I huddled on another chair while Emery collected Lyric's information and weight. Then Emery perched on a stool to gather Lyric's history. As if making the baby wasn't intimate, this took us to another level of our relationship.

"Okay," Emery said after she'd asked a million questions. "Dr. Abdallah will be right in." She paused and smiled. "Is it getting real now?"

"A little bit," Lyric admitted. "But it's weird. I feel fuller in my abdomen, but other than changing my habits a little, like no alcohol and stuff, I don't feel different."

Emery smiled, her expression nostalgic. "With Avery, I didn't show until I was past the five-month mark. I wore my regular scrubs for over six months, and I had this cute little round belly. Then boom. Beach ball belly for the last two months. With the other three, I had to break out the maternity scrubs earlier and earlier. Then this one." She rolled her eyes, but her grin stayed in place. "But Holden's a lot taller and bigger than Henry, so the experience is different."

"Getting ready for a ten-pound baby?" I asked with no other way to contribute to the conversation.

Emery laughed. "I wouldn't be surprised." She rose and dug around in a cupboard drawer, then laid some faded fabric on the exam bed. "So, this visit is a full exam, and Dr. Abdallah likes to do some labs right away too. She'll also try to listen to the heartbeat. After she's done with you, I'll come back with some new-parent education materials. And in case I forget to tell you—if you leave and have questions, just give me a call."

We were closed into the room by ourselves. Lyric slapped her knees and rose. "Guess I'll get changed. Do you want to be in here when she does the exam?"

"I've seen it all already." My voice had turned gruff; we were in the least sexy place I'd ever been.

"Not in full light with someone else digging around." She winced. "That makes it sound like there's a s'mores chance in hell that it's not uncomfortable."

"Where do you want me?"

She hugged the clothing to herself. "Here. But don't look." She held up the whitest cloth in the pile. "I'll have a sheet over me, but my ass will be hanging off the bed."

"No peeking. I promise."

I kept my head down and scrolled through my phone

while she undressed and put the exam robe on. Shortly after she was settled, Dr. Abdallah came in, her long dress swishing under her white lab coat. She greeted Lyric like they hadn't just seen each other yesterday at work and introduced herself to me. This was the first time we'd met. Dr. Abdallah was a few years older than me, but she and her family had moved to Coal Haven for the job. I'd seen her around. The physicians were akin to celebrities in our small town.

There were more questions, and it was like I didn't exist until Dr. Abdallah asked Lyric if she was okay with me in the room for the exam.

"He said he was fine," Lyric answered.

The doctor gave me a smile. "All right, then. Let's get started."

I did the phone scroll thing the whole time, but I didn't pay attention to the ten-day forecast I had looked up or the vacation photos an old classmate posted.

When Dr. Abdallah scooted the blanket below Lyric's abdomen and produced a little device, I tucked my phone away. Nervous anticipation ran through me. This was it.

"All right. Time to hear Baby." The doctor angled herself so I could see, but we were all poised to listen. She concentrated as she moved the wand.

A steady *whoosh woosh* filled the room. Elation made me sit straighter. Was that it?

Dr. Abdallah smiled at Lyric. "That's your heartbeat. Baby's will be much faster." She continued moving the handheld device. "It can be hard to hear Baby's heartbeat at this stage. These fetal Dopplers are great, but they have their limits. We may need to *see* the heartbeat instead. I'll give Lilith a call."

Lyric spared me a glance. "She's the tech who does ultrasounds."

"She might be able to get to you right away, but if not, do you two have some time to spare? Or we can always set up an appointment."

Lyric looked at me. She'd made the appointment on her day off so she didn't have to rush in and out of the exam room to get back to work and afterward we could grab a bite to eat and talk about what we'd learned. I'd gotten up earlier than normal to accomplish my tasks.

"I've got as much time as you need." I wasn't letting Lyric down by rushing off to tend to cattle that often had the audacity to give birth in the middle of a blizzard.

"Okay." Dr. Abdallah tucked her device away. She helped Lyric cover her stomach and gave her a hand to sit up. "You'll come back here after the ultrasound, then Emery will be in with the prenatal information." Her warm-brown eyes were friendly but searching as her gaze moved between me and Lyric. "Any questions? Concerns?"

I shook my head.

I had a ton of questions. Was this normal? Was everything all right? Did this Lilith know what she was doing? The ultrasound tech was another person I didn't really know. She'd moved here for the job.

But the clash of questions was only new-dad anxiety, and Lyric looked as mellow as my old Pyrenees on a sunny day when he sprawled over the green grass.

Lyric dressed once the doctor had left the room. She led me down a long hallway, past the lab, where she waved to one of the techs, and to a separate waiting room on the other side of a door with a sign that read Radiology.

A few minutes later, a girl around Lyric's age popped out, a grin plastered on her face. "Ready, Lyric?" She lifted her gaze to me, her eyes flaring with wariness as I stood. The tech was barely over five feet tall. Compared to her, I looked like I'd jumped off a beanstalk and demanded to know who had my golden egg.

"This is Stetson," Lyric said quickly. "He's with me."

Lilith's trepidation diminished but didn't disappear. I rarely experienced being around someone taller than me, and if they were, it was by only an inch or two. People got antsy around me. For so long, I had thought it was because of my last name, but it was a relief and a frustration when I realized my size intimidated others. I couldn't do anything about it, but also, not everything in my life came down to my parents.

"Hi, Lilith. How's it going in the ultrasound world today?"

She relaxed a little more. "Good. Come on back." She led us to a dim room with a screen on the wall. "Lyric, you get the bed. Stetson, there's a chair beside it." The machine Lilith sat behind made her look like a figurine.

Lyric and I kept our gazes glued to the monitor on the wall. A little white arrow zoomed across the screen.

"That little nugget"—Lilith tapped a button—"is the baby." A picture printed from one of the slots on the machine. "See the steady flicker?" She grinned. "Baby's heartbeat."

I couldn't take my eyes off the tiny, pulsing organ. Baby Barron resembled a peanut more than they did a human, but they were there.

A baby.

Why did seeing the image make things seem like they were serious now? As if Lyric and I hadn't been navigating some deep shit. But this was why. For a bean in her belly.

Fuck me, I was gonna be a dad.

Lyric squeezed my hand. When had I grabbed it?

Lilith brandished a flimsy black-and-white photo and handed it to Lyric with a towel to wipe her belly off. "You two are ready to go back to see Dr. Abdallah. I'll let Emery know you're heading back. She said you can just go into the same exam room."

I walked out of the room with Lyric, still in a daze. She was staring at the picture. "It's real."

"I know. Fucking amazing."

She chuckled. "Makes my head spin."

"You make my head spin." I didn't care that we were in the middle of a clinic hallway. I pulled her to me and pressed my lips on hers for a solid kiss. "I love you."

A squeak at the end of the hall caught my attention.

Krystal.

Tears glittered in her eyes, and she darted into the break room. Dammit. I hadn't wanted to hurt Krystal, but because I let us go on too long, she was still dealing with emotions. And they were spilling over onto Lyric and me.

Lyric sighed. "Can't we get just one momentous moment to ourselves without dealing with everyone else's reactions?"

"I'm sorry."

"It's not your fault."

"Some of it is." I wrapped an arm around her shoulder. "But it won't be like this all the time."

Lyric stared up at me as we walked. "Promise?"

Her vulnerability cut through the moment. She wasn't joking. There was no humor in that one word. She wanted me to promise that the shit she was dealing with because of my parents, because of my ex, because of who I was, wasn't going to continue to happen.

"I promise." It was the only time I wasn't sure of myself.

* * *

Lyric

"So that's Baby?" Mom held the photo with both hands while I witnessed her go full grandma. Her expression said that this baby would never hear *no* from her if at all humanly possible.

Stetson leaned against the cash register. The bell on the door dinged as it opened.

Mom glanced up. "Hattie. Come look at my grandbaby."

Hattie shuffled over, delight on her face. I hadn't been around a lot of adults while they interacted with their grandkids. My dad's parents had been older and had passed away years ago after listening to my dad go on about how toxic my mom and I were. And Mom's parents had died before I was born. One reason she'd been so scared to be a single mom.

Would I have felt the same if things between me and Stetson hadn't worked out? I had Mom, and that was more than she'd had when she learned she was pregnant with me.

Hattie beamed and looked up from the photo. "Congratulations. I've pestered Liam for new baby pictures so much that he pulls out his phone as soon as he walks into the store."

Mom and Stetson chuckled. Hattie now gave zero fucks about anything Barron after Naomi had tried to close down her store. The shopkeeper had partnered with Liam to sell his welded decor; that was as far as her Barron tolerance went. However, I wasn't surprised she didn't hold hostility toward Stetson. He would've worked to ensure she didn't hold a grudge against him no matter how much his parents had upset her.

"If you've got company, I'll catch you later." Hattie tilted her head as she grinned. I could always tell it was her from a distance due to the way she cocked her head.

"No," I said. "Stetson and I aren't staying. We wanted to show Mom the picture and update her on the due date." March, like I had calculated.

"I'll lock up behind you." Mom grabbed her keys as Stetson and I started for the door. It was Thursday, and our tradition had faltered thanks to work for both of us, but she'd assured me each week that it was fine.

It's time for you to start new traditions with your family. When the dust dies down, we can still get together here and there for Thursday dinners.

My guilt had given way to the realization that she was releasing me from the nest. I gave Mom a quick hug at the door.

"Now what?" Stetson asked after we climbed into the pickup.

"Isla has the farmers' market, but I feel like showing off this peanut." I'd take the picture to work and show Joan and my other coworkers. I couldn't quit looking at the photo of the tiny bump in my belly.

"Invite some friends over. I can get the firepit going and leave you alone."

"You mean like a girls' night?"

He nodded and adjusted the brim of his hat. "Sure. I mean, we could invite Holden and Emery, but if both of them come, they'd have to bring the kids. I love 'em, but it's okay to have adult time too."

The idea got better the more I thought about it. It was my home too, and I wouldn't be ditching him. But there was still the great divide to work with. I'd like to chat with the whole group and not base attendance on who was friends with Liam. For me, that meant whether Isla was along or not. She didn't interact with Liam. There were several years between them, and while she was friendly with Kennedy, they weren't exactly friends.

But Isla had the farmers' market tonight. Would Emery be free? "I could call Aspen too. Maybe Kennedy and Laney could come over. Nora?"

"Whoever." He didn't have to ask about Isla. The man was more knowledgeable about Barron logistics than me. "Want to do supper or just roast marshmallows? Or would you rather just use the bar downstairs?"

I liked his basement. It had an exterior door that kept it from feeling closed off from the world, but the living area of his house was large enough. I didn't have much need to go beyond the main floor.

I loved the outside as much as the inside, and I hadn't had friends over. It was time to change that. "The firepit sounds fun." I took out my phone and sent a group message. I wasn't sure any of them could make it. Kennedy and Aspen probably had to teach tomorrow, Delaney got up early with her chickens, and Emery was pregnant, with four kids.

Replies came immediately. Emery bowed out. **Sorry, school night drama. Why not tell me about homework five minutes before bed? Thanks for the invite tho.** I could picture her eye roll and subtle smirk.

Kennedy sent her reply separately. **Are you sure it's okay I'm there?**

Understandable reaction. **Stetson offered to start the firepit for us. You're more than welcome**. And she always would be if I had any say.

Wasn't that a lingering issue? Submerged just below conscious thought was the worry that I didn't have any say, that Stetson had power over my living arrangement.

I shook off those concerns. The worry would eventually

be buried under my own experiences with this house and people who were important to me. The more Stetson and I lived our life together, the more I'd trust this thing between us.

Going to the upstairs linen closet, I grabbed extra blankets in case it got cold. I peeked out the window. Stetson was setting chairs out. Five of them.

I hated not including Isla. This feud wasn't mine. I sent her a message. **Having the girls over—Laney, Kennedy, and Nora. Drop in when you're done**.

There. Guilt didn't often bother me when I hung out with groups that didn't include Isla. She preferred to avoid awkwardness and potential drama. Being her mother's daughter hadn't offered a lot of togetherness with supportive women. But this was her brother's place, and it'd kill him if she didn't feel welcome here.

Her reply came. **Soft pass, but thanks for the invite. I'm going to bury my head in the covers and pretend I never signed up to be market manager.**

That bad?

Same bickering. Gets old.

We'll have s'mores later. I had sent her a photo of the baby picture earlier.

By the time Stetson had the fire roaring, Nora was pulling in.

I didn't know it was her until she got out of the beat-up farm truck. "New wheels?"

She rolled her eyes. "Colt will tell you how right he was about my engine burning oil."

"Oh, no."

"Oh, yes. I out stubborned him, and he won. It wasn't a game of chicken. One day, the engine just stopped. No oil. No more car."

"That sucks."

"Not as much as the way he laughs when he sees me in this thing—which he got running before my car died."

"Colt laughs?"

"It's in his eyes," she practically hissed, but a smile played on her lips.

Kennedy and Laney arrived a few minutes later in the pickup I usually saw Archer driving. Aspen pulled up behind them in her little sports coupe.

Some of the group were dressed in jeans and hoodies. The chill of the night could be warded off by the fire, but Aspen wore suede ankle boots, white pants, and a knit sweater with a scarf around her neck. If she'd ever dressed down, I'd never seen it. I had on insulated leggings since my jeans were getting too snug around the belly.

I'd worked this weekend, but Isla was going with me to buy maternity clothes in Bismarck next weekend. I had ordered a few pieces already, along with some baggier scrubs.

"Hey." I waved the photo. Everyone piled around me.

This wasn't my normal. Growing up, Isla and I had been a pair, and not many other girls our age had talked to us. Now I had a group. Friends. And I still had my best friend.

The next couple of hours went by. Stetson occasionally stopped by to tease us as he stoked the fire, but he hung out in the shop and kept the dogs from sniffing around our treats. None of us were drinking.

Water and juice would have to be added to our grocery list, along with ingredients to make those goodies we'd talked about freezing. I wanted to be prepared for more nights like this.

"Y'all are gonna give me baby fever," Laney grumbled. She was tucked into an old quilt Stetson's grandma had made. Her blond ponytail hung out the back.

"Y'all?" Nora giggled.

Laney grinned. "Blame Archer—it's a convenient word. But I lied. I have baby fever; I'm just..." She blew out a breath. "It hasn't happened yet. And that's okay. Ma tried for a few years to have Kane, and I was an accident a ways down the line. But damn. We've got the land, the chickens, the goats. Of course, the cattle. If I keep adding on, I'm going to have to have five kids to help with all the chores, and I need to get started."

Kennedy adjusted her maroon blanket on her lap. "We're discussing how close we want the kids. There're six years between the boys and Ginny. I don't want to go that long, but I can't imagine being pregnant again right now."

Laney snorted. "As often as he has his hands on you, the odds are not in your favor."

Kennedy's playful scowl made us all laugh.

Nora spread her hands out. "I am not in this race."

"You and me both," said Aspen.

"I wasn't either, but sometimes the race picks you when you aren't wearing your bib," I said. Laughter ringed the fire.

Stetson appeared with an armload of wood. After losing my home, I hadn't been sure I'd enjoy the smell of woodsmoke, but it wasn't the acrid electrical smell of the trailer fire. This was nice. In so many ways.

He squatted and set the wood down. "I feel like I walked in at a bad time."

"We were only partially talking about you," I said.

He glanced over his shoulder at me, his eyes crinkling. The firelight sharpened his rough edges. He looked like the hard guy people assumed he was when they didn't know him. Turning his attention back to the fire, he put his ball cap on backward and added new wood, working his firepit magic.

"Stetson?"

My heart dropped right out of my chest at Cameron's scandalized tone. My gaze jerked right to Kennedy. She was stiff, same as Laney.

Stetson rose and twisted toward his dad in one smooth motion. "Dad. Hey, didn't know you were stopping by or I would've gotten some peanut butter to add to the crackers."

Cameron's gaze narrowed as if Stetson had given away the refinery's top secret information. He was dressed like he'd just come from work in his typical perfectly tailored charcoal-gray suit and cowboy boots. "What's going on?"

How did Stetson manage a casual shrug? "Lyric's having some friends over, and I'm their fire guy."

Cameron's gaze swept the group, hardening to ice when it touched on Kennedy and Laney, and going glacial when it landed on me. With precision, he shifted his focus to his son. "Your mother and I need to talk to you. We'll wait for you in the house."

"Or I can swing by in the morning." His tone was full of warning.

"Tonight." The word was curt, cutting through the night harsher than the chilly wind. He spun on a booted heel and strode over the grass and around the side of the house.

Silence descended around the fire.

"Sorry," I said, not wishing to prolong the discomfort.

"Don't worry," Kennedy said, shaking her blanket out and folding it. "I was thinking it was time to get going."

"You're welcome to stay." Stetson's smile was tight. "Any explosions will take place far away from the fire."

She smiled. "Thanks for taking care of us, Stetson. It's nice to see you again." To others, it would be an odd thing to say when they lived in the same town and she was married to his half brother. But this might have been their first real interaction since her first husband had been alive. "I hope there are more firepit nights in the future, but the mornings can get hectic, and I need to get to bed."

Laney set her folded quilt on top of Kennedy's. "I'm charged with getting the schoolteacher home at a decent hour. The other schoolteacher doesn't have a curfew."

Aspen rewrapped her scarf around her neck. "The other schoolteacher doesn't have to face kids until the morning recess bell rings." Her warm smile was sympathetic. "Thanks for inviting me."

My smile was strained. Why did Cameron and Naomi pick tonight? Did they have a radar for how to make the biggest scene without making an actual scene? "Thanks for coming."

Nora gave us a wave, but her parting look at Stetson brimmed with pity.

When we were alone, he gestured to all the items we had readied for the company that had vanished in a minute. "Leave it." His jaw was tight enough to compress coal, but he quickly kissed my lips. "I'll be right back."

"I think it's a conversation we should have together." Both his parents were here. This wasn't just ranch talk. The chocolate I'd had with my s'mores curdled in my stomach. It hadn't been his idea to ask me to leave when we'd announced the paternity test results. Would he ask me to stay out of it now? Would it be a giant fracture in what we were building together?

He spun his hat around the right way and sighed. "Me too."

I stalled my relief. I had to make sure. "They won't want me there."

"I want you there." He said it like it should matter, but we both knew that what he wanted didn't factor into his parents' consideration. "We're in this together."

The party cleanup would have to wait. Stetson always said he'd deal with it. He'd probably said the same to Cameron and Naomi about me. But we would all pile into his house, and Stetson and I would face them. He'd said he'd handle it, but he had to know he no longer had to do it alone.

Seventeen

STETSON

When I walked through the mudroom, my feet dragged like I was walking through two feet of fine sand. Lyric's presence bolstered me. This was my house. My home. Where I lived with my family.

She shut the door behind her. When we came around the corner, Mom and Dad sat at the dining room table. Mom's face was wan, her expression haggard but determined. Dad sat on a stool, his shoulders uncharacteristically slumped.

"Everything okay?" Had they come here because Isla was home? They didn't want her to witness their sledgehammer tactics.

"No." A terse, quiet word from Mom. "Does she have to be here?"

"Yes." I refused to budge on running Lyric off again. As much as I didn't want her to get shit from my parents, this was our life together. We needed to be a united front. "This is her home too."

I pulled a chair out for Lyric, the farthest away from the mushrooming emotions of my parents.

Taking a seat next to her, I folded my arms. "What's up?"

I knew the answer. I wasn't the compliant son.

"You've been talking to Liam?" Mom spoke barely above a whisper.

Ah, hell. Somehow my half brother tied into why they were here, but it wasn't the sole reason. A dull ache started at my temples. "Yes." I didn't bother to defend my actions more than that. We all knew who Liam was to me and who he wasn't supposed to be.

"You allow his kids to call you uncle? In public?" This time her voice shook.

"Yes."

She made a disgusted noise and avoided looking at me. Tears glittered in her eyes. She'd be sobbing if Lyric wasn't here.

"Didn't you listen to a thing we said when you told us the paternity results?" Dad asked.

Out of the corner of my eye, I saw Lyric's gaze whip to me. I hadn't told her word for word the rest of the conversation after she walked out. "I did. And then I made my own decision about the people who are going to be my family."

Mom's eyes flared. "You're going to marry her?"

A discussion of marriage was supposed to be private. It was supposed to be a romantic topic that caused excitement. I met Lyric's gaze. I wanted her to know I was serious about forever, but fuck, I didn't want it to be like this. "I haven't asked yet."

Mom pressed her hands on the tabletop. "She's upsetting everything, Stetson."

Lyric's quiet scoff drew the force of Mom's glare.

The dam holding my temper back bulged. "No, Mom. Krystal upset everything, and you tolerated her until it got embarrassing. I'm proud of Lyric, and I like who I am with her." I liked who I could be with her. I wasn't a guy in his thirties doing what his parents told him to do. I was a man taking care of my loved ones, free to get to know the rest of my family.

"Krystal wasn't an enabler," Mom protested. "None of your girlfriends pressured you to go against the wishes of your family. Then *she* comes along, and you've lost all your good sense."

"About what?" I almost shouted. "She lured me into not being an asshole to my brother?" Mom gasped, and Dad squeezed his eyes shut. "My nephews? You know what? They're good people. So's Archer. And Uncle Bruce has even turned over a new leaf of not being a giant dick."

"Stetson Cameron Barron, don't you dare swear at me."

"I'm not swearing at you." Said like a petulant teen, but Mom liked to use her language reprimands as another tool to control others. Police someone's language and appear like she was on higher ground. "But you get my point. I'm an adult. Liam's an adult. They're my family too, and looking around, the line you've drawn between us and them is getting pushed back and there's fewer people standing on our side."

"You've never talked like this before." Mom shook her head. She squeezed Dad's bicep like she was lending him strength.

Dad stared at her hand a moment. When he spoke, it was slowly. "I told you we can't risk everything we have."

He almost looked...uneasy. Unsure. That wasn't Dad. I stayed quiet, waiting for him to swing the hammer so I knew how much damage I had to deal with.

"With the way you're behaving, I can't guarantee that you'll follow through with a prenuptial agreement."

I cocked my head. Why would I want to? I had a nice savings and investments. From what Lyric had said, she was building her own retirement fund from her work. My share, with the house, would still be more, but I didn't plan on divorcing the only woman I'd ever fallen in love with.

"You would've gotten everything, Stetson." Dad's jaw hardened as he ground his teeth together. "Everything."

Lyric's back hit the chair. "You're cutting him off?"

My brain was sluggish to keep up. Cut me off? From what?

"Our land, this ranch, has been in our family for *generations*." Dad's voice was razor sharp. "My father tasked me with its care."

Why would he think I didn't care as much as him? That I wasn't invested? "And I haven't been helping you since I was old enough to walk? This place is my life." I had made it my life. I had made them my life. The throb spread until a pressure headache set in.

Dad shook his head. "Do you know how it starts? One divorce, and we lose a couple of sections of land. Another divorce, and there goes another quarter. Maybe two? Income from the oil wells gets split. Your cousin marries a woman with four kids. Then what? Do they each get some when Holden passes?"

"By then, you won't be around to know. Why do you care?" My volume rose with my frustration.

Dad stabbed his finger into the table. Lyric jumped, but Dad, thankfully, ignored her. "I almost lost it all once. My parents taught me a hard lesson, and I'm...I'm doing the same for you."

What was the lesson? He'd stayed with Mom. He'd

humiliated Liam's mom so badly, so publicly, she'd been too distraught to drive, and she'd crashed. He and Mom...

"You loved her," Lyric said, slight accusation in her tone.

I stared at the two people I thought I knew so well, betrayal flush with hurt and anger. It couldn't be true.

"You were in love with Liam's mom," Lyric continued. "But you couldn't divorce or you would've lost everything. Your parents—"

"Enough," Mom said.

I picked up where Lyric left off. What the hell had happened all those years ago? I knew the fallout, but why was the shadow smothering this family? "You were going to leave Mom, and your parents forbade it?" When Dad had taken over after Grandpa Barron died, he'd ruled Barron Ranch with more iron in his fist than an oil well. I'd been determined to be different, but Dad had been just as intent on seeing me do the same.

"Every marriage has hard times," Mom said, her words stilted. "We worked it out."

"Because you had to," I pointed out. "Because you both would've had no place to go. Why wasn't the refinery enough?"

"I loved my wife." The muscles in Dad's jaw flexed, and there was a flicker of conflict in his hazel eyes. He was a man raised being told he had everything. It was all his by right of birth. Then he'd fallen for his assistant, and he'd wanted her too. Why not? Everything else was his. And reality had slammed into him hard. He'd faced going from golden boy to absolutely nothing. A disgraced CEO, yet another one who couldn't keep it in his pants? The humiliation hadn't been tolerable.

And Mom. The girl who'd settled, and because of it, she would've been left with nothing in the divorce. She had been in the position I was in now. My parents had all the assets. Nothing was mine but the house, and the land encapsulating it like an island in the ocean was theirs.

I would lose it all. The future I'd been working for. My job. I'd have my house, but if Dad wanted to push it, he could make living here difficult for me. Devastation wasn't a strong enough word for the emotion rebounding through me.

"We love you." Mom clasped Dad's hand and leaned forward. "We want what's best for you, and she isn't it."

Instant anger made me rise so swiftly I nearly knocked my chair over. Lyric caught it, saving me from terrifying my mom into an early heart attack. "Why do you keep insisting that?"

Mom's gaze landed on Lyric for a moment. Then met mine. "I explained it before. I've seen the signs. Her presence in your life is already tearing our family apart."

"*She's* not doing anything!" I yelled and sucked in a breath to control my temper. "And the baby?"

Mom straightened. I didn't have to see her hand to know her knuckles were white. She deliberately avoided looking at Lyric. "We already talked about custody."

"You did?" Lyric pushed back in her chair. She'd gone pale. Shit. I should've told her every detail of the conversation that night. "You guys covered a lot in the few minutes after I left."

"Lyric—"

"No." She put her hand up. Floof meowed from the kitchen, curving for Lyric as if he sensed her turmoil. "You didn't tell me about the paternity test. You didn't tell me they wanted to take the baby if we didn't work out. You didn't tell me they alluded to cutting you off. And you still haven't told them to fuck off." She stooped and picked up the cat, hugging him close, his gray fur sticking out in tufts around her arms.

"This is complicated, Lyric," I said, trying to intervene before Mom chided her about her language and shit went from reactive to nuclear.

"It shouldn't be. That's the point you don't see, Stetson. I was so afraid of becoming an obligation like my mom was to my dad that I made justifications for your devout loyalty to your parents. It's a problem. You know it. They know it." She huffed a scornful laugh. "I know it, and I don't want any part of it." She directed her gaze at my parents. "You got what you wanted. He's all yours now."

Blood roared between my ears until I worried my brain would explode, but I didn't fucking care. I'd been trying so hard to hold all the parts of my life together and now the biggest piece was walking out? I shook my head. She couldn't be serious. We were in this together.

Mom released Dad's hand. "The baby—"

Lyric whirled so fast a meow escaped Floof. "I don't have Barron money, but I will fight for what's best for this kid. And that's something you don't have experience with. You only do what's right for you." She breezed out of the dining room toward the bedroom.

Mom swiveled to me. "Stetson, how can you let her—"

"You two need to leave," I said, my voice as menacingly calm as Dad's had been earlier. Nothing mattered until I talked to Lyric.

Dad nodded and rose. Mom opened her mouth like she was going to fight it, but Dad offered his hand. A united pair. Thanks to a decision forced on them decades ago.

I waited until they were out of the house, then I went in search of the woman who'd announced she was leaving me and taking the cat with her.

* * *

Lyric

I dumped an armload of toiletries into a tote bag. Floof twined around my feet. My emotions were all over the place, and it worked him up too.

The bedroom door eased open. "Lyric, we need to talk."

I barked an empty laugh and stormed into the closet. "You missed that boat, Stetson."

"Come on. I didn't want to upset you."

I stomped out with an armload of clothes and another tote bag. I dumped everything on the bed. "They upset me when they insult me. They upset me when they descend on this house and scare all my friends away. They upset me when they order a paternity test so they can decide whether to take the kid away from me or not."

"They can't. I won't let them."

"I know. You'll handle it," I said bitterly. I hastily stuffed my clothes into my bag, riding my anger before debilitating tears started. Anguish deep in my chest was brewing, and I wanted to be far away from here before I crumbled.

"They're not taking the baby away from us." He reached for my tote bag like he was going to unpack it. I snagged one of his flannels that had gotten mixed up with my scrubs and tossed it at him. He caught it before it hit his face.

"What are you going to do?" I propped my hands on my hips. "You going to go look for a job? You know that's what he meant, right?"

"I know," he said, his quiet tone smothering all the feelings he'd been ignoring his entire life as he put his parents' wants and needs first.

"And you won't get anything that you've worked for? Not one head of cattle? Not one acre of land?" I punctuated each question with a fling of my hand. He'd been upset at how they spoke to me, but what about him? They treated him worse than an employee. A worker could leave with what they had, but they were trying to take everything from him.

"He won't..." He sighed. A tiny beat of satisfaction hit me. He couldn't say his dad wasn't serious without lying to himself and knowing it.

"He and your mom are obviously willing to do a lot to keep their pride and reputation intact."

"Rich, isn't it? I can't imagine Mom and Dad fighting for the reputation they have now if they had known what it'd turn out like then."

"It is rich, Stetson." My adrenaline was crashing. I had to keep moving. "Just like they are."

I hooked the bag over my shoulder. Stetson's dark gaze swept up the clinic logo on the tote to my belly. "You're really leaving?"

"Did you tell them to fuck right off, that you and I were tamperproof?" I knew he hadn't, but my heart dangled on a hook, hoping he'd cradle it in his hands and take it to shore.

"It's not that simple." There went my heart, released to go hide in the reeds and nurse its wounds. "It's everything I have, Ricky."

"Don't." I couldn't hear the intimate name and keep my hormones from swaying my resolve.

"I can't take care of you and our baby without an income. Even the pickup is owned by the ranch."

He could buy them out. Or was that oil money in his savings too precious? "Then I guess that's it, then."

"It's not it." He towered over me. I wanted to swaddle myself in his strength. I wanted to believe he'd deal with his parents. That he'd handle it. I refused to let him put off handling me.

"This baby won't be another little Barron running

around." It wasn't as if I'd been keeping this topic to myself. My silence was nothing like Stetson's.

His brow crinkled. "What?"

"Look, we weren't going to get married before the kid was born, and I wasn't assuming this baby would be born a Barron." I rubbed my swelling stomach. "This is Baby Finnegan. You're its father. I'd like you to be a part of its life. But it won't be a Barron. I can't let this kid walk around with the name of a family that cuts off children as easily as they have them."

"Dammit, Lyric. I'm not cutting the kid out of my life. I would never do that."

"The thing is, Stetson"—I held my arms out to the sides and let them drop, as helpless as I felt—"I don't know that. You're choosing everything that comes with the name instead of being with me."

He worked his jaw. I lifted the other bag, and he tracked my movements, his gaze jumping from tote bag to tote bag.

I could stay. We could talk this out. Make a game plan of how to deal with his family. But it wasn't right. I loved him. So damn much. But I deserved better. Maybe that was what had kept me from pursuing him once I returned from college. I had grown up with the family. I'd seen the power of their influence, and I'd seen how it hurt others.

Our kid shouldn't have to grow up in a tug-of-war. We could co-parent, and I'd be able to limit Naomi and Cameron's interference. If they cared at all.

"I love you, Stetson." I almost choked on the words. Holding my breakdown at bay was sapping a lot of energy. I loved him so much, yet I'd learned it wasn't enough. "But I refuse to endure the toxic relationship you have with them." I had my dad to thank for my wariness and lack of trust when it came to relationships. How much heartache had it saved me? More than tonight was causing?

"You've been ready to walk out the door since you stepped foot in here."

The subject change was like a pop quiz I hadn't studied for. "What?"

"Two tote bags. You've been here for a couple of months, Lyric. You *live* here. Yet that's all you have." He gestured to Floof. "The cat's stuff takes up more room than your belongings."

Confusion was almost a reprieve from the destruction of the evening. "I lost it all in the fire."

"We've made trips to buy things. I've offered to buy you stuff. We've talked about redecorating. You haven't moved a thing in the guest room. You've been waiting for an excuse."

"An excuse for what?" I said tightly. Why was he turning this on me? I was leaving because of the way he refused to handle his parents. He was the only one with sway over them, too afraid to take his eye off the carrot they'd dangled instead of having faith that he and I could succeed without them.

"To leave." He ground his teeth, his expression growing more decisive. "It was easy to want to be with me when it was my fault I wasn't hitting on you. But you're just like the rest of the girls I dated."

Cold washed through my veins. How could he compare me to his exes?

"I thought you were different, but you're not willing to stick with me through the hard times. You didn't want to be an obligation, Lyric? Well, I didn't want one more girl yelling at me when I didn't change for them. Yet here we are."

My gasp echoed throughout the room. Was I more pissed he'd implied I was someone he felt he had to be with or that he was comparing me to someone like Krystal? The ex who'd been exactly right about him. Maybe that stung more.

I had to leave. I blinked, trying to hold back a flood of tears. "I'm going to load this up, and I'll be back to get Floof."

He made a disgusted noise. "Leave the cat. Get settled, and then I can drop him off."

That was it, then. Taking Floof would've meant coming back into the house. It would've meant seeing Stetson again. My heart was already broken. I didn't need to crack it wider open than it was.

But leaving without my cat meant I was well and truly on my own. I had nowhere to go and only myself to get there.

Eighteen

LYRIC

There was no snow gathered on the ground, but flurries melted as they hit my skin. Zelda unlocked the door to the still-vacant top-floor apartment. Her short curly hair stuck out over the collar of her puffy coat. I wore my heavier jacket too. I hadn't been warm in the week since I'd left Stetson.

I went inside and dropped my tote bags by the door. I had added a third bag, thanks to Mom. My little pile of belongings highlighted what Stetson had said when I left last week.

Isla crowded in behind me, stepping out of her boots to keep from tracking snow across the clean but empty place.

Zelda set keys and a few forms on the kitchen counter. "Go ahead and fill these out whenever you can. Drop them in my box by the door."

"Thanks, Zelda." Tears burned the backs of my eyes as I stared at the tidy stack on the counter. My own place. What should be a joyous milestone left me empty and aching.

Zelda left, and I blew out a breath.

"It's still cute." Isla stuck her hands into the pockets of her fleece coat. We hadn't had much of a chance to talk since I'd left Stetson. I'd worked the weekend and had gone in to draw blood and run tests so many times during the night I'd had to sleep when I could.

It was the best-case scenario for a breakup. I was too tired and busy to think about how my life had imploded. Work had kept me absorbed in other people's serious medical issues, and I'd cried about my own only two or three times a day instead of the entire day.

I'd spent the first half of the week recovering, then arranging this apartment. When I had called, Zelda had said two prospective renters fell through. *It's your lucky day.*

Yay...

I'd called Mom when I left Stetson's, but I had checked into the motel. It'd been late, and her place was so small. I was on my own. Just like I had assumed I always would be.

I chewed my lower lip, increasing the pressure of my teeth until the pain burned the tears away.

"You wanna talk?" Isla hadn't pushed for the story. She'd probably sensed the tension between her parents and Stetson or overheard enough to glean why I'd left.

"No." The backs of my eyes stung again. I sniffled and studied my new home. "Yes? Have a seat, and we'll talk."

She skeptically glanced around my empty living room and the kitchen with no table or chairs.

Laughter sputtered out of me, and she snickered. Tears rolled down my cheeks. The situation was absurd, my heart was broken, and it was possible to laugh and cry.

I dropped next to my bags on the floor and buried my face in my hands. "So, what do you know?"

"I can figure out most of it just because." She sank to the floor a few feet away from me. "Nothing about what actually happened. Stetson's impossible to be around. I heard one of the vendors at the market mention she'd heard Stetson chew Joss out. I ordered takeout from Rattler's, and Remington asked if he was okay. Mom and Dad clam up when I walk into the room. What did they do?"

"They did exactly what I expected them to do," I said, knowing Isla wouldn't be offended. I traced the grain of the wood flooring. It wasn't real wood, but it looked nice. "So did Stetson."

"Oh, no. I'm so sorry, Lyric."

Her lack of surprise eased my anxiety that I'd overreacted. The story poured out of me. I let it all out. I doubted Naomi or Cameron wanted Isla to know they would've divorced long before she was born, but it wasn't a secret I was willing to keep. Their family secrets had done nothing but continue to hurt generations down the line.

"I heard Grandpa was a hard guy to deal with," she said, sadness lining her expression. "But I had no idea he'd do that to Mom and Dad. To Liam."

In the man's mind, he had two generations of heirs. Liam was a threat to the line and to the family's reputation. When his mom had died, the entire family had cemented their commitment to shunning Liam and his grandparents.

"Do you think…" I had stopped before recounting what had been said between me and Stetson. *You've been ready to walk out the door since you stepped foot in here.* "Do you think I sabotaged the relationship?"

Isla frowned, making me feel a smidgen better that she needed to think about it. "How so?"

"He pointed out that I only had these for belongings." I swept my arm toward the bags. "And Floof, but he offered to keep him until I was settled." I missed my cat. I missed the man even more.

"All your stuff was lost in the fire." Her gaze flicked to the stash of totes, unable to hide the question in her eyes. "Why don't you have more, though?"

I let out a sigh. Hadn't I been asking the same question? I wasn't liking the answers I was unraveling. "I was waiting to see if we were going to work. I thought I was moving out."

"That was like the first week or two," she said softly.

Yeah. "I didn't feel like I needed more?"

She ducked her head to peer at me. "Are you asking me or telling me?"

"I don't know." More tears cascaded down my face. "After Dad left, it was just me and Mom. She didn't date. She wasn't interested in getting married. I thought…"

"You thought it was because no one was interested." She scooted closer until our knees almost touched. "You thought no one wanted her—or you."

I blinked back a new onslaught of tears. It sounded childish. I should've known better. "I'm an adult. I'm not a kid."

"We're all left dealing with the baggage of our pasts."

I had told Stetson the same thing. I had urged him to change. And when he hadn't, I left.

"But that doesn't mean that you shouldn't come first with Stetson." Isla could read me better than almost anyone. Which was why what Stetson had said continued to bother me. I hadn't been as close to him for as long as I had been with his sister, but he had read me.

"Do you think he would've done it? Left everything?"

"I don't know. He's been nothing but a farm kid. A Barron. Everything he's done has revolved around our last name. He wouldn't just get cut off from Mom and Dad but Aunt Kira. Who knows about Uncle Bruce? He's already on

Dad's shit list." She shrugged, her light hazel eyes understanding—for her brother—and for me. "But there's Holden and Emery."

"Do you think I should've given him more time?" The question had cost me hours of sleep.

Her expression lost all contemplation. I'd never seen her so serious. "No. Mom and Dad won't quit. They've got their minds made up about you. It's not a game of chicken. It's about power. They sacrificed. Everyone else should too, no matter how unhappy we all are."

I dissolved into sobs. "I really love him, Isla."

She dragged me to her, hugging her arms around me. I cried, a little less alone than I had been all week.

When the worst had passed, I kept my head on her shoulder. "And I still have to raise a kid with him."

"All I can say is that he'll do as right by you and the baby as he can."

It'd be so much easier if I could walk away. If I didn't have to go into every business and wonder if I would run into him. "What if..." She waited for me to finish. I couldn't believe I was speaking out loud. "What if I moved away?"

She pulled away. "Really?"

I brushed at my eyes and straightened. "I haven't thought about it. Until now. But I could."

She watched me carefully. In this moment, she wasn't just my best friend. She was the sister of my baby's daddy.

"Not to be vindictive," I stressed. "Please understand that. But I think about the future, being single, and, well, Mom doesn't need me here. Bismarck is only an hour away, and there're more options there. Every lab is so short of techs, I might land a mostly day shift." If I was scheduled on weekends, Mom would help. And Stetson. "The pay would be better." And I wouldn't be surrounded by Barrons.

"You wouldn't find a cute, cheap apartment like this."

"It is cute, but I also wouldn't have steep stairs right outside the door with a kid learning to walk."

She squeezed my hand. "You need to do what you need to do. We both know you haven't heard the last of Mom and Dad."

"Maybe I have. If Stetson married someone they approve of and had a kid, they probably would've written this baby off anyway." The words soured on my tongue.

Hurt tightened her features, but she nodded. "I think you're right. I keep wanting to say they aren't horrible people, but...they kind of are." She sucked in a long, cleansing breath. "We need to get you some supplies so you can camp out for the night. Let's make a run to the store and see what they have."

They'd have literal camping stuff. My lack of planning would give me a sore back by morning, but I had to start somewhere, and this was it.

* * *

Stetson

I sat alone at the round table in Rattler's. I'd growled at everyone who'd stopped by. Sienna had smiled and started toward me. I couldn't see my expression, but she'd veered off.

Remington spun the chair next to me, sat, and propped his arms across the back. "I'm one glare away from kicking you out of here."

I scowled at him. I was fucking hungry, but I hadn't gotten groceries for two weeks. The weekend after Lyric left, I'd chewed out Joss after he asked what Dad had said about the harvester. *Ask him your own fucking self if it's so damn important. And I'd better not hear about that damn tractor the next time I see you or I'm taking all of my business to Beulah.*

That could've gone better.

Since then, I'd done my work, cooked from the freezer, and was really tired of pasta and hamburger concoctions. The recipes made so much food, I ended up having leftovers for lunch and enough for breakfast the next morning—after I pried the damn cat off my face.

I didn't know who was needier—me or him.

"I'm a paying customer," I grumbled. I took a swig of my iced water. I'd fucked up my life enough. I didn't need to nurse a broken heart with alcohol.

"Who's scaring off other paying customers. Since last week, everyone's afraid to sit here. I caught the hostess pushing together two tables for a party of seven. This table was empty, but she was afraid you'd stomp in and glower at her."

I sucked my lips against my teeth. The comment irritated me. I was a good customer when I was the fun guy. How dare I be cranky? I'd grown tired of the standard I was held to. A level I put myself on and everyone expected. "I was just leaving anyway." I shoved back from the table.

Remington stopped the trek of my chair with his black shoe. "Have you talked to someone?"

"Don't need to."

He held up his hands. "I get it, man. I've been through some shitty breakups myself, and I've worked in enough bars and restaurants to have witnessed some downward spirals."

"And that's what you're seeing now?" I sat in my chair like a sandbag. No energy to make it look like I gave a shit.

"No, and that's what worries me. You usually shrug off a

breakup. You're back, laughing and drinking. You're Stetson. Here for a good time."

"Okay?" I regretted not ordering a few meals to go for the rest of the week. I wasn't going to stay here longer to wait for three different variations of steak and potatoes while Remington told me how pathetic I was.

"I think we're seeing the real you, and that worries me. Because it was like you knew the real you would turn into your dad and that was why we got the bigger-than-life Stetson. You're not spiraling. You've reached a stasis that I don't know you'll come out of."

"You're telling me not to be myself. Doesn't that go against all the advice these days?"

"This isn't the Stetson who makes you happy. But maybe the other guy wasn't either."

I swallowed hard. Remington was a lot like me. He was *on* all the time out of a self-imposed necessity. He had a business that came first, and he kissed every customer's ass to ensure they kept coming back to spend money. It wasn't duplicitous. It was just a dominant part of his personality.

"It's not just the breakup." Everything was the breakup. My days were now about going through the motions. I had deluded myself into thinking I'd been working for my future family. Get up at dawn, run a business, build a home, and, when the right girl came along—when the right girl told me to fuck her already in the back of a barn—I'd have it all.

I'd had it all.

Now I had a cat that about an hour ago Isla had messaged me about. I couldn't bring myself to reply.

"It's what the breakup showed me," I finished. "It's all been for nothing, and it cost me everything."

The young hostess approached but stopped several booths away, hovering.

Remington nodded but held up a finger at her. "Some

things cost so much they're invaluable. Takes a lot of pressure to make a diamond." He stood and twirled the chair back into place.

What the fuck did that mean?

Another message from Isla lit up my phone. **If I don't hear from you, I'll just swing by and grab Floof and his things.**

I dialed and didn't wait for her hello before I said, "Why isn't she coming to pick him up?"

A beat of silence greeted me. "She needs some time, and you have to understand why your house isn't a place she wants to go right now."

The thought clotheslined me. The house wasn't the same without her. "Fine. I'm in town. You can let yourself in. I just changed the litter, and his toys are scattered in the living room. There're a few downstairs. He likes sleeping on top of the dryer when we're not home. His food is in the cupboard by the pantry. Take the whole container—that's what I bought it for. Oh, and his brushes are by the couch." He liked to be groomed while I watched TV.

Another quiet stretch went by. Yeah, I'd heard myself.

"Okay," she said carefully.

That was all she'd called for, but I wasn't ready to let her off the phone. I hadn't heard from Lyric other than short messages telling me she had an apartment and would be ready for Floof soon. "How...how is she?"

"Getting by."

"She can call." I'd endure more emotional torture to hear her voice. "It's not like I'm going to yell at her."

"I'm sure she will, eventually. She said there's another prenatal visit in a couple of weeks. One that's still in Coal Haven."

I sat forward, my elbows slamming onto the tabletop. I

was focused on nothing but what Isla had to say. "What do you mean 'still in Coal Haven'?"

"N-nothing."

"Isla."

"Stetson, it's not my place."

"So there's something you're not telling me?"

Her breath gusted over the line. "Shit. Okay, but listen. You talk to her. *Talk.* You don't storm her apartment. You don't sic Mom and Dad on her." My chest nearly imploded waiting for her to finish. "She's looking for a job in Bismarck."

What the fuck for? She couldn't leave. But she'd already left me. Still, it didn't make sense—or I didn't want it to. "She said none of those would work for her."

"Circumstances changed."

It was me. I was circumstances. "When?"

"I don't know. She doesn't either, but she's been looking at doctors there. Better to get set up there earlier than later."

"She's leaving." She couldn't. She wouldn't. But what else was keeping her here? She had a car. Visiting her mom wasn't an issue.

"Maybe. You can't blame her. It won't be easy for her here. The talk and speculation. Watching you get on with life like she's been doing for years."

I pinched the bridge of my nose. "Fuck, Isla."

"I know." Said with the heaviness of a person who understood. "Look, I'll get Floof. You gonna be okay?"

I grunted my answer and hung up. Lyric was going to move? How could she think I'd carry on like life was a party? How could she think this place wasn't her home?

How could she leave me?

I wanted to leave my sorry ass right now.

Customers in booths and tables cast furtive glances my way. People at the bar murmured to each other, then glanced at me. I had to leave. But I couldn't go home. I couldn't be around to watch that damn cat leave.

I wasn't going to be the guy jealous of a cat because he was going home to his woman.

So what was I going to do?

The answer formed in my mind as if it'd been there all along. And it had. I knew what I fucking had to do. But I'd need some help.

Nineteen

STETSON

When I approached Holden's place, I groaned. He had company. Archer's pickup was parked next to Liam's.

I didn't see kids running around. Was it just the guys there?

Did that change anything? I had come to talk to Holden, but the reason I was here wasn't ordinary. Archer and Liam would have unique insight into the topic. Without thinking too hard, I turned down his drive and lined my pickup alongside the others.

The big shop door was open. I could make out each guy. Colt was there too. I nearly pulled away. Colt wasn't a talker, but he was Aunt Kira's employee. She wasn't the type to keep a secret confidant, but if she did, it wouldn't be a guy. Growing up under a harsh man with a controlling older brother had to be why Holden's dad, Nora's dad, and any other guys were absent from her life.

Talking to Holden about what I had on my mind

would be hard enough. Archer and Liam weren't deal breakers, but Colt could be. If I had seen his pickup, I might've driven by. He'd probably ridden his horse, Cutter, over since the snow would make it hard to ride soon. I was about to back out when Holden stepped onto the big concrete slab in front of his shop. The rumble of my engine had announced my arrival before I could retreat.

He lifted his chin in greeting but cocked his head when I didn't get out right away.

I opened the door, each movement wrenching my stomach harder. This was only the first step. If I chickened out of this, then my breakup with Lyric had been the right thing. We wouldn't have worked for all the reasons she had stated. Our argument, her leaving, and my empty house didn't feel like the right path.

Bolstered, I shoved my hands into the pockets of my pants. Holden assessed the drag in my boots and the hunch of my shoulders.

"You want to go in the house for a few minutes?" he asked. The guys' voices and laughter reached me.

The offer was tempting, one the old Stetson would've taken. But the old Stetson had fucked up, and privacy hadn't helped him. "Nah. Everyone might as well hear. It'll get around soon enough."

He gave me a measured look before leading me to the shop. Talking ceased when I walked in.

Archer and Liam watched me quietly. If they worked to keep judgment off their faces, I couldn't tell. Their gazes were cautious, but also curious. Colt's brow crinkled. He'd steered clear of me after his first post-breakup encounter with me when I'd growled in place of a greeting. No one had been able to stand me. I could hardly stand myself.

Holden leaned against the workshop bench, stretching

his legs out, as if he knew I wasn't going to chicken out. "What's up?"

Holden's confidence that I'd talk in front of everyone helped me spill the details. "Mom and Dad said they'd cut me out of everything if I stayed with Lyric. And when I didn't immediately walk away from it all, Lyric left."

Liam's expression turned to stone. Archer's eyes widened, and Holden shook his head. Nothing surprised him about our family anymore. When I looked at each of them, it dawned on me. They'd all been in my position. Liam had been cut off before he was born. Archer almost the same, and he hadn't been allowed in when he'd chased his wife to Coal Haven. And Aunt Kira had done her best to manipulate Holden the same way as my dad.

And they all were living the life I wanted.

Colt slapped Holden on the shoulder. "I ain't touching this conversation. Your mom has a way of finding this shit out, and these jobs don't grow on trees." He walked toward the big open door but paused next to me. "My useless input?"

I'd take anything, but for once, an emotion other than lonely devastation crept in. Curiosity. Colt shot the shit; he didn't give his two cents. I nodded.

He cleared his throat. "I've lost everything once. And I started over. It ain't easy, but it can be done, and you might even come away a better man than you were before. Sometimes having it all taken away removes the bullshit you used to cover up all the reasons to change."

His boots hit the concrete in a steady beat as he left.

I wasn't just worried about being a better man. I wanted to be a better father than what I had. A better husband than what I'd seen growing up.

"What exactly are you upset about?" Liam asked, his gaze touching on the door as if he'd leave depending on my answer. "What your parents said? Or that Lyric wouldn't put up with it?"

"Both," I said, turning an empty five-gallon bucket over and sitting on it. I scrubbed my face with my hands like I could wipe away the sight of Lyric and her packed bags leaving my house. "I shouldn't have to make a decision like that."

"Since Lyric broke up with you," Liam said, the challenge in his tone unrelenting. "I'd say you made your decision."

I ground my teeth. "I wanted time to think."

"Did you think you could figure out a way around it?" Holden asked.

"Yes, dammit. I've always been able to. I thought so, anyway, but I've been doing their bidding all along." Anger and determination pushed past my broken heart. "Fuck this, and fuck them. I love Lyric. I'm so fucking in love with her, and I can't believe I messed it all up. If there's a chance she'll take me back, I'll walk away from it all." I couldn't believe I'd been too afraid to earlier. I had enough to start fresh. Lyric was already doing it. I wanted us to make our new lives together.

"And if there's not a chance she'll take you back?" Liam crossed his arms, unimpressed with my outburst. "Lyric has a sensitive bullshit meter. I was surprised she even gave life with you a chance knowing the family like she does. So if you're only doing this to get her back, she's going to think it's a bluff. Just another ultimatum, just like your parents hand out, only dressed up in standard Stetson niceness."

Any other time, I might've been pissed. I might've written off his claim as nothing but resentment. But his insight was why I had decided to stay. Why I had walked into this shop knowing the brother and the cousin who should hate me wouldn't tiptoe around my sorry ass.

"I'm done with it all." I hadn't realized it until the words were out of my mouth. "Fucking done. That's what I came here to talk to you about."

Holden pushed off the bench, his face a mask of disbelief. "What?"

"I'll put my house up for sale. If Lyric will take me, I'll move in with her. I'll...shit, I don't know. Get a job somewhere?" I ran a hand over my face. "Isla said Lyric was talking about finding a job outside of Coal Haven. I'll go with her."

Holden stared at me with disbelief.

"You know," Archer said, his tone low, introspective, "when my dad got cut off, it was rough. Not for the first few years. He had the money they bought him out with. But he had no support. He wasn't Cameron. He'd been told what to do, not taught how to do it or why. I guess what I'm saying is—you need a plan. You need to make sure you know what you're going to do when the new road you're traveling gets tough, so your family doesn't suffer."

I hadn't been raised with the militant precision of Grandpa Barron, but I'd had the advantage of being a ranch manager for most of my adult life. With his job at the refinery, Dad had no choice but to let me learn and grow. I didn't yet know how I'd transfer my knowledge and experience to an outside job, one with benefits, but I'd try. "I'll keep that in mind."

"So you're just going to sell?" Holden burst out.

He'd been with me every step of the way when I built my place. He knew what it had meant to me. My announcement had to shock him more than the other two. All he had to do was imagine walking away from everything he had during his pre-Emery days and we'd be in the same boat.

"I don't know who'll buy a house right smack in the middle of Barron property, but if it sits empty, it sits empty." I'd built that house for a family, but if my family wouldn't be happy in it, I didn't want it.

"I know I haven't talked about it much," Holden said, his tone as serious as his expression, "but I'm little more than a coworker with my mom anymore. Avery, Landon, Afton, and Riley are a threat to whatever the fuck she thinks her legacy is. And I've gotta decide what to do about her when Emery has the baby. I'm not letting Mom treat that kid like a prince while she ignores the others." He shrugged. "Honestly, she'll probably ignore her grandbaby too. She only cares about biology when it comes to inheritance, and she'll likely bypass me because I'll include the older four in my will. They're *all* my family. Fuck my mother."

It wouldn't be just me and Lyric. It'd be us and Holden. Liam and Kennedy. Archer and Laney. Even Uncle Bruce.

"Our parents love us, but the love they learned was conditional." I lifted my gaze to Archer. Then to Liam. "I really wanted a brother." The corners of his jaw flexed. "I think they sensed that, and it's why Isla finally came along. A sibling to keep me occupied, but I should've been smarter than that. Stronger. You should've never had to go through what you did."

I didn't expect Liam to forget, and I felt I needed to earn his forgiveness for another three decades to make up for ignoring him, but his eyes shone with appreciation. "I didn't have a choice. You do, and that's not what they're used to. I'm not gonna lie—I feel for the position you're in, but a huge part of me is going to be grinning when I think of this going down."

"I have no right to ask anything of you"—I tipped my head toward Archer—"or you. But if you've got a few minutes, I could use some help figuring out what I need to plan for. If I'm going to win the love of my life back, I need to have my shit together."

* * *

Lyric

It was Friday, and I was running the weekend's list through my head while Isla drove so we could grab a bite to eat in Crocus Valley. I still needed a bed. A real one, not an air mattress that had seemed like a good idea when I didn't have Floof and his claws that turned into talons in the apartment.

And it was time to shop for baby gear. I rubbed my growing bump. I had changed out of my scrubs. In my larger leggings and a flowing shirt, it was easier to tell I was expecting.

A tug of longing pulled at my heart. I missed sharing this with Stetson. With each week, I had expected the pain of the breakup to decrease, but I maintained a steady level of hurt that spiked way too often. We'd have to talk soon. We'd have to do more than message quick updates about the next prenatal visit and the cat. I'd have to let him know I was moving once I had more information, but the anticipation of talking to him was nearly as bad as not hearing his voice.

"I can't believe Krystal got fired." It was the third time I'd said it. Joan had told me this morning. As soon as Joan suspected Krystal was snooping around coworkers' medical records, she'd talked to management. They'd audited the records Krystal had logged on to and found way more employees than me—employees who didn't see the doctor at the clinic but at one of the other satellite labs or the main clinic in Bismarck. There'd been no way for her to justify her actions, and she'd been fired at the end of her shift yesterday.

"You won't have to worry about her hollering your lab results in public again."

I smiled, still relieved I could go to work and not see her.

"Or the way she'd track us down if she thought we didn't pay for a pop we took from the break room fridge."

"This time she shouldn't get hired back." Isla executed a turn that wasn't in the direction of Crocus Valley. "I'm not going to lie. I'm really in the mood for a Rem burger."

I groaned and gave her a *Do we have to?* look. Remington's burgers were good, but they weren't worth venturing into Rattler's and seeing Stetson in his natural environment—one that didn't include me.

She flashed a sympathetic smile toward me. "It's been almost a month, Lyric. Can we just try it tonight?"

Almost a month. Technically, it'd been three weeks and one day. Next Thursday would be four weeks. Yet the breakup didn't feel like almost a month ago. Five months, maybe. Yesterday. Depended on which level of heartbreak I was on.

I missed Rattler's food, but I was also pinching my pennies. I had started applying for jobs. Once the decision had been made, I was anxious to get moved and settled before the baby arrived. I'd had a long talk with Joan about how I should handle my pregnancy and a potential new employer. She was supportive, and I was ready.

I shouldn't be too scared to go into Rattler's.

Shouldn't be. I was supposed to meet Stetson on Monday for the next prenatal appointment. I didn't think he had to come, but we'd probably hear the heartbeat, and I didn't want to deprive him of that.

Isla pulled into Rattler's and parked way too close to the building. I hadn't answered her yet, but here we were. Acid bubbled in my belly as I looked around for a familiar pickup.

She noticed what I was doing. "I don't know what my brother's doing tonight, but I saw his pickup outside his house. We should at least be able to grab some food before he stops in."

There was a tone to her voice that usually wasn't there. Was she not as confident as she wanted me to think that her brother wouldn't show up tonight? I didn't want a full restaurant to witness my first interaction with him since the breakup. The clinic offered more privacy, and my coworkers supported me.

I stared at the entrance to the restaurant. The dinner crowd was arriving. If we wanted a decent seat, we had to get inside.

All right. I'd go in. I'd order a Rem burger, and if Stetson showed, I'd rip the bandage off my heart and cry myself to sleep tonight. Again.

"Fine."

Her smile had an edge I wasn't familiar with.

"You planned this," I accused. Alarm flashed in her eyes, but I shook my head. "You're either the worst friend ever or the best."

"Let's go find out which one I am."

She rushed to the door. I nearly had to trot to keep up with her long legs. Inside, she smiled at the hostess.

As if she'd been expecting us, the young girl grabbed two menus. "Come on back."

I avoided everyone as I walked down the row of booths. I could be only so brave. The last three weeks, I'd shamelessly let Mom buy my groceries, and I'd picked them up from her after work and paid her back.

The hostess led us all the way to the back of the restaurant. To the round table.

Before I could ask why the hell she'd seated us here, she laid the menus down and scurried away.

"I don't want to sit here," I said stubbornly.

Isla pulled out a chair. "It'll be fine."

I remained standing. "No." If he decided to come to Rattler's tonight, he'd head right here. And I'd be at the damn table. "Let's get a booth."

"Lyric." Isla let her exasperation out. "It's fine. We'll just order and eat quick."

Ugh. How big of a scene was I willing to make over this? Stiffly, I shrugged out of my coat and hung it on the back of the chair.

"Lyric?"

I had been so terrified of facing Stetson, I wasn't prepared for my ex. "Cole?"

The man I had dated for a few months before I hooked up with Stetson stared at me, his gaze traveling to my stomach. It was like a bubble full of calculations materialized over his head. A divot formed between his blond brows. "That isn't—"

"Nope." Suddenly sick of all men's shit, I slammed a hand onto my hip. "I have the paternity test to prove it."

"But how far along are you?"

"I didn't cheat on you, if that's what you're asking—no matter how many times you told me you could do better."

Defensiveness entered his expression. He squared his shoulders and lifted his chin. I used to hate when he did that, like he was trying to intimidate me into being impressed. He wasn't a cobra, and I wasn't impressed. "And you think you did better?"

I had thought I'd done so much better.

As much as Cole tried to puff himself up, he couldn't hide the giant of a man approaching behind him. A man whose features were carved from angry marble. "I'd like to think she did a lot fucking better."

My heart crawled into my throat as if it was trying to get a better look while I was deciding whether I could believe what I was seeing.

Cole sneered and glanced over his shoulder, doing a double take when he saw it was Stetson. His cobra flare withered. "You're the dad?" He rounded on me. "I knew you had a thing for him. Were you fucking him—"

Stetson's big hand landed on his shoulder. "She answered you already, but she can't make you understand." Stetson spun Cole around and slapped him on the back in the universal *Time for you to go* sign. "Now, if you don't mind, since this woman has already suffered your bullshit, I'd like to tell her that I'll be the best man she's ever fucking dreamed of if she gives me one more chance."

I blinked. What did he just say?

Cole stumbled, confusion crinkling his brow. By the time Stetson turned to face me, Remington was dealing with Cole.

Isla rose and scooted around the table. "I'll be at the bar."

"You planned *this*?" Isla had tricked me? I'd barely registered my interaction with Cole, and now Stetson was right in front of me. All the humor he usually showed on his face when he was in Rattler's was gone. His face was all harsh angles, but he wore his black jeans and a forest-green sweater. His dark hair was neatly combed to the side, making him look like a model instead of a rugged rancher. He was missing his cowboy hat, and he looked like he had the day we'd first had sex during Holden's wedding reception. Why was he dressed up?

"I asked for her help." He sounded almost apologetic. "Can we talk?"

"Here?"

"I want you to see I'm serious about what I'm going to tell you."

At Rattler's? I still hadn't sat down. Neither had he. There was practically a spotlight on us, but I couldn't pay attention to the other customers or I'd run. Yet if Cole tried to intrude on this moment, I'd donkey kick him out of my view.

I crossed my arms, attempting to look more defiant and less like I was giving myself a comfort hug. "Okay. What do you have to say?"

He'd been serious before, but his expression hardened. "I talked to my parents yesterday. Told them I quit and I'm selling the house."

I laughed. None of what he said made sense. His job was his life, and his house was everything to him.

"I'm serious, Lyric."

It should've been exactly what I wanted to hear, but it wasn't even a case of too little, too late. His parents were playing along. I'd take him back like I so desperately wanted to and then we'd slowly merge back to where we'd been. "It doesn't matter."

"I'm moving with or without you." He took a step closer. "But I'd much rather be with you. You and the baby are all I want." His gaze dropped to my rounded belly. Stark yearning darkened his eyes. "I want to be with my family, and I'll do anything I have to in order to make that happen."

My voice shook. "I'm moving." Was he too late? Would he refuse to leave Coal Haven?

There wasn't a single flicker of surprise. Isla had told him, and she'd kept it from me. Maybe I'd be irritated after I was finished being grateful. "Wherever you go, I'm there."

Tempting. So dangerously tempting. "You expect me to believe you'd actually walk away from Barron Ranch?"

He pulled a sheet of paper out of his pocket, unfolded it, and handed it over. I took it, and a quiet gasp escaped me. A picture of his house was on the front. A price printed across the top and all the details listed underneath. He'd listed his house for sale.

A separate fissure cracked my heart a little more. That house. The view. The porch he'd told me he loved me on, would be someone else's dream.

"I talked to Mom and Dad last night. Told them I was done. That whether or not you took me back, they were never allowed to control my life again. Once I move my things out of the house and find a new car, all ties are cut." He swallowed hard. "You'd think it should be hard to cleave myself from everything I knew, but I have surprisingly few ties to the family business."

"Oh, Stetson." Sympathy filled my voice. The realization must've gutted him.

"Once I got over the shock, the answer was clear, Ricky. And if you hadn't left me, I might not have seen it." He shoved a hand through his hair, ruffling the neat strands. "With the sale of the house, I'll have some money to last us for a while. And if it sits on the market, I have what's in savings. I'll still need to find a job with decent benefits, but I'll be able to support us."

He was serious. There was nothing but resolve in his determined features and his unflinching body language. His mind was made up. He was going his own way—with or without me.

His decision was huge. It couldn't have been an easy one to come to, and it would be an even harder one to carry out. But he had started the journey on his own.

I wanted it to be with me. "Well, I mean, you won't have to worry about benefits. I have health and dental through my work, and retirement." I bobbed my head like this was the most casual conversation in the world when in fact it was the most pivotal.

A slow smile spread across his face, but he didn't move. "Oh, yeah? Do you maybe have a place to live? Because I don't quite have that yet either."

I grinned in return. "It's a bring-your-own-bed situation, but yeah, I've got a place."

His expression suddenly went serious. "Ricky, don't mess with me. I want it all. I want to be your husband. I want to be there to raise our baby and, if you'll let me, knock you up again. And again and again until you tell me enough. Hell, I don't have a job. I'll be a stay-at-home dad. I also don't fucking care what last name the baby has or even if you take mine—God knows I won't blame you if you don't—as long as we're together."

It was everything I wanted to hear, but more importantly, he radiated sincerity. "Yes."

He took another step closer, his expression taut. "Yes to what, Ricky?"

"To everything."

He whooped and picked me up. I lost track of everything when his mouth landed on mine. Clapping registered in my brain, a cheer from Isla, but I didn't let it stop me from kissing him. From feeling every inch of him against me. From hugging him as if my life depended on how tight I could hold him.

When he finally released me, he was grinning. "I'm so fucking in love with you."

Sudden shyness stole over me. "I've been in love with you forever."

Isla appeared at my side. "So, that makes me the best friend and not the worst, right?"

* * *

Stetson

. . .

I practically ran up the stairs behind Lyric. She let us into her place, and once the door clicked shut, I took her into my arms. "I'm going to keep you up all night." But if she wanted to sleep, my prayers would be answered holding her all night just the same.

"Lucky I don't work tomorrow." She tugged her coat off and hung it on a hook by the door.

I wasn't wearing a jacket. If she had rejected me, the cold couldn't have hurt me worse. "I know. I kept track of your schedule."

"You did?"

"I've thought about you every second of every day, Ricky." I toed my boots off and left them on the rug. I tugged her to me, but when I turned us, searching for a place for us to sit, I frowned. "I forgot Isla mentioned that you didn't have much furniture."

A round wicker chair with a giant pad for a seat was pushed into the corner. An iron stand with a polished wooden top was next to it. I had seen enough of Liam's work to recognize his creations. In the kitchen was a folding table with only two chairs around it.

"I've just gotten enough to get me by, but Floof keeps poking holes in my air mattress."

The cat twined around my legs. I stooped to give him a scratch behind the ears. She'd been sleeping on an air mattress all this time? No more. I didn't care how much money we'd have in our life, but she'd always be taken care of. "In the morning, I'll grab furniture from the house. Until then, I'll be your chair, bed, and pillow."

She ran her chilly hands under my shirt until I hissed. "I like the sound of that."

"I clearly need to warm you up." I flipped the light off, cloaking us in shadows. There were thin blinds on the windows, and I didn't want witnesses to what I was going to do to her. "Wait here."

Leaving her by the front door, I needed only a handful of strides to get to the back bedroom. I didn't bother with the light switch. Her half-deflated air mattress was by the wall, under the sloped roof. I crouched and gathered her blankets.

Back in the living room, I spread them out. "Come here."

She had a small smile. "This is almost romantic." Headlights flashed from a car making a turn a few blocks away, the beam strong enough to reach the second-floor windows. "I guess that's our candlelight."

"I'll give you candles and romance, Lyric. But all I want to do is hold you." Our commitment to each other wouldn't feel real until her body was pressed to mine. "To be with you, inside you, over you—that part will wait for a bed. I'm not smashing you against the floor."

She yanked her loose top over her head and dropped it at her feet. I glued my gaze to the mound her stomach made. She rolled her leggings and underwear down. I was helpless to move as her bra came off.

She walked to the edge of the blanket. I was still dressed, but I dropped to my knees and splayed my hand across her waist. Her flesh was warm and firm at the roundest part. "I missed so much."

"It was barely a month. But it felt like forever," she murmured.

"It was forever." I pressed my lips to her belly. Kissed her to the left of her belly button. To the right. Then under. And lower. "Hang on to me."

She gripped my shoulders. I nudged her legs apart. It was an awkward angle, but I'd contort myself into a damn pretzel to taste her. I licked a path to her clit; her special flavor hit my tongue, and I groaned. I never wanted to go a day without her again. I'd dedicate my life to making sure she never had a reason to leave me.

She bucked against me. I gripped her ass, ensuring she didn't lose her balance, and devoured her. She hit her peak in seconds, her fingers digging into my shirt. As soon as she'd crested, I pulled away and swept her legs out from under her.

She yelped, still sounding breathless, and clung to me. I laid her down and ripped my fly open. I shoved my pants down far enough to keep the material from digging into her, but then I growled and rose to my knees.

There was too much goddamn shit between us. I yanked my sweater over my head, threw it God knew where, and wrestled myself out of my pants and socks. Finally naked, I stretched out next to her. "I like seeing you spread out on the living room floor, flushed from your orgasm."

"I like my orgasms too." She wiggled to her side and danced her fingertips over my chest.

I caught her hand and kissed each of her fingers. Then I rolled to my back and pulled her over me. "I don't want to crush you."

She pressed her knees to the floor and scooted down my torso until her wet, warm center hovered over me. When she wrapped her hand around my cock, pleasure tightened my balls, and I rocked my hips up. She scowled at me as if to tell me to hold still.

My body shook as she slowly impaled herself on me. I wanted to thrust like the building would detonate if I didn't get off in twenty seconds, but I also wanted to savor this moment.

When I was fully inside her, she spread her hands on my stomach and inhaled. "I can't believe you're giving everything up." Vulnerability shone in her eyes. The darkness couldn't hide it.

"No, I'm getting everything. Don't ever doubt my decision. I would make the same one a thousand more times."

She rocked and I grabbed her hips like I was going to prompt her to go faster or hold her in place so I could last longer. "I didn't think... You were right. I had one foot out the door."

She might've, but I hadn't given her reason not to. "No again, Ricky. You were right to worry. But I'm going to move more than three fucking tote bags in here with you. You're not going to know where you end and I begin." Electricity raced through my body, making my cock twitch inside her until I was ready to explode. "You'd better get moving or I'm going to finish just staring at your tits."

She palmed the creamy globes. "They've gotten bigger."

"Yeah, they have." I'd been intent on her when I'd entered Rattler's. And I'd been focused on driving Cole away, the insulting bastard. But I'd noticed the delectable extra padding on her curves and the way her boobs rounded against her shirt.

Enough. I took over, and as soon as I urged her to ride me, she didn't need my encouragement.

This position kept her open to me. I loved watching her bounce on top of me, but I curled up to a sitting position. The last few weeks couldn't be shed by a couple orgasms. I had almost lost her, and I needed to hold her. Her freedom for riding me was hindered, but there was enough friction. Her walls clamped around me.

Doubting I could hang on until she came again from just my cock, I slipped a hand between us. Hot, wet heat met my fingertips, and all it took was resting a pad on her nub. She hung her head back and moaned. A few circles, and my name ripped from her lips.

At last, I let myself go. Power racing through my body and into hers.

Tremors shook my body—or maybe it was her trembles—but I didn't ease my hold around her. The sex was off the charts, but it was who I was with that made all the difference. Being alone had sucked, but I hadn't wanted anyone else. "I love you."

She shoved her hands into my hair. "I love you too."

"But I am going to have to throw my clothes on and run home to grab my bed."

When she didn't answer, I lifted my head. She feathered her fingers over my forehead. I had missed this so damn much. Just the two of us, in the dark.

"You said 'home.'"

My decision to be with Lyric had been easy. That didn't mean the details were. "It'll take me a while to quit calling it that."

"I'm going to miss that house."

"I thought you didn't like it."

She frowned. "Because I didn't have anything in it?"

"And you didn't change anything."

"There was no need to. The nursery, yes. But the rest of your house? It's gorgeous. It's simple, it's peaceful, and it's... perfect." Her eyes glittered. "I'm sorry."

I breathed through the weight on my chest. "We'll build the perfect home again someday."

She stroked her hand down my face. Her eyes said she heard everything I wasn't saying. That I'd miss my home no matter what we built, where we built, or when. Knowing she understood helped—as long as she knew that I had everything because we were together.

Twenty

STETSON

With a final heave, I pushed the recliner up the stairs, and Holden angled it to move through the door. We wrestled the chair into place.

Holden stood back, took his hat off and ran a hand through his hair, then stuffed it back into place. "That's the last of it."

I sprawled in the recliner. "Yup. Thanks for your help."

"Anytime."

"You need a hand tomorrow?" I had nothing else to do at the house. It was in nearly perfect condition. I wouldn't move the remaining furniture until the place sold. Lyric and I had talked about moving, and we'd decided to wait until after the baby was born. Winter would be done, and she wouldn't have to start a new job only to go on maternity leave just as her training was wrapping up.

"I do not, but you might want to steer clear of Mom for a while."

I winced. I hadn't talked to Aunt Kira since before the breakup. "That bad?"

"Not good, but also not your problem."

Aunt Kira wasn't a warm and cuddly aunt. She was as prickly as an Arizona cactus and as hard as the rock in our fields. But she'd talked to me like an adult since the day I was born, and while I wouldn't call her kind or caring, I'd at least been accepted. One of the few people I could be around without pretense. She knew exactly what Dad was like and didn't expect an apology for it. "Sorry you got dragged into it."

"I wasn't dragged into it, and I won't be. Mom's treading lightly around me, but she exploded about you. I think it's transference or whatever. I scared her spitless when I was willing to move if Emery had to. Then you go and ditch everything. Maybe she thinks Emery and I will pull up stakes and leave too."

"Not when you just added on to your house to fit all them kids. Want a beer?"

He waved me to stay seated. "I'll grab 'em. It's five o'clock somewhere."

Not in Coal Haven. We had a few hours yet. Holden had been helping me move furniture all morning.

He retrieved two beers from the fridge, popped the tops off, and returned to the living room. He handed me a longneck.

"I heard it was a spectacle at Rattler's," he said, amusement lifting his lips as he sat and propped an ankle over his knee.

"It wouldn't have been if her ex hadn't been there. I always hated that guy."

"I could tell. I warned Nora away from him before he got his claws into Lyric."

"Nora doesn't date."

"Nope. I used to prefer it that way, but the longer she's at home, the more I'm worried I'll show up to the house and she'll have become another Mom."

"Oof. I don't know what to tell you. Couldn't she find a job?"

"Didn't you hear? She's getting a master's."

"But she's living at home."

Holden nodded, his expression perplexed. "Online. Why the hell would you go online when you could get away from Mom?"

Aunt Kira treated Nora like she was clueless, but the girl was smart. She had to be planning something. Or biding her time. Maybe her drama would take the focus off me. I doubted Isla would. She was less industrious than Nora.

I loved my sister, but I worried. Without me around, would our parents grind down on her? Would they crush the vibrant spirit that had survived an oppressive childhood?

She was turning twenty-five soon. She'd receive her trust. Maybe she was the one biding her time.

I took a long pull of my beer and studied the cold bottle. "I don't know what to do with my days." Saying the words was like unzipping myself and exposing my insides for Holden to poke at. He wouldn't. It was why I trusted him to say something. "I'll start buying nursery stuff, but Lyric, of course, wants to be there when we purchase it. So, working around her schedule gives me a metric ton of time." I peeked at my watch.

"Got somewhere to be?"

"My agent said someone's looking at the house at four."

"That sucks."

"Yeah." Strangers walking around my home. The place I'd built for me and my family. How many people would walk through it just to be nosy? I'd locked up every document and scrap of paper possible. I'd put the pictures in a closet with a blanket over them, and I'd brought all my clothing here to Lyric's. It was too much for this place, but it was temporary until the house sold. I refused to have buyers walk through the house hoping to get an inside glimpse of Barron life. No one would even know what size boxer briefs I wore.

I was still a Barron. I liked my privacy.

"It wouldn't burn so bad if I was selling because we had to move." I couldn't bring myself to change the subject. This was the first viewing. It'd get easier. "If there was no other way for us."

"But you have a couple of stubborn assholes for parents."

I set the beer on the end table that used to be in my living room. "It's weird. I would've stopped by their house at least three times since I moved out. I would've messaged Dad with updates—about the cattle, the equipment, or even articles I'd read. Mom might've asked me what she should paint the downstairs bathroom." It'd been less than a week of radio silence. A giant piece of my life had been neatly carved out of me. An empty hole that could never be replaced. We weren't an affectionate family, but we'd been close.

"I hope things change for you. I really do."

I nodded. We both knew they wouldn't. There was nothing that could coax a change of heart in my parents.

My phone buzzed. Uncle Bruce's name popped up. I flashed the screen to Holden. His brows lifted. A couple years ago, Uncle Bruce would've been like his sister. But now? I answered.

"Stetson, hi. Hey..." The other end went quiet, and I waited, my heart slowly climbing into my throat. Was Dad using him to lay into me? I hadn't counted on Uncle Bruce's support until I worried I didn't have it. "Hey, uh, I heard about, you know."

The only reason my anxiety decreased a few levels was because Uncle Bruce was like Dad when he was unhappy. He spread that negative feeling as freely as frosting on a cake. But emotions stopped him up. Admitting his feelings was too new. "I'd be surprised if someone hadn't."

"What are you— Do you have plans?" He cleared his throat. "I ask because— Listen, me and the cold don't get along like we used to. I could use a hand around here if you've got nothing else lined up."

I stared at Holden. I also hadn't counted on how grateful I would be to Uncle Bruce for wanting me to lend a hand. My cousin hadn't heard what was said, but he sat forward, gleaning that something had been uttered to stun me. "What are you thinking? Wait—are you sure? Having me out there? Wouldn't that—"

"My brother has no say over my land. I'm getting clearer and clearer on that subject, Stetson." His voice resonated like the old Uncle Bruce, the guy who used to have as much authority as my dad. "Will he get upset? You bet. But this is my business, and I can hire whoever I want."

"You don't have to pay me. I'll be fine until Lyric and I get settled." Fuck, I hated the thought of moving. I'd make the same decision all over again, but it was going to take me time to mourn what I'd lost. Even longer since Lyric and I shouldn't have been put into this position.

"I'm paying you. I'll pay you triple what it'd cost to hire some guy off the street. Quadruple. Trust me. It'll be my pleasure." He huffed. "I don't agree with what my brother's doing."

"Lyric and I plan to move after the baby's born." The

idea was easier. I wasn't excited, but it'd be a relief when we were finally settled.

"I don't blame you. I'll take you as long as I can. And Willow would love to see you more often."

Working for Uncle Bruce would be like a balm on my raw, empty spaces. "I'm not going to lie, it sounds better than staring at these four walls. Can I talk to Lyric first?"

"Of course. Give me a call anytime. And if you don't take the job, no hard feelings." There was a beat of heavy silence. "I drove one son away and I lost another. I can't go back in time, but moving forward, I can be a different Barron. I can be someone that maybe..." A long, weary exhale echoed through the phone.

"I wanna be a different Barron too, Uncle Bruce."

"You and Holden are good kids. I worried about you for a little bit, but you two, Liam, and Archer? You're our future. And I hope the girls can be as strong or stronger than you."

It was the first time I'd heard the older generation talk about our sisters as being part of the family, part of the Barron legacy, or whatever bullshit they'd been taught to spout. Uncle Bruce had really changed.

I was included in his list of decent guys. Not because I'd been nice to him or because I'd balanced where I spent my money. Uncle Bruce had no reason to reach out—and if he didn't want a headache, he wouldn't—but he'd included me in his list of decent guys, and for once, I was proud to be a Barron.

I was going to make sure it stayed that way.

* * *

Lyric

· · ·

The afternoon was quiet, a nice reward for a busy morning in the lab. I'd finished verifying results in the computer that didn't autorelease. Joan was in the office, Arwyn was on break, and I clicked through some continuing education about platelet function.

I had tried to go through the lessons and take the quizzes a month ago before Stetson wooed me back, but I hadn't been able to concentrate. I adjusted my seat, my scrub top pulling tight over my stomach. I should've gotten a bigger variety of sizes, but Stetson and I were running to Bismarck this weekend.

Whenever we went to Bismarck, we looked at places to live and narrowed neighborhoods to buy a house in once his house sold. So far, he hadn't had any offers, and I hated dreading that he would get one. I didn't want to yank Stetson out of his hometown. The transition was hard enough for him. He'd been helping Bruce, shoveling snow for the entire block, and Zelda had even run out of projects for him to do, but eventually he'd need more.

I clicked to another tab. Open positions in the state were listed down the screen. I kept an eye on med tech positions, especially those around Coal Haven. We didn't have to move to Bismarck. We could go anywhere.

The problem was that neither of us wanted to. We'd talked about moving back eventually, but we'd agreed that leaving for a few years might be best for us.

The steps of a patient approaching in the hallway reached me. They weren't the shuffling or stilted steps of someone older or in pain. The footfalls hit strong and confident. I closed out of the computer tabs I'd been in and went to the window to greet the patient.

Cameron.

My heart thudded, threatening to stop if I didn't run. This was inevitable, but for some reason I had been under the impression I'd be able to prepare. Like I'd be in the store and have a premonition or something. I'd see him or Naomi and be able to walk by, ignoring them.

I couldn't hide behind an aisle here, and my pride wouldn't allow me to run and get Joan to deal with him. Stetson and I were in Coal Haven until at least after my maternity leave was over. I'd face Cameron.

The slight turndown of his mouth took his gaze from flat to incensed and, if I wanted to delude myself, a hefty dose of what looked closest to grief. His jaw was so hard, his teeth would crack if he didn't relax.

Instead of greeting him, I held my hand out.

He handed me a sheet with his patient demographics. I nodded my head in the direction of the blood-draw room, leaning on my trained professionalism as much as possible. "Have a seat. I'll be right in."

He didn't give me a second glance but did as I asked. By the time I'd pulled his orders, printed labels, and breezed into the room like this wasn't the last thing either of us wanted to do, he had finished rolling up the sleeve of his shirt.

I laid the labels down and rubbed sanitizer onto my hands. I willed my voice not to shake. "Can you give me your name and birthday?"

He rattled off the information, his voice rough. I made sure it matched his labels as I put my gloves on. He glared at the wall while I readied my supplies. I sucked in a long breath to steady my heart rate and my hands before I brought the needle and tubes to the drawing chair. I didn't think I'd be as nervous with Naomi. I had spoken my mind around her enough. Cameron had been a dark cloud, hovering on the edges of Isla's existence when I was around, and he wasn't much different when I wasn't.

He put his arm flat. I tied the tourniquet around his

biceps. His muscle twitched when my gloved fingers grazed his arm. We both wanted this over with. "Make a fist for me, please."

He didn't flinch when I stuck the needle into his antecubital vein. All I had to get was two tubes. The draw was over in less than a minute, and I placed a bandage over the site.

"You're free to go," I said as I labeled the tubes.

He rolled his sleeve back down. I thought he'd be gone by now. He could put his suit coat back on in the hallway. But he took his time buttoning his sleeve.

I had to wait until he left. We couldn't leave patients alone in the drawing room—needles and syringes appealed to a certain crowd—but I wasn't sitting at the reception desk where I could monitor the room. I had to prep and test Cameron's samples.

"I heard you're thinking of moving," he finally said, a rough edge to his voice, but he spoke as if this was a casual conversation.

I nearly jumped when he spoke. I wasn't ready for him to make conversation. "We thought it was for the best."

His brows drew together. "And you think you know what's best for my son?"

It turned out talking to Cameron was a lot like conversing with Naomi. This was our first one-on-one, and my tension freed the filter around my vocal cords. "No, but I think we can talk about it and he can decide for himself."

His jaw worked. "He'll come back."

I couldn't speak without thinking. He thrived on yanking the carpet out from under a person. He could read people. It was how he'd been so successful in his professional life and with pushing people to their limits in his private life.

So I spoke the truth. He might not like it, but he'd respect it. "He would've worked for you forever, Cameron.

Stetson wants nothing but to make a good, honest living and have a quiet life where people don't hate him. He wants a family to come home to every night, and he doesn't want a life of fighting his family."

He shrugged into his suit coat. "Naomi and I don't expect you to understand."

"I understand more than you think. You know, when my dad walked out, I spent years wondering what I did wrong. I spent so many years wondering what was so wrong with me that a dad could walk out of my life. But finally, I realized it had nothing to do with me. It was him. Just like it's you. You've cut your brother out of your life. Liam." Muscles jumped in his jaw. "And now Stetson. Three people, and you're the common factor. You might blame your parents for the way you are. Their parents. Maybe you tell yourself it's gotta be this way, but in the end, it's your choice, and you don't have many people left before you end up alone in the end. I understand that clearly. So does Stetson."

"Not many would dare talk to me that way." His anger floated on the air between us.

"That's been a lot of the problem."

He tilted his head, like he was the scientist and I was the specimen he needed to identify. "What do you think you're going to do without the money that comes with the Barron name?"

"The same thing I would've done with the Barron money. A job I really enjoy and am proud of."

"I'd like to believe that," he said and stepped around me to leave.

"I doubt it," I said to his broad back. "Then you'd have to admit you were wrong, and that's something you've never been able to do."

His stride faltered, but he continued walking. I sagged against the counter, his two tubes of warm blood in my hand.

That just happened.

I put Cameron's chemistry tube in the blue plastic rack by the centrifuge to spin later and carried the other vial to the heme analyzer. After inverting the tube a few times, I pushed it into the machine. I leaned against the counter as the analyzer clicked and whirred while it calculated hemoglobin and cell counts.

My pulse was settling down. I held a hand flat in front of me. Its slight tremble was the last of my adrenaline energizing me.

I had told off Cameron Barron. There was no satisfaction. Just a grim realization this was how it was. How they had ordered it.

When I'd fantasized about being with Stetson, I had never taken his parents into account. Part of me thought they'd accept me. Their son had, so why wouldn't they?

Not so, but still... I wished for a different outcome. For Stetson.

The tube was kicked out of the analyzer, and I took it to the fridge, setting it in the rack of other blood drawn throughout the day. The printer fired up. Frowning, I crossed to see what was wrong. Results only printed for abnormal results.

The flag listed on Cameron's results was "abnormal lymphocytes." Sometimes the flag was due to precursor cells that often signified something wrong and nothing good. Or there was an internal issue making some white blood cells appear different to the analyzer. But it was often a false alarm. The analyzer erred on the side of being too sensitive.

Looking at the cell counts the analyzer had produced, I frowned. His white blood cell count was way too high, along with the percentage of lymphocytes. "Abnormal lymphs, huh?"

I'd have to do a manual cell count and check the morphology. I grabbed the tube from the fridge, made blood smears on a couple of microscope slides, and ran them through the staining process.

While I waited for everything to dry, I had another patient to draw. Finally, I was able to sit down with Cameron's smear at the microscope. I started at the lowest resolution.

Pinkish-red-colored red blood cells were scattered across my field of view, and among them were the pink-, purple-, and blue-stained white blood cells. The smaller granular purple puffs of platelets were dotted between them all.

Several deeper-blue cells caught my gaze. There were a lot of lymphocytes in Cameron's smear. A lot.

I switched to a more powerful lens. "Damn." Cells with a dark, cracked middle filled my view. The analyzer was correct. I didn't make diagnoses. I could only report what I saw, but Cameron Barron's fatigue wasn't from some bug.

Damn. As if things weren't hard enough for Stetson.

"Joan? Can you come look at this?" I could report it out, but given my contentious relationship with Cameron and our recent conversation, I wanted to cover my bases.

She popped out of the back office. "What's up?"

"Can you take a peek and tell me what you think?"

I moved, and she took my seat at the scope. She peered at the smear. "Mmm. Soccer balls." Her tone said everything. The inside of the cells resembled soccer balls. They were indeed abnormal lymphocytes, with the hallmark cracks of chronic lymphocytic leukemia in their nuclei.

She pushed back and peered at the label. As soon as she read the name, her gaze shot to mine.

I nodded, my throat constricting. "That's why I wanted

you to look at it. I can finish the differential and make more slides. I'm sure the doc will want to send smears to the pathologist."

She nodded. "He'll be referred to Bismarck once his doctor gets the results. He's got a long road ahead of him."

What was I going to tell Stetson?

Nothing. I couldn't risk my job. He had some money in savings, but thanks to what his parents had done, we needed this income and the benefits more than ever. Besides, this news was for Cameron to tell his loved ones when he had all the information. I just wished he had gone to the doctor earlier. I wished he would've realized he was seriously ill and then maybe he wouldn't have issued an ultimatum. I wished something like this would soften a hard man like Cameron, but I had quit believing people like him and my dad ever changed.

* * *

Stetson

A tabletop Christmas tree sparkled in the window of our apartment. Snow fell outside. Lyric didn't have to work this holiday, so we'd had our own cozy Christmas dinner with Erin. I picked up the dishes from the folding table. I hadn't dragged my big set up the narrow stairs. Holden and I had hauled only enough to get us through the first half of next year.

Then come summer, my life would change. We'd move. I wouldn't work for Bruce anymore. If we moved to Bismarck or Dickinson, I could pop back to Coal Haven and lend a hand. If we moved farther away...seeing any of my family would be sporadic.

The thought of leaving was getting easier, and it wasn't just because it was Christmas. I had learned a lot about myself over the last two months. I had learned who cared about me as a person and who'd only wanted to keep the Barron accounts. I bought my Coke where I felt like it. Joss didn't approach me in public, but his technician, Damon, had stopped to tell me good luck with the move and that he was striking out on his own. He hadn't known I was working for Uncle Bruce, so I'd landed Damon his first account. I gave zero fucks who it pissed off.

That by itself was a gift, and I was ready to rain presents down on Lyric. "I got you something."

"You got me a lot of things." She gestured to the little tree. The evergreen might be small, but underneath the table was a stack of wrapped presents. I had wrapped only a few presents in my lifetime. If I had gotten something for Holden, I'd just given it to him. Mom and Dad had everything, so my labor was their gift. One year, Mom had wanted a new stall built in the barn. I had knocked it out over a weekend. The only presents I'd wrapped had been for Isla.

A few of the gifts under the table were mine. We'd watched Erin open her gift after we'd eaten, and I helped her load it into her car. She had refused my offer to follow her the few blocks to her apartment and carry the item upstairs. I'd always liked Erin, and I was glad she was now part of my family. She accepted me just as I was.

Her gift was one of the lamps Liam had made. Lyric had talked to Hattie and obtained her insider knowledge of what Erin really wanted. With her new, much smaller place, Lyric wanted to make sure the gift was intentional and useful.

Our apartment was small, but I didn't share the same reservations.

I pulled out the biggest box, not caring that my taped

seams were uneven or that the paper bunched in each corner. "Open this first."

Lyric dug her teeth into her lower lip like she was biting back a smile. She dove for the present and ripped off the red paper full of candy canes.

"Seat covers for my car?" Her confusion was valid. Who got seat covers from their boyfriend for their first Christmas together?

"Open them up."

She peeled the plastic away and unfolded a cover. I had kept the color black to match the seats in her car, but it was the words printed on them that made me grin like I was five years old again.

"'Titrate or Die,'" she said, laughing. Her laughter bubbled louder. When it died down, her smile stayed in place. "Not many people can say their shirts match their car seat covers."

"Look at the other one."

Her grin widened as she held them up, side by side. The second cover read "Calm Down and Dilute." Her two favorite science shirt sayings. On the seat pad of each cover was an image of a test tube and a syringe.

She snickered. "Cops are going to look inside my vehicle and think I'm cooking meth or something."

"They'll be shocked when you tell them what their cholesterol levels are instead."

Her delight over the first gift made me bypass the rest and grab the little square box I had hidden under the table by the wall, figuring a woman over six months pregnant wasn't going to be crawling around on all fours, snooping through gifts.

She sat forward on the recliner, absentmindedly petting Floof as he poked through stray wrapping paper. I crossed to her, knelt down, and handed her the box. After the conversation at the table with my parents, I was determined to make this romantic. Significant.

It worked for me. Emotions zinged inside me like a pinball game. Excitement that I could surprise her. Giddiness that I thought she'd say yes. And nerves that made it easy to stay on my knees.

Her humor was gone, replaced by stunned disbelief. She took a moment, as if she had to steel herself for whatever was inside. My wrapping job was nearly as bad as with the first present, but it gave her enough places to get a good hold and tear the paper off.

She worked slowly, methodically, until the velvet box was revealed.

"Stetson," she breathed.

I held my breath as she opened the lid. Her lips parted as the princess-cut diamond in a platinum setting was revealed. A simple band with a simple diamond.

"Lyric, will you marry me?"

She flipped the lid closed and launched out of the chair. I caught her as she wrapped her arms around my neck. A muffled "yes" was loud enough to make me cheer. Oops. We were in an apartment now. I couldn't be loud.

"You don't know how happy I am," I said.

She pulled back and wiped her eyes. We were both on our knees, and Floof mewed, confused. "I love you, and I want to spend my life with you."

This was officially the best Christmas ever. I tapped a finger on the velvet box, encouraging her to open it again. "I asked Isla about what I should get. I wanted to make sure you'd like it."

"She never said a word. I should start worrying how well she can suddenly keep secrets." She lifted the ring out and admired the way it sparkled in the lamplight. "It's gorgeous, Stetson. And the perfect size. I can still wear it at work without knocking it on everything or getting my gloves caught on it."

I gently took the ring from her and slipped it onto her left ring finger, my satisfaction swelling until the ring was seated in place. A perfect fit. My sister had known exactly the style and size I had needed to buy. *We've only been talking about this since we were kids*, Isla had said. *Only I didn't know for way too long that the groom in her mind was you. But I couldn't imagine her with anyone else.*

"It's perfect." She held her hand out, fondness etched into her features. "You're perfect." Her expression fell. "I'm sorry our situation isn't perfect."

"I'm not." Eventually, the sadness that tainted holidays and happy news would pass. "We're still together."

"Let's get married soon."

"We don't have—"

"I know. But I want to. A small gathering, maybe in January, then we can have something to celebrate in the dead of winter."

I'd marry her tomorrow if I could. "I'll do whatever you want."

"I was thinking about the name thing," she said hesitantly, "and what you told me Bruce had said about not being *that* Barron. I'm going to take your name, and this will be a little Barron running around. One of the *new* Barrons. There are more Barrons than Finnegans, and I want our kid to have the support you and I didn't."

This woman destroyed me. I touched my forehead to hers. It wasn't about the name but about who would stand next to our child like my cousins had banded around me. "You're amazing, but through all this I realized it's not the name that matters, it's who we are that does."

She rubbed a hand over her belly. Her eyes lit up, and

she grabbed my wrist. Spreading my hand under hers on her stomach, she concentrated. "Can you feel that yet?"

We both went still for several seconds. Finally, I shook my head. "Soon, though." I couldn't wait. It was trippy enough to see her belly growing bigger and bigger with our baby. To feel them? Couldn't. Fucking. Wait.

"Ready to open the rest of the gifts?" I asked.

She laughed. "I'm afraid my gifts will be nothing compared to this."

"I absolutely disagree." I lowered my voice to a purr. "But you can always strip down and let me inside you, you know, just in case."

Her scowl was playful, and the blush that stole across her cheeks made me chuckle. I couldn't get enough of her. My fiancée.

Damn, that had a good ring to it.

I was about to grab the next gift when the outside stairs creaked. I glanced at Lyric, but she was frowning at the door.

"Are you expecting someone?" she asked.

"On Christmas Day? Maybe Isla's stopping by?"

I went to the door and opened it, unconcerned about who was going to surprise us on a cold holiday night. Surprise crossed Dad's face as if he hadn't expected me to answer at all, much less before he knocked.

Astonishment sealed my lips. My gaze jumped from him to Mom standing next to him. Her hands were shoved into the deep pockets of her long coat, and a scarf was secured tightly around the collar. Her expression was pensive, almost contrite.

Dad looked tired. Worse than when I'd seen him last time.

A meow cut through my stunned immobility. I gently

toed Floof away from the door. "What are you two doing here?" I asked with only curiosity in my tone.

"We need to talk," Dad said. I couldn't detect a trace of hostility in his voice.

I studied Mom, trying to determine any underlying motives that would somehow lead to Lyric being insulted. When I could find none, I checked with Lyric.

She had stayed seated, her hands resting on her bump, but her back ramrod straight. Her brows were lifted, but she didn't say no. I stepped back to let them in.

Cold air swirled around my parents when they entered. They didn't make a move to step off the welcome mat or to take their coats off and hang them on the hook by the door. I didn't offer. There was no point in getting cozy when I might have to kick them out as soon as they opened their mouths.

"What's going on?" I worked with Uncle Bruce every day. I'd have heard if something was wrong with a member of the family. Dad hadn't quit talking to Uncle Bruce, but in the last month, they hadn't done more than exchange text messages. Same with Aunt Kira. But between Holden and Uncle Bruce, I would've heard if there was a disaster looming on the horizon.

Dad's attention went to Lyric, and the corners of his mouth turned farther down. Shit. Was it going to get bad this quickly?

"I suppose you've told him," he said.

Told me what? The foreboding that had set in when I opened the door grew larger.

Lyric gave a slight shake of her head. When her gaze met mine, sincere regret darkened her blue irises. "I couldn't."

My patience balanced on an edge. I didn't want a reason to be upset with Lyric, not on a night that was supposed to be nothing but a good memory we told our kids and grandkids about when we were in our golden years. But what were they talking about? What had Lyric hidden from me?

She gestured for Dad to go first. "I still can't say. I can't risk my job, not now. If you want anyone to know, it needs to come from your mouth."

A grudging respect I had rarely witnessed entered Dad's expression. Mom hugged her arms around one of Dad's and tucked her face into his shoulder. Dread clawed up my spine. Whatever was going on, it wasn't good.

"Dad?"

"I'm sick, Stetson. Leukemia. I'm sure Lyric can explain it better than I can."

No. Fuck no. He couldn't be sick. Dad was a constant. I could rely on him to be Dad. Even if we never spoke again, I'd know he was there. What did he mean Lyric could explain it?

Lyric rose and tucked herself into my side much like Mom had done with Dad. "I'm so sorry I couldn't tell you."

"You knew?" I asked more out of confusion. Did she know from working in the lab? And why wouldn't she tell me?

"I was pretty sure after I saw his results. But after Krystal was fired, I wasn't diving back into his chart to check on the official diagnosis. I don't do that with any other patients, and I certainly wasn't going to do it with a Barron. I wanted to tell you about it all, but I couldn't risk my job when we're both relying on it. I knew I'd be under more scrutiny—"

I placed a quick kiss on her lips. "I understand. It's not your risk to take. Something like this I needed to hear from Dad." I shifted my attention to my parents. My next words came out stilted. "Thank you for telling me."

A band tightened around my chest. I hadn't wanted my last interaction with him to be like this. Were we going to leave it at *I might die, I might not?* I had so many questions.

How bad was the leukemia? Did they give it stages or levels or some other bullshit? Was he given a countdown? Fuck, I didn't know.

Dad put his arm around Mom, mirroring us. "That's not the only reason why we're here." He still didn't move to take his coat off or to get comfortable. "The diagnosis has forced us to think." He squeezed Mom tighter, and she nodded, as if she knew he needed the encouragement to continue. "We don't want to lose you, Stetson. Isla's not interested in continuing the ranch. She's not attached to it like you are."

"Like I *was*." I didn't mean to add salt to the wound, but I wanted to be real about the situation we were in. He'd showed up to tell me he was sick. I was his son. The news was devastating, but I'd tabled my emotions until I knew whether Dad was using his illness as another lever to flip.

He worked his jaw. "We want you to come back. Reject any offers on your house, move back in, keep ranching. You and Lyric."

Disbelief crowded into my brain. It was everything I had wanted to hear two months ago. But these were still my parents I was talking to. "What happens if you get better? Will I get another ultimatum the next time we disagree?"

Mom's voice was barely above a whisper when she spoke. "We realize we should have handled things differently."

No shit. "You said some pretty hurtful things to Lyric, and that's not something I'm willing to put her through in the future. I can't just come back and pretend like nothing happened."

Mom stared at the tips of her shiny black boots. "I wasn't ready for the change. I wasn't ready for someone else to be more important to my son. I've tolerated Lyric for so many years, just like I tolerate Kira and Willow. She's actually been a part of our family for years, and that made it seem, well, it made it seem like more of a betrayal. But I've had some time to consider it, and I honestly don't think I could choose a better person for this family." Mom lifted her chin, determination etched into the thin line of her lips. "You might assume I'm lying or I'm only saying what you want to hear, so I'll tell you exactly what I mean. Lyric hasn't spread any gossip about our family. She doesn't tell anyone our business. She's proven she can maintain confidence. To me, those are the most important qualities. The rest, I guess, is up to you."

If Mom had gushed about welcoming Lyric as another daughter or simpered over how good we were together in her speech, I wouldn't have believed her. But she'd compared Lyric to Kira and Willow using the word *tolerate*. That made it more genuine.

She'd been threatened by Lyric, the one woman I was willing to do anything for. Mom wasn't warm and fuzzy. She'd never welcome Lyric with open arms. She wouldn't welcome anyone with open arms.

"We want to sign it over," Dad said. "All of it. Get the paperwork going just in case..."

"Shit, Dad. How bad is it?"

His eyes crinkled at the corners. His version of a weary smile. "It could be worse. They've taken a ton of blood. The results are coming back—genetic tests and things like that. I've started on some medicine. If that doesn't work, or begins to no longer work, there are still more options. But there's a chance things can change and get...worse."

I blew out a hard breath. Merry fucking Christmas.

"So you see," Dad continued, "I thought I was thinking about the future, trying to keep this family strong, but now I'm really thinking about the future, and how short it could be. You need to come home. The place is yours."

"It's not just me."

"I know." Dad looked a decade older than he had a couple months ago. "This should be a happy time, but it's like history repeating itself, and it shouldn't have. You didn't make my mistakes. I should've tried to be a better father than—" He clenched his jaw.

It was almost like saying the words was sacrilegious. The man was in his late fifties, but he was afraid to speak ill of his dad.

"We also want you to know, Stetson," Mom added, "that your dad and I love each other very much. When we recommitted to each other, we meant it. But those years..." She fiddled with the end of her scarf. "They were hard. I felt like I gave up everything for nothing, and your dad felt trapped. We were a perfect match on paper. Still are, but our families encouraged our marriage more than we each did." She gazed at Dad, and his expression softened. I didn't get to see this side of them very often. "So maybe you and Lyric being opposites on paper means you can skip past the hurt we caused each other."

"I plan to spend my life proving it." I thought about what they said. Their standard glint was gone. The air of authority. I'd never seen them shattered like this. I wasn't making the decision without Lyric, but I needed to get all the information. "I'm not doing the prenup bullshit."

"We assumed so." Mom's gaze dropped to the new ring on Lyric's finger. "While I still recommend it no matter who you marry, your children may not choose to have one. Their children. Your grandparents wanted the Barron Ranch to withstand the test of time, but it won't if we push you away." She nodded, as if to prove to herself her decision was resolute.

My parents waited for my answer. This was real. Their offer legitimate. But I was cautious. "Lyric and I will discuss this and get back to you," I said. I grasped her hand in mine. "I'm not going to change who I socialize with or who I call family."

"We understand," Dad said. "Trust me, after all this, it's the least of our concerns." He put his hand on Mom's lower back and led her to the door. "Just know that we're sincere. We don't want to lose you."

I was rigid until they left. Once they were out the door, we didn't speak until their footsteps were no longer heard on the stairs.

"There's no need for a decision tonight." I had to process Dad's illness. Their offer. Lyric was going to be my wife, and she had as much say in this decision as me. "We can wait to talk."

"We don't need to." Lyric put her hands on my chest. "This has been hard for you. We both know it. Just because we were willing to endure what we had to in order to be together doesn't mean we *have* to. And I'll sign a prenup." I was about to argue when she shook her head. "No. I don't plan on divorcing you, so it doesn't matter. But if something happens, I have my reserves, you have yours. Mom taught me to always have my own accounts. As long as our children aren't cut off from you, that's all I'm worried about."

I wanted my old life back, but not if it'd be harder on her. Fuck the prenup. "We should talk more—"

She cupped my face. "I love you, Stetson. This place is cute and all, but I love your house. I'd like to make it our home. I'd like to see our kids playing in the pastures and helping you do chores. You miss your job, you miss your house, you miss your parents. If we moved, I'd miss your house, I'd miss my job, and I'd miss my mom."

I hadn't had any offers on the house, thanks to the place being encapsulated by Cameron Barron's land. All I had to do was cancel the listing and move us back in. By the New Year, I could have my fiancée in my house. By Valentine's Day, she'd be my wife and the nursery would be ready. When March rolled around, it would be baby time. Lyric could rest and heal on maternity leave without the cloud of moving and changing jobs hanging over her head. "Okay. We'll do it. On our terms."

Twenty-One

LYRIC

I pried my eyelids open. From the place I was nestled in my blankets, I could see only a hint of sunlight peeking around the blinds. "It's too early," I groaned.

"I know, babe." Stetson's voice registered in my sleep deprivation. "But you have all the parts. I don't."

A baby's fussing roused me the rest of the way. Marina's *I'm hungry NOW* sound was becoming easier to recognize. Both my mom and Willow had pointed it out.

I wasn't sure which one stopped by more often to be on baby-rocking duty so I could sleep between feedings. My mother probably beat Willow, but only because Willow made rounds to all the Barron babies like it was her part-time job.

I scooted into a sitting position. Stetson handed me the nursing pillow and helped me situate Marina. She latched on like she was going to blow away in a tornado. I adjusted her so I could lean against the headboard. For some feedings, moving to the rocking chair took too much effort. I yawned and blinked down at the nursing pink-faced baby.

"Good thing she's cute," I murmured.

"Yeah, she is."

It was too damn early for Stetson to look so good, and the way he'd taken to fatherhood made him sexier. When I wanted to cry, he had a smile and danced with her around the house. When I was about to refuse to wake up for another middle-of-the-night feeding, he was my cheerleader. And when he'd caught me crying over the washing machine because *How tired could one person be?* he'd stayed home so I could have a few moments to myself. I often caught him fluttering his fingers in her dark hair when he was rocking our daughter, Marina Erin Barron.

He'd suggested the name. It reminded him of the mariner's compass on my back. Marina would be able to go anywhere and do anything she wanted, including staying right here. We'd make sure of it.

"Need me to stay in this morning?" he asked quietly, like he was afraid to wake someone when sleep was a precious commodity under this roof lately.

"No. Willow's coming by. Emery went back to work yesterday, and I think Willow is already missing the extra baby snuggles."

He nodded to my phone on the nightstand. "Isla was blowing up your phone last night."

"Oh, crap, I missed her."

"No worries. I called her, but she said it would wait." He stretched across the bed, dressed for the day in a clean but worn pair of jeans and a T-shirt under an old Drillers sweater. Prebaby, he'd be out the door by now. It was calving season. But Bruce, Archer, and Liam were helping Stetson and Holden with their duties.

Stetson had worried about leaving Bruce after he'd said he'd help, but he ran to Bruce's place most days to lend a hand. Holden was getting additional help at his place. Avery was turning out to be a country girl down to her bones, and Landon had to perfect whatever his big sister was good at. Afton and Riley were content helping Emery with their new little brother, Grady.

Another yawn attacked me. "I'll call her before lunch."

"You should go out some night. Marina and I will be fine for a couple hours."

Marina popped off the nipple, and I switched her to the other side. This had been the center of my world for the last six weeks. Stetson had done all the errands, and I'd been content to stay home. Ever since we moved back into the house, I'd embraced my new home.

The closet was half-full of my clothing. Same with the dresser. I had maternity clothing I'd store away, and I had a variety of items available for figuring out what worked best when I was ready to get out of my pajamas. Mom had stocked me up really well, and I might've gone on some online shopping sprees the last few weeks.

Stetson and I had worked on the nursery together. His old mobile hung above the crib, and Isla had found a big stuffed rocking horse. Playing off the horse theme, Isla had painted the Barron Ranch brand on the wall opposite the crib and a giant sunflower on the wall the crib was bumped up against. Mom had tracked down crib bedding mottled in the black and white of Holstein cows. Stetson had joked that our kids might turn the ranch into a dairy farm because of that bedding.

I had left the rest the way it was. The house was perfect, and it was ours. Stetson was already planning a playroom in one of the empty rooms downstairs.

"Maybe I will." The idea sounded better the more I thought about it. "What do you think Isla's up to?"

"Mom and Dad are wondering the same thing. She got her trust fund money, and she refuses to tell them what she's doing with it."

Isla hadn't clued me in either. Perhaps she hadn't wanted me to worry, but more likely she hadn't been sure herself. What her parents saw as flighty indecisiveness was actually a highly contemplative personality. Isla wasn't a gambler. If she thought she'd fail, she wouldn't do it; otherwise, why risk the wrath of her parents or the embarrassment of public judgment?

"Whatever she's planning, it's going to drive your parents crazy."

"Yup. Oh, that reminds me—Mom gave me some baby outfits yesterday."

Cameron and Naomi weren't attentive grandparents, and no one thought they would be, but when each of them had first seen Marina, there'd been a change. One that might never be recognized or acknowledged by others, but I'd seen it and so had Stetson. Something had softened inside each of them. A long-held belief had shattered.

When they wanted to see Marina, Stetson packed her up and drove over. They weren't comfortable coming here yet, and that was fine. I wasn't pounding on their door to visit. Baby steps with the baby.

I wasn't pushing them, and they weren't pushing me. "I'll make sure to get some pictures for you to show them."

"One's a literal princess dress," he warned.

Naomi's style was the opposite of mine. "I didn't expect less. But we can find socks that look like Converses to go with it."

He grinned. "She didn't know what to think of the 'Titrate or Die' onesie."

"It's an inside joke."

"Ricky, I don't even get the inside joke. I have no idea what titrate means in your world." Yet, he'd used the saying on my custom car seat covers and had special baby clothing made. "But I'm not in this halfway. You're my everything."

I used to fantasize about him telling me those very words, and now I was getting to live my dream.

* * *

Isla

The building in front of me was old. The brick had lost its luster, the roof leaked, and weeds grew in and around cracks in the concrete sidewalk and the pavers by the flower beds. But the bones...

The old train station had character. It had promise. The place had seen a lot of failed attempts in its life. One of the previous owners had purchased this abandoned station from the railroad company—or the railroad company had gladly dumped the property—but nothing had come of it.

That would change.

My real estate agent had already left, but I stayed, staring at my acquisition.

So it began.

Everything I had been planning for revolved around this building.

My phone continuously vibrated, but I ignored the call like I did the others during the rest of the day. My parents had learned what I was doing with the oil trust fund money my grandparents had left me, and they would likely have more than questions. Demands. Ultimatums. I didn't want to hear them.

My plans had been in the making since college. I had bided my time. I'd done my research. I'd learned everything possible. It was time to execute.

I let out a long exhale.

Digging my phone out of my pocket, I bypassed the missed call notifications and dialed a different person. A woman who'd been nothing but supportive, helpful, and knowledgeable. I was paying her, but still. It was more than I'd had while growing up.

When Sylvia answered, I said, "It's done. It's mine."

Her mature, rich voice oozed over the line. "Now it's time to celebrate. Securing the facility is a huge step, and for you to be able to purchase the place outright? It's almost unheard of. You are going to do so well in this venture. I know it."

I preened under her praise. The old train station was mine, but I didn't know how I would celebrate. I should take my wins when I could. There'd be enough complications to bog me down in the future. But after years of toeing the line, I had finally entered the race. "Have you settled on a time line for when your crew will be here?"

Sylvia McDaniel lived and worked in Colorado. Her company, McDaniel Contractors, did specialty construction. Breweries. And I had hired her to build mine after years of research. The older woman had an impressive record, and she was genuine.

To cover my bases, I'd queried several companies. Many hadn't called me back. Others had talked to me like they'd pat me on the head and tell me I must be a smart girl if I'd been next to them. All of them had been men, and so many of them had reminded me of Dad. I wasn't doing business with a guy like my dad. I'd had enough of over-confident C-suite guys who thought their opinions were policy.

"I wanted to talk to you about that," she said, her tone serious compared with her exuberance from seconds ago.

Tension stole across my body. I spun until my back was to the train station, as if I didn't want the place to hear any complications or doubts. This project was going to be successful. I was putting everything into it. If I failed, I would be stuck at home for years to come, broke and humiliated.

Not much different from how I'd been living since I'd come home from college, other than I would've lost seven figures.

"It's not bad news." Sylvia chuckled, reading my silence correctly. "I'm sorry I scared you. There'll be plenty of bumps in the road, but this isn't one of them. I only wanted to talk to you about who I'd like to lead the crew."

Relief washed away the concern, and I pivoted to face my future brewery and event center. "Okay."

"The crew I send will have many workers who've been with me for years. But what I had wanted to talk about is the manager. He's not new to either industry—construction or brewing. He's very experienced at both, and I'd like him to take lead on this project. You'd be working very closely with him."

Disappointment filtered into me. I hadn't expected Sylvia to come in person and lead the crew, but a part of me had hoped.

"What's his name?" I had buried myself in industry information over the years. I wouldn't be surprised if I recognized his name.

Sylvia's pause stretched. Finally, she said, "McCoy Cunningham."

I sifted through all the names and places I had delved into during my research. "McCoy Cunningham? Any relation to Hannah Cunningham?"

I had paid close attention to female CEOs, especially those in the beer and brewing industry. Hannah Cunningham's name had started to appear in articles and online forums a little over a year ago. She had taken over the trendy Blue Steel brewery in Nashville. Her sours were shipped all over the world, and her batches were in such high demand she couldn't keep up, which drove her profit margins sky high. I could hope for only a fraction of her success.

"You'd have to ask McCoy," Sylvia continued, so quickly I shrugged off the connection. If this McCoy knew Hannah in any way, maybe he'd have some specific expertise to add to the project. And if he didn't, then it didn't matter.

Sylvia had an excellent reputation and was featured in all the top-ten lists for brewery contractors. I trusted her, but in the end, this was my legacy on the line, and I didn't want to ignorantly bumble through the process. "So when you say he's going to be the crew leader, he's going to oversee both the construction side and the assembly side?"

"McCoy's well rounded in all aspects of this business. He can help you with anything. You're okay with his arrival?"

I dug at a loose pebble in the old, cracked concrete of the parking area I stood in. "Can you tell me more about what makes him well rounded?"

"He hasn't led a team, but he's been a part of the company for years. When he was going to college and doing his brewery internship, he'd work on a crew during his time off. After his schooling, he worked in several breweries before opening his own. He just left the place he was with to come work for us. This would be his first leadership position, though, which was why I wanted to talk to you. He'd be a new crew lead, but he has deeper knowledge of the process."

Her explanation unknotted the tangle in my belly. Why hadn't she led with that? "He sounds like a great asset for the team."

"Perfect. He's available sooner than the rest of the crew. They're wrapping up a project in the Springs area, but McCoy has immediate availability. I'll send him on down, and he can look the place over, go over any changes he might recommend, and when the rest of the crew arrive, they'll be ready to hit the ground running."

"Sounds good. I'll be ready to hear from him."

"Are you excited?"

I grinned, keeping both feet planted. This was one of many reasons I'd decided on Sylvia. I wasn't just an account. She saw the person behind the build. She also didn't talk down to me. I wanted to jump around and flail my arms, but I'd wait until I hung up. My mom accused me of being childish; I wasn't giving Sylvia a reason to. "Yes. Very excited."

"Good. McCoy will likely be on a flight by the end of the week. Congratulations, Isla."

"Thank you."

A notification of a missed call from Dad flashed across the screen. I ignored it and shoved the phone into my pocket. I had the building. I'd hired a crew. And now I was getting a manager who sounded like the perfect fit for this project. I couldn't wait to get started.

Thanks for reading!

Isla has big dreams but not everyone's supportive, and

when a grumpy contractor shows up to take charge, she has to make sure she knows exactly what she wants. But the problem is...it might just be him in Make Me Exhale.

For all the latest news, sneak peeks, free bonus content sign up for my newsletter and receive an **extra epilogue** for Stetson and Lyric.

About the Author

Marie Johnston writes paranormal and contemporary romance and has collected several awards in both genres. Before she was a writer, she was a microbiologist. Depending on the situation, she can be oddly unconcerned about germs or weirdly phobic. She's also a licensed medical technician and has worked as a public health microbiologist and as a lab tech in hospital and clinic labs. Marie's been a volunteer EMT, a college instructor, a security guard, a phlebotomist, a hotel clerk, and a coffee pourer in a bingo hall. All fodder for a writer!! She has four kids, cats, and a half blind Corgie.

mariejohnstonwriter.com

Follow me:

Also by Marie Johnston